The Life and Death Of My Best Friend

Davy Crockett

Daniel Carlson

The Life and Death of My Best Friend, Davy Crockett

Copyright © 2023 Daniel Carlson

This book is a work of fiction based upon factual and historical events.

All rights reserved. No part of this book may be reproduced in any form or by any electronic or mechanical means, including information storage and retrieval systems, without permission in writing from the author, except by reviewers, who may quote brief passages in a review.

ISBN 9798863853277

Cover by Carl Goodall

All rights reserved.

The Life and Death of My Best Friend, Davy Crockett

Chapter 1 – Humble Beginnings

I grew up with Davy in the mainly unexplored and unknown wilderness of Hawkins, Tennessee, where silent streams and vast forests shared there treasures with plentiful game and countless Indian tribes. Here rifles and bows supplied the food and the axe, saw and hard labor were the only means of obtaining shelter.

Crockett senior, John and his three small boys had constructed a small log shanty alongside the northwestern banks of a small river located in east Tennessee. Similar to my own father's home the Crockett's cabin was a single story one room and one-window building with a soil floor and a small stove fireplace. Void of any luxuries, only bear skins and buffalo hides provided couches and bedding.

My first memory of Davy was when we were about five years old and we were playing on the banks of the Nolichucky River. Four of us, ignorant young boys, chose to amuse ourselves by pranking Davy and daring to steal a canoe and set afloat down the river while he, with his back towards us, was still trying to light a campfire. Without any knowledge of how to direct the canoe, we plied the paddles with great excitable haste, but within only a few minutes we were caught up in a strong current that dragged us rapidly towards a deep waterfall where the water dropped thirty feet and foamed noisily over huge rocks with unabated fury. Heading towards our doom with a great speed we paddled and screamed for help, until recognizing our looming peril, Davy ran with all his might to a nearby cornfield where he convinced a field worker to come to our aid.

The Life and Death of My Best Friend, Davy Crockett

Stripping almost naked, the man and Davy plunged into the cold water and swam with all their vigor until they seized the canoe, and then with absolute exertions they managed to drag us to the shore. Being unable to swim the man and young Davy saved my life and so at that young age, I decided I would repay Davy with my loyalty for the rest of my life.

I don't recall much fun as a youngster, mainly we labored every day, collected wood, foraged for berries, and tended to our father's vegetation fields. When we did have fun it was when one of Davy's uncles paid his occasional visitation. Joseph Hawkins, the brother to Davy's mum, was a war veteran who fought alongside his brother-in-law John Crockett in the war for American independence and he was one of the Overmountain men who defeated the English at King's mountain.

Davy's, Uncle Joseph found it difficult to settle down after the war, and working as a trapper he would disappear for months at a time only returning when he had furs and pelts to sell. It was said he could see and smell things in the forest that no other white man could, we called it Indian sense. Upon his rare appearances, he taught us how to hunt, stitch clothes from pelts, and make coonskin hats. He could spin a yarn of exaggerated tales, occupy an ear all night, and given the opportunity he could drink cask after cask of the strongest homesteaders throat burner.

My last recollection of Uncle Joseph was when an accident occurred. One early morning when the dew was still as thick as fog he took us out hunting, still red-eyed and rather unsteady on his feet as a result of Crockett seniors home brew, Uncle Joseph soon got impatient and upon the indication of a rustle in the dense thicket he raised his gun and rushed a shot in desperation and hope rather than good fortune.

The Life and Death of My Best Friend, Davy Crockett

After the thunder died down and the powder cleared we were to hear the scream of a man. Rushing to the spot of the target to our shock and dismay, writhing around in agony in the dirt was our neighbor, Ben Symons. The three of us hauled the earsplitting Mister Symons back to the Crockett's cabin where Davy's mother, Elizabeth inspected and tendered to the wound. Noticing the ball had entered, but not exited the man's fleshy side, quickly Elizabeth used a gun rod and a silk scarf the push the ball out through Mister Symons rear. Such was her tenacity and her skill for mixing herbs and salt water her patient made a full recovery, but Uncle Joseph had disappeared over the mountain range before any retribution could be administered. I'm not sure if it was a coincidence or if Uncle Joseph met with an unfortunate happenstance while he was out in the wilderness because we never saw or heard from him again.

A few years after the shooting incident, when Davy was about eight years old his family was forced to live with us for a short while when a flood swept away most of the valley including the Crockett's homestead. It was during this time I became aware of Crockett senior's fondness for liquor. Everyone learned to keep away from him whilst he was swigging from the casks due to his intemperate nature, profane and often brutal ways. However, when he was not red-eyed and in a degraded condition he was an honest hard-working friend of my fathers and soon after the rains stopped and the ground dried sufficiently to permit travel both our families uprooted and move deeper into the wilderness, crossing the green ranges until we reach a small scattering of log cabins in a place named Morristown.

The Life and Death of My Best Friend, Davy Crockett

Whilst my father continued to pursue a livelihood from managing the land and rearing livestock, Davy's father, John opened a tavern which he used to encourage hunters and travelling immigrants to stay and rest up. Teamsters could rest their travel-weary cattle and hardy pioneers could enjoy a night's sleep and find protection from the wild elements whilst under the cover of a solid roof. Here grilled steaks often scented the earthy fragrance as John enhanced his earnings by offering the choicest venison and corn-pounded 'journey cakes'.

The Crockett's small tavern was over three miles away from our homestead and it was secluded in the dense woods, so to avoid the cry of the grizzlies and the howling of the wolves during the dark early nights I was allowed to stay over week after week and work alongside Davy's siblings to raise additional funds from foraging and hunting. In return, Davy would replicate by volunteering to work in our fields throughout the long warm summer nights.

Another event I vividly remember is when, James Crockett, another one of Davy's uncles wandered into the tavern. With long shiny crow hair and looking like no white man I knew or had ever seen before, James had been taken prisoner as a boy when Davy's grandparent's home had been attacked by the Creeks. Davy's father was on duty with the militia when the Indians attacked his home and slaughtered his vulnerable parents. Abducting James, everyone presumed he had also been murdered, but astoundingly he escaped the Creeks seventeen years later and found his way to his brother's tavern.

Lengthy and boisterous celebrations were held and James became a spectacle as curious neighbors from miles around visited the tavern to buy the hero a drink and convey their good wishes by bequeathing gifts

The Life and Death of My Best Friend, Davy Crockett

ranging from clothes to pigs. As with Uncle Joseph, James didn't stay too long at the tavern and one day he too vanished into the wilderness without notifying anyone of his whereabouts.

One particular year we were allowed to leave our chores once per week and join the other local boys and girls on the walk to Miss Diskin's cabin for half a day's tutoring in numbers and lettering. As an enticement, Miss Diskin offered a fat slice of fruit pie to the pupil who at the end of the class had remembered most of her teachings. Neither I nor Davy ever got close to tasting any of that appealing-looking pie.

Along with all the other boys and girls we had no fancies and barely any clothes, most of the time our legs and feet were bare, and our backsides were covered with only a deer hide tabard. However, we enjoyed our time in the company of our classmates until our schooling came to an abrupt end. At the age of twelve, our parents hired us out to pay their dues to a Dutch drover who was desperate for help. Although nervous I and Davy could not wait to leave the damp valley in search of far-off adventures, little did we know or realize the four hundred-mile trek to Virginia proved to be nothing more than tedium with blisters from long hours of work and endless uncomfortable nights spent under cold layers of pelts which did little to protect us from the continual rain-bearing clouds.

It wasn't until many years later I realized that we had been sold off into slavery by our parents who knew only how to teach and administer stern and implicit obedience and were void of displaying any kind of love or affection towards their children.

The Life and Death of My Best Friend, Davy Crockett

The toilsome journey lasted over two months and led us over miles of knee-deep marshland and bog mires. There were frequent storms and we were often drenched and left shivering for days due to our inadequate garments. The Dutchman, Jacob Siler was a man mean of heart, he offered us no comforts and only meager scraps of food which was barely enough to keep us alive. We slept the Indian way, on beds made from leaves and moss, each lost in our own thoughts until the noise of nature in the darkness slowly lulled us to sleep.

Luckily Davy, being a good shot managed to keep up our fortitude by shooting game and roasting or broiling the meat over our derisory campfire, when the conditions allowed. Mainly everything was so drenched by the constant downpour that it was impossible to ignite a spark, and so day after day we journeyed on through the thick mud without the warmth and comfort of a night flame to gladden us. To survive the damp chill of the long nights Davy and I slept back to back and on many occasions, we induced a couple of the camp dogs to snuggle in tight, covering our heads under the worn tarps we tried to block out the calls of the unnerving night beasts.

All too infrequent was the luxury of finding enough pieces of dry bark to set ablaze and warm the soles of our sore and ailing feet and to protect us from the cutting wind and dry us between the ferocious periods of cold rain.

At the end of our tenure winter had set and Siler was reluctant to let us return home. The boorish man wished us no harm and was so pleased with our vitality and obedience that he offered to retain our services with an offer of a few dollars per day. After long considerations with much debate and plenty of deliberations, for I wanted to stay and see out the

The Life and Death of My Best Friend, Davy Crockett

winter and Davy was restless and persistent, claiming his affectionate heart dearly missed his mother and he was anxious to return home.

To avoid another lecture from the persuasive Siler we sneaked out of his cabin door in the middle of the night and trod knee-deep in fresh falling Virginia snow. With a winter gale blowing against our necks, we trudged slowly in the moonless night and waded for seven miles across rutted mud which had frozen into ridges overnight, and being as hard as iron we had to tread carefully, for one slip could have easily broken an ankle. Finally we chanced upon a family of traveling merchants who were harnessing up their cattle in the dawning light. Astounded by our sudden appearance the family, called Dunn kindly warmed us by their fire, shared some hot bacon fat and revitalized us with a fresh supply of boiling coffee.

Listening to our tale with a sympathetic ear and concern they offered tenderness by insisting we should accompany their encumbered wagons on the track to Knoxville. Day after day we walked beside the sluggish turns of the wagon's wheels advancing through the heavy snow with difficulty due to the constant storms and battery of strong gales however, we were privileged by the kindly merchants who permitted us to sleep amongst their trade in the rear of one of the wagons come nightfall.

After several weeks of bone-numbing travel, the track split and we parted ways with the generous merchants. We walked for several miles until we happened upon a drover who was returning to Knoxville with his herd of horses. Unfortunately, I cannot recall the name of this fellow with the compassionate soul who allowed us to join him and then extended his kindness by stating our scrawny weight would be no burden for one of his strong mounts and he led us towards one of his mules.

The Life and Death of My Best Friend, Davy Crockett

We traversed with this friendly fellow across the diverse wilderness for another couple of weeks until we bade him farewell where the road diverged about fifteen miles from our valley. Here the shoots of spring prettied the final part of our journey home and the fragrant prairie breeze increased our fervor.

Our stay at home didn't last very long. Numerous new emigrants had settled in the region and many new smoking chimneys dotted the landscape. Miss Diskin had married and moved state and with the increased population a school house had been erected for the first time and a full-time teaching master employed, a man named Horace Kitch. The learning classes were extended, but we found them dull and the room claustrophobic after getting accustomed to the vast expanse of the frontier land.

During Miss Diskin's teachings, Davy was popular with his fellow chums, they enjoyed his joviality and his pranks, but now neither of us fitted in too well with newcomers, and then, one day after school Davy whipped the classroom bully when the antagonist roused his anger. Davy was not a big fellow for his age nor mean, but he was ferocious and fearless and that afternoon he spanked the older boy so hard he had to be carried home in the back of a cart.

Anxious to return to the school due to the severe punishment that would be administered by Kitch, Davy played truant for several days and kept the beating a secret from his father, but after a few days, Kitch announced himself on the Crockett's doorstep to enquire if the boy's illness had bated enough for him to return to school. Davy was called to account and fueled by excess alcohol John Crockett raged with humiliation and uncontrolled anger. He took a grip of a stout hickory stick and lunged forward swinging

The Life and Death of My Best Friend, Davy Crockett

the stick in his son's direction. Knowing there would be no reasoning or leniency shown by his drunken father Davy ducked low and spun away from the powerful, but untimely swings until he was able to flee out of the tavern and sprint the three miles over the fields and through woodlands to our cabin. He spent that evening sleeping in our cattle barn concealed from my parents as he pondered what to do next and the following morning instead of returning home to the beating that awaited him he told me that he intended to enroll with another drover, called Jesse Creek, and head to Virginia. Before he left, he asked me to sneak back across the valley and inform his Ma of his decision and tell her not to worry. Duly I performed his request all the time being careful to avoid any contact with his father, but on my return home, I was ambushed by his older brother Nathan who insisted he also wanted to leave home and join Davy on the adventure. Discussing their plans together it didn't take me thirty seconds for me to decide I was also going on the journey, and so leaving my own Ma a goodbye letter I joined the Crockett brothers on the track over to Jesse Creeks homestead.

Herding and transporting the cattle was basically a repeat of the preceding journey we had embarked upon only a few months earlier with Jacob Siler however, Creek used a different route and we passed through different frontier regions and a few large towns the size and populous of which we had never experienced before. We gaped in amazement at the displays of opulence. We saw gentlemen dressed in long coats and tall hats, and ladies adorned in high-waisted fashionable dresses and bonnets, all a far cry from our everyday rags in which we never changed.

The Life and Death of My Best Friend, Davy Crockett

Upon reaching our destination at Front Royal in Warren County the drove was soon sold and the three of us were rewarded with our small earnings. With a few dollars in our pouches, we continued on for a further week until blisters and rawness prevented any further progression. We hunkered down for a few day's rest on the outskirts of a small settlement and upgraded our moleskin slippers for a fine pair of sturdy boots which unfortunately cost us most of our earnings.

By now sullenness had developed within Nathan and he talked a lot about missing home, it came as no surprise to us that a few days later he told Davy he missed his Ma dearly and that he was going to return home. He urged Davy to do the same and join him. At length Davy considered the proposition, he too missed his Ma, but he knew his father's anger would not have abated he declared he was not going to return home just yet instead, he confirmed he was going to seek out employment which would take him on another journey much further away from Morristown.

Hitching a ride with a wagoner we passed through a few towns until we eventually found work as laborers for John Gray in a small settlement called Gerrardstown.

We worked hard for our 25 cents a day until the following spring when finally bored of the daily chores and dull farming life Davy announced to me that he wanted to travel more and so after a short while he secured us both employment as toilers for a flour delivery company. All was well with our duties until one day in Ellicott's mill we encountered deaths chill breath over us. During a routine delivery the wagon horses became suddenly spooked and in their panic, they broke the tongue strap off the wagon releasing full barrels of flour to whirl in every direction. Wood split and flour clouded the air thick with choking dust and Davy vanished from

The Life and Death of My Best Friend, Davy Crockett

my view at the rear of the cart. Rendered useless by fear I gaped into the swirling mass of white cloud for a few moments until I saw Davy emerge from the white flurry of powder like a ghost. Once the fear subsided and the coughing stopped we laughed until our insides hurt and our cheeks ached. It was at that time we reflected on the danger that I first encountered one of Davy's allegories and his idea of God's will.

"If a fellow is born to be hung, he will not drown." He mouthed spitting out breaths of white powder.

After wiping Davy free from the covering we managed to make temporary repairs to the wagon and hire another one to drag the wreak behind us all the way to Baltimore, where we found ourselves amazed by our first sight of a great harbor and the array of towering masts which bobbed up and down on its swells in the distance.

Never before had we seen so many long lines of red brick buildings, sky-reaching churches, and huge mansions surrounded by a majestic expanding civilization whose tongue we could barely understand. Before us lay an expanse of water which spread its entrancing blue free from hindrance until it merged with the horizon. It was the first time either of us had seen the sea or heard the sound of a rustling forest which was bare of any trees.

Curiosity soon conquered our thoughts and at dusk, we ventured onto one of the harbored ships unfortunately, whilst sneaking amongst the crates we were discovered by one of the shipmates whose strong arm presented us with force in front of the Captain. Surprised by the calm reception we soon found out the Captain desired to increase his crew and he asked us if we wanted to enter his service and take a long voyage to London.

The Life and Death of My Best Friend, Davy Crockett

Eagerly agreeing he asked us a few rudimentary questions and completed the enlisting documents, then afterward we were fed and shown to our hammocks which hung from a low roof in the dankness of the lower deck.

By first light, we had changed our minds. The lack of sleep by the scurrying rats and the claustrophobic surroundings which we were not accustomed to was not in accordance with our expectations, but mainly we both got the jitters once we looked out of the small window at the vast blackness and felt the sharp salty breeze upon our cheeks. We were familiar with only mud and high trees and so shivers of trepidation claimed us as we watched the low moons reflection dancing on the ripples.

In fear of being captured and punished for abandoning our duties and deserting the ship we immediately left Baltimore and re-entered the wilderness again walking and hitching rides to transport us as far from Baltimore as possible with great urgency. In desperate need of money, we stopped at a small collection of cabins near Montgomery, and here we stayed for the next two years working in various industries as laborers, hat makers, and coopers until the yearning to see our mothers outweighed the prospect of the leather strap and could not be ignored any longer.

The Life and Death of My Best Friend, Davy Crockett

Chapter 2 - The Return

Sleeping where we worked, eventually, we earned enough money to fund our journey back to far-distant Tennessee. Again we trudged day after day, over bone aching hard rock dried by the exhausting scorching sun and through rain and grueling mud, until our advance was stopped by a broad stream that was swollen by heaving rain. Fueled by gales, angry waves ploughed deep into the banks surface making it too dangerous to cross the wide expanse we stowed away on an abandoned canoe which was unsuitable for such a perilous journey.

Blown south by the gusty billows we soon found ourselves unable to navigate the crossing as planned and knowing our only salvation was to duck down low and hold tight we clung onto the canoe as it bobbed perilously across the top of the surging waves and forceful current. Within a few minutes, the canoe was half full with icy water and the pair of us was drenched and shivering. In desperation, we hung our hands into the water to steer us into a collision with a muddy rise two miles beyond our intended disembarkment post. Breaking out from the canoe, sinking ankle deep into the mud, and urged on by the blustery cold gales battering our backs and quivering us to the bone we ran with all our strength deep into the seclusion of the tall pines and oaks in search of protection and warmth. Lucky for us after only a few hundred yards we stumbled across an empty hunter's lean-to where we could light a fire and dry our clothes. Davy trapped a couple of rabbits and we skewered them to roast over the redeeming flames.

The Life and Death of My Best Friend, Davy Crockett

That night whilst chewing on that red hot stringy meat and gnawing on those little mites dainty bones I knew we would never starve whilst out in the wilderness, although we were both decent enough hunters Davy displayed a natural instinct for being able to turn his hand to anything. He did not ponder or dwell on decisions, and using logic he set his mind quickly, whereas I labored with my judgments.

He could set traps with ease, strike up a fire even in damp conditions and he knew what berries and foliage we could eat without causing illness so throughout the rest of the journey whilst I gathered wood to erect a night cover Davy would supply the food and the means to cook it.

Two months later our humble cabins were within our sight. The route upon which we walked led us directly to my home first, but finding my home locked and seemingly deserted we quickly moved on to reach Davy's home before sunset knowing John Crockett would have a forwarding whereabouts. Outside crowding the taverns sward were several wagons and a dozen tethered horses, all indicating inside there was considerable activity.

As expected, the small cabin's fetid and tobacco reeking small interior was so congested no one noticed us enter and so whilst the men ate and drank we squatted ourselves in the corner next to the fire. After a few minutes Rebecca Crockett, Davy's younger sister asked us if we required food or drink, to our astonishment in the dim light she did not recognize us, and taking our order she simply confirmed the food would be sent over in just a few minutes.

The Life and Death of My Best Friend, Davy Crockett

Little did we realise how much we had grown and how our appearance changed over the passing two years. Still, we sat and watched Davy's ma and his sister cooking food in the pots that hung above the fire whilst leaning on a barrel John Crockett smoked his pipe and chattered amongst the assembly of storytellers, hunters, travelers, and farmers. After a few minutes of listening and watching the gossipers Davy's sister returned with two bowls and some biscuits which she placed at the end of a large table, then following behind her Davy's ma approached carrying a large pot and a ladle. Taking our seats on the bench and filling our nostrils with the lure of the streaming broth we hadn't dunked our biscuits nor taken our first mouthful of game when suddenly Rebecca astonishingly called out.

"Davy?"

We both looked up to see her frown and squint as she observed the resemblance to her missing brother.

"Davy. Is that you?"

John Crockett heard his daughter's exclamation, and he swiveled at the waist to see her gazing down upon the strangers. He grabbed the nearest lamp and shouldered his way through the crowd from the other end of the room.

"That you son?" His eyes rounded wide and bulged as he held the yellow flickering light to Davy's soiled face. "Is it really you?"

Davy's ma shrieked loudly and fell to her knees at my friend's side, then after flashing a quizzical look in my direction she tenderly raised Davy's face to the light with her cupped palm.

The Life and Death of My Best Friend, Davy Crockett

"We thought the Lord had taken you." She cried.

Before Davy had time to speak he was surrounded and clasped tight in embraces from his ma and sister, but anxiously he peered through the limbs to study his father's reaction.

"Well, I'll be." John's face beamed delight, "Get out the bourbon." He called out over his shoulder.

Noting his father was not reaching out for the hickory stick, I saw Davy's mouth curl into a smile for the first time in many months before it disappeared again in a family hug.

After drying our feet, being well fed and plied with strong liquor, John wrapped his arm across my shoulder and accompanied by a sympathetic and consoling Missis Crockett, he led me outside and explained my parent's sudden passing. I was told they both succumbed to a fever and died within a week of each other, and then he promised that early the following day he would take me to visit their resting hollow. Unable to hide my despair, good wife Crockett kindly confirmed that I was welcome to stay with them until I found suitable employ with lodgings.

Both Davy and I knew feeding an additional two adolescent males would put a strain on the Crockett's resources and it came as no surprise when after only a few days John Crockett informed us he had found us both employment and secured us a six-month bond to work for a local farmer named Abel Wilson. Still weary from our wanderings we were both apprehensive, however we were in no position to object and so we reluctantly consented to the arrangement and confirmed we would fulfill our obligations.

The Life and Death of My Best Friend, Davy Crockett

It was not until several months later when we asked for our pay that we learned John Crockett owed Wilson thirty-six dollars and our labor was in lieu of the dept. When the six months were completed, John Crockett's debt was cleared with Wilson, but we were homeless and out of work. However, we were not idle for long and soon found work with a Quaker called John Kennedy, who had emigrated from North Carolina and needed farm laborers to help him establish his homestead. For the next few months, we cleared and worked the lands and managed cattle. At the end of the term, he fulfilled his undertaking and paid us with an obligation note.

Now fully understanding that John had encountered several misfortunes, and he lived on borrowed wherewithals, Davy duly decided to give his father the note to help clear his escalating debts and ease his burdens. Shocked by his son's unexpected aid, John admitted to Davy that he was desperately short of funds and was on the brink of abandoning his enterprise to seek out and find other means of survival. The offer was kindly welcomed and accepted, albeit with embarrassment, this was the only time I saw old man Crockett's stern countenance and bullish affront yield, as with his head bowed and his hands raised to obstruct the flow of tears, he took the gift. Unfortunately Davy's relationship with his father soon soured. His eldest sister had been dispatched by his father to work and live on homestead some twenty miles distant. With her earnings for lodgings deducted, all monies were to be paid directly John Crockett. However after only seven months she returned home when she fell pregnant to the land owner.

The Life and Death of My Best Friend, Davy Crockett

John Crockett, both incensed and humiliated refused to accept that she had been raped by his friend and he abandoned her to seek refuse in a nearby chapel. By the time the news reached us and Davy had the opportunity to return home his sister had died giving birth.

Davy was incensed when he found out his father had not believed his sister account and he was sickened when he found out that his mother had not supported her daughter in her hours of desperation. With an uncontrollable rage poisoning in his veins he galloped the twenty miles intent on administering his own justice. When I saw Davy the following day, with his knuckles purple and skinned he told me that he had ensured the fiend would never lay with another women. A few years later he told me that his retribution consisted of good beating followed by a cauldron of scolding water being poured over his man parts.

For the next year, we continued to work for the Quaker with a live-in arrangement due to the distance from Crockett's tavern. Unfortunately, our food and mattresses were deducted from our misery earnings.

Quaker Kennedy's abode was quite a grand affair compared to the rest of the cabins surrounding our community. Constructed from huge logs and stone, the Quaker's home consisted of two levels with designated sleeping quarters for all members of the family, including a small garret that Davy and I shared. We worked hard and without rest during the day, but in the evenings we would wait until we could hear the old man snoring, then we'd sneak out of the gable end window to relieve the monotony and seek fun. Being as nimble as wild cat we could scale up and down the cabin walls undetected to meet up with my older cousin Bart, and frolic with the three sisters who lived in the next dale.

The Life and Death of My Best Friend, Davy Crockett

Davy had the natural gift of a sweet tongue, and he could talk to anyone with ease. This confident exuberance made him popular with the girls, and they flirted shamelessly to gain his attention. During those warm summer nights we'd stay out making merriment as long as possible and almost every day we watched with the girls the huge orange ball peak over the eastern horizon and flood the valleys and forests with its warmth steaming away the hanging dew.

We became intimate with those girls in ways I could never have imagined and I throughout the day as I worked, my mind was occupied with womanly imaginations and I yearned for the haste of the night. Although puffy-eyed and at times sluggish, we worked as hard as we could knowing that at sundown we would be as excited and alert as pole cats. My heart beat so fast I was sure it could be heard pounding and leaping inside my chest.

Each one of us took our favorite girl and bonded romantically and affectionately, almost as naturally as bees to the honey pot. The six of us talked fervently and openly about the promising future, often planning to take our nuptials together in a daisy-filled meadow. We were the happiest boys in the whole created world. We earned money, we hunted freely and we each had the prettiest sweetheart linked around our arms. However, our dreamy exploits came to an abrupt end.

As I've mentioned previously, Davy had a natural skill for shooting and with practice, he became a first-class marksman at the shooting contests, which were regularly held in our region.

The Life and Death of My Best Friend, Davy Crockett

Gradually he built up a reputation as the number one shootist in the whole of Greene, Hamblen and Jefferson County and soon gamblers and vagrants, idlers and swindlers of all types were encouraging Davy to enter shooting contests in neighboring townships.

Whilst we were away, traveling far throughout Tennessee, entering rewarding shooting contests my cousin, Bart began a flirtatious relationship with Davy's girl. Succumbing to Bart's devious and wicked tongue she became smitten with the boy and together during our absences they secretly deceived Davy.

It was my girl who eventually, when Davy had returned to Greene County to share with us his five-dollar winnings that embarrassingly told him about the affair. With a broken spirit and a bruised heart, expletives and cusses were exchanged between Bart and Davy but, Bart insisted he loved the girl and that he wanted to marry her. The news hit Davy like a clap of thunder and his pride was shattered. I was annoyed with myself, although I never did admit it to Davy, because I suspected the secret cajoling and I kept it from Davy until it was too late for him to intervene.

Never again did we sneak out from the old Quakers window and we never saw the sisters nor my cousin again. I heard some years later he had married the girl and moved back east, but of their whereabouts and presence to this day I have no knowledge.

Over the next few weeks, we distracted ourselves with daily chores and we found new employment with a farmer called John Canady, who allowed us to travel far and wide to shoot in as many contests as we desired, but Davy was not yet excitable and he was still disconsolate. He was quieter than usual, normal volubility and character had lost its spark.

The Life and Death of My Best Friend, Davy Crockett

He was in a state of great dejection and daily he suffered from the sickness of a broken heart. To remedy his agitated spirit and to help him forget about the little varmint I eventually convinced him to join me at the 'reaping frolic' where I informed him all the County's prettiest girls would be in attendance, all of them on the lookout for a handsome soulmate. Using stern words intended to rally his needs, I told him that he must rid himself of all self-pity to catch the eyes of the sweetest maidens, for I knew the power of a new affection would rid him of the melancholy of rejection.

We strode through the browns and greens of the forest that summer day with vigour and a newfound purpose. Our faces washed and hair parted, rifles resting over our shoulders, necks stretched high and chests puffed out to the full, we bore a grin of optimism that reached from ear to ear. It was not too long before the distant fiddler's chords and the sound of clapping and whooping injected our imaginations and emotions with an appetite for a lusty encounter. Our curiosities and impetuousness beckoned forth through the forest with an increased urgency.

The welcoming we received was not one we had anticipated or envisaged. By arriving late, it appeared to us that all of the appealing darlings were already partnered and being lavished upon by suitors with the same intentions as Davy and I.

For the best part of the afternoon we sauntered about and loitered around the moonshine tent unaware that all of the time Davy was being oddly observed by an older woman.

The Life and Death of My Best Friend, Davy Crockett

Eventually, when the woman approached us, she complimented Davy regarding his reputation for being a hard laborer and upon his notoriety for being a skilled triggerman. The women spoke with the rapidity of the Irish and Davy, being naturally conversational equalled her free-flowing words.

With amused interest and a great curiosity I listened to the teasing banter until after hearing enough from Davy she smiled a farewell and moved over to another lonely young fellow who was leant upon a tree. Stirred up I watched the desirable women saunter from one salacious male to another until it finally dawned upon me that the woman was checking out would be suitors for her daughter. I ridiculed Davy for his naive misunderstanding and laughed until my belly ached, however to my surprise Davy's reddened cheeks had not banished when she unexpectedly returned.

Again she complimented Davy for his assured confidence and his honesty for he had unknowingly impressed the women with his integrity by telling the women he had attended the frolic not so much flirt nor to have merrymaking, but he intended to find a suitable and more importantly, a loving partner with whom he could devote upon and should the opportunity arise, wed. The woman told Davy that she had exactly the sweetheart he sought, but she was in a yonder tent being teased and harassed by an undesirable bruiser who lived across the river.

With his natural certitude, Davy marched over to the tent and pulled open the canvas to immediately fall in love at first sight as a rosy-cheeked and embarrassed smile greeted his timely intervention. Pressing his intentions upon the delicate maiden the young man angrily pulled away from the embrace to turn and face the intruder. To his surprise, he had to calm his

The Life and Death of My Best Friend, Davy Crockett

rage and embarrassingly scatter from the tent at full speed as there before him stood the boy who had given him a good beating in the schoolyard a few years earlier.

No formal introduction was offered. Instead, Davy took the girl's shaking hand and escorted her out of the tent to join in with the dancing. Her discomfiture was forgotten in an instant as the couple of sweethearts joined in the vigorous 'double shuffle' and the 'two-step gig' to dance the afternoon away. By dark, the couple was worn out and they collapsed upon a fallen tree to talk away the remainder of their time together. As always when enticed and occupied with pure pleasure, time seems to speed up and pass by quickly and so still seated on the huge trunk Davy and his darling called Polly, greeted the encroaching darkness of night with the desire for countless more encounters.

As for me, I spent the afternoon unsuccessfully swilling away my misery until the Irish woman, who I leant was called Jean Finley decided she would invite herself to chew my ear off with her nonstop annoying chatter.

Finally, in a haze as the dimness and the strong spirits blurred my vision I watched the Irish women part Davy reluctantly from his new acquaintance and disappear into the black shafts of the forest. I'd never seen Davy so happy, and I never did again.

The Life and Death of My Best Friend, Davy Crockett

Chapter 3 – Marriage

From that night henceforth he dreamed and talked about owing his own land, livestock and a rural matrimony. He and Polly immediately loved each other, but needing to regularly visit his future wife of twenty miles away and engage in a lengthy courtship Davy had to deposit his old rifle against a horse.

Words soon spread of the planned wedding and his brothers and sister pledged themselves to making the day the sweetest memorable day for the angel-faced bride and the proud groom, however Davy's future mother-in-law had developed concerns regarding Davy's ability to provide for her daughter. He had no land, livestock or any kind of wealth, he didn't even own an axe in which to build them a cabin and so she withdrew her consent for the marriage stating that she wanted to find a more ambitious suitor for the allegiance with her only daughter.

One Sunday when Davy came to conduct his regular visiting and courting, the Irish women met him at the door and with a savage wrath she commanded that he must call off the wedding and never call upon her daughter again. However, Davy noticed to his delight a yearning in the girl's watery eyes, and standing firm he opposed the infuriated woman with a restrained disposition to inform her that he would be bringing the wedding date hither closer and that he would return next Thursday to escort the bride to the justice of the peace for the wedding to be legalized. The door slamming in his face did not deter Davy from his intentions and he rode away to inform his family and friends of the incident and his unyielding defiance.

The Life and Death of My Best Friend, Davy Crockett

As per the custom in our whereabouts, family, friends and neighbour's all gather for such an occasion and escort the groom to the bride's home in a long procession. Horses are decorated to suit the occasion with threaded ropes, floral blankets, and ringlets of flowers for the bride. The poor young folk including me and Davy had only one outfit consisting of deerskin moccasins, leather breeches, and a homespun shirt so we cleaned them up the best we could with Yucca soap which John had the foresight to trade from the local Creeks, then Davy's ma and sister placarded our shirts with ringlets of the season's flowers. Our ladies made an effort to brush up in coarse homespun gowns of wool and they stitched buckskin shoes and gloves to match. To enhance their ensemble they made their hair fashionable with pins and they colored their cheeks and lips with berry pulp.

Together we traveled the tree-winding narrow trail on the horse path with a giddy interchange of jokes, pranks, and songs boasting of gallant lovemaking, bewitching maidens, and graceless amorists.

Upon reaching a mile distant from the bride's house it was customary for two of the groom's family or friends to race to the house where the awaiting father-in-law would present the race winner with a keg of whiskey for him to take to the groom's party to quell any nerves.

With a shrill and savage yell Davy's older brother William and I thundered along the root-breached path, swerved precipitously around the slopes, conquered steep ravines, and waded through the deep waters until a plumb of chimney smoke became visible through the tall brown trunks and canopy's of greenery, by which time I had gained a narrow advantage and was able, with great delight to seize the jar from stationary awaiting hands to triumphantly proceed with a calmer return.

The Life and Death of My Best Friend, Davy Crockett

Another Indian yell announced my success, and I presented Davy with the jug, which he readily accepted with a pleasurable mouth stretch, then he proceeded to immediately take a huge swig of the throat burner before passing the pleasurable venom to his nearest companion. This practice continued until the whole procession had taken a long draw. We repeated the satisfying act of wildness until the fire water was spent by which time we had reached the bride's cabin.

The sour-faced Irish woman and her husband appeared in the frame of the opened door and blocked the view inside. Davy dismounted and made his approach as the women ignored his smile and looked beyond him to study the size and characters of the congregation. Words were exchanged at length on the threshold and eventually, relenting from her disapproval, she nudged her husband forward with her elbow. After a delay of slight hesitation, the man embarrassingly stepped out into the bright midday light, and being accustomed to his wife's bitter tongue and her harsh way with words he perceived the change in her manner and called out for all to hear.

"Our wish is that you should stay here to be married as is only right and proper." Bowing his head slightly he continued. "Forgive my woman. She has much tongue and you ought not to mind her."

A few gasps could be heard amongst the creaking of branches as Davy pluckily replied. "The marriage will be at the Justice of Peace's unless good wife Finley steps out here and apologizes to me for the discomfort she has laden upon me and my darling Polly."

As soon as the words left his mouth, the cabin door slammed shut with Jean Finley behind it.

The Life and Death of My Best Friend, Davy Crockett

Old man Finley shook his reddened face and pleaded. "Please give me one minute."

From beyond the timbers, much persuasion could be heard and after a short time the door crept open and Jean Finley appeared. Displaying a red blotchy face with a distinct white hand mark, she leaned out and said.

"I'm sorry."

"I can't hear you." Davy cut in. "Come out here if you have anything to say to me."

Slowly and sullenly, keeping her eyes cast downwards Missis Finley edged away from the door and it was not sweat from the hot sun which beaded on her forehead.

"I said I am sorry for the words I have spoken to you." There was a noticeable quiver in her hushed tones. "Polly is my only daughter and I cannot bear to see her go off and marry in this way. Please be welcomed to my home and married here as it should be."

At first, Davy did not reply. He shot a glance at me then another toward his mother as if he awaited her approval.

"I will do the best I can for you." Jean Finley pleaded.

Davy shouted over his shoulder to me "Leander! Go get the Justice of the Peace." Davy spun at the waist as he consented. "The wedding will be held here." He hollered with an accompanying huge smile.

Relieved and with good nature the wedding contingent sped in all directions. Quickly without hesitation or debate, they agreed upon the

The Life and Death of My Best Friend, Davy Crockett

supply of all celebratory provisions and as I heeled in the direction of the Magistrate the others sought out food, fiddles, and lots of liquor.

Within two hours the nuptial knot was tied with all the pomp and splendor the locals could grant. Copious amounts of homebrew, substantial repasts of pork, turkey, and bear meat roasted over spittle's and warm cornbread, potage, and vegetables awaited the hungry on a large slab of timber which was utilized as the grand table.

Great hilarity soon prevailed, course jokes soured the air, and bouts of laughter and jollity echoed distant. Darkness eventually enclosed, but by the light of a huge fire, the fiddler and the dancing continued until late into the night. Davy and Polly slipped away in the midst of the uproar to find solace with each other in Finley's loft as the revelry continued outside.

It was only when the dawning goldened the tops of the spruces that the weary revelers collapsed into a stupor, their limp limbs thronged and cramping every conceivable space in the small cabin, wood store, and barn.

By midmorning, I awoke Davy with a greeting of liberation to regenerate his faculties. Downing the whiskey in one gulp he burst up from beneath the covering of deer skins and ignited into a state of panic. He grabbed me by the shoulders to lead my weary body down from the loft and out of the cabin with uncontrolled haste.

"What's wrong?" I repeated several times, not knowing the cause of his agitation, but assuming it was of a delicate sexual nature I kept my tone low so as not to wake the others.

The Life and Death of My Best Friend, Davy Crockett

"I've got my wife and thought I was a complete man, but I've got nothing." He gasped.

"What?"

"I've got everything I ever wanted, but I've got nothing." He led us to the horses.

Confused I could only repeat my befuddlement, but mumbling Davy led us away then as we sped from the cabin and into the woods he finally settled to admit he thought he had made a mistake by taking a wife whilst he had no cabin, no land, no furniture, and that his only possession was an old horse. After a good while I managed to calm his trepidation and desperation by convincing him that the newlyweds could survive for a short while with his family until a suitable dwelling could be sought. Eventually, Davy calmed and concluded this was the only logical option available, and we turned to trundle back to the awakening and fatigued loafers at the cabin.

Greeting us with an unexpected smile Jean Finley left us open-mouthed by announcing that Mister Finley and herself were giving Davy and Polly two cows and two calf's as a wedding gift. This dowry which was not expected gave Davy the start he needed and living between the Crockett's tavern and Quaker Kennedy's cabin Davy continued to work hard until he had saved enough money to rent an neglected cabin on John Canady's land.

Being extremely fond of Davy due to his honest approach and his work ethic John also loaned Davy fifteen dollars to pay for furnishings and essentials which he could not manufacture by his own hand.

The Life and Death of My Best Friend, Davy Crockett

By the winter Davy, Polly and I had weatherproofed the lodging and established a homestead of such prosperity that it equalled most of his neighbors and friends.

During the winter months when the snow was deep and travelling was impossible, I worked and stayed with John Canady and I did not see too much of Davy, that was the first time in many years we had been apart for such a length of time, but I was content knowing that both of us did not want for food, a shelter or a warm fireside where we could pleasantly rest.

When I returned to the Crockett's cabin three months later, Davy had invested in a spinning wheel. It was the only one in the region and the first cloth maker I had ever seen. Polly had also, being industrious by nature become apt at spinning a fine web of cloth suitable for either selling or trading.

During the next two years, I saved up enough money to put down a deposit to rent a small holding just six miles north of Greene County and I married Polly's cousin, Annabelle. Although I no longer laboured alongside Davy, we'd cross the dense woodlands to go out for a ramble and chatter once in a while. Eager to escape the drudgery of farming and back-breaking logging, we would return to our boyish pranks and foolery far away from prying and condescending eyes.

 Often we would hunt, attend shooting matches and make hilarity with our friends and neighbors. In the harvest season, we would help each other with the arduous duties and during the long winter months, we would converse with messages delivered by passing neighbors or travellers.

The Life and Death of My Best Friend, Davy Crockett

Whilst Anna and I never received God's blessing for fertility Davy's and Polly's responsibilities increased when in their second summer John Wesley was born then fifteen months later in the winter of 1808 Polly birthed William Finley and soon after Davy's resources started to strain due to the inadequate size of his acreage.

Davy and I seldom argued, I can only recall but two occasions when we had a difference of opinions, the second came much later when a dire situation arose which we could never have imagined in our worst nightmares, but the first was in the winter of 1811.

Davy had disclosed to me that he feared he was beginning to fail with his obligations as a father and now with the extended family having four mouths to feed his small holding was not sufficient to healthy satisfy the family's basic demands and that he had no way of improving his fortune to ensure his loved ones did not starve the following winter. I suggested that he loaned additional lands from John Canady, but already embarrassed by accepting Canady's charity he was too humble to ask for further handouts. Davy told me he had received word that beyond the Cumberland Mountains in west Tennessee, the US government had declared they would give any American settler the title ownership to four hundred acres of land so long as they built a small abode and planted corn.

Not wanting to upset Polly I rendezvoused at his father's tavern to check his sanity. I reminded him that not many years earlier the Cherokees had exterminated all white settlers who ventured into that pathless wilderness. Women had been raped in front of their helpless husbands before being murdered and all hamlets and cabins had been pillaged and burnt to ash. No man with sane faculties would venture over the towering mountains, never mind uproot his whole family to emigrate there.

The Life and Death of My Best Friend, Davy Crockett

To describe Davy as stubborn is an understatement and plead with him the best we could neither me, his father nor his distraught mother could alter his way of thinking and come the fairer weather the following spring he packed up his worldly belongings on a couple of horses and set about the four hundred mile trek over unbridged rivers, rugged mountains and through dense forests, where Indian trails had seldom if ever been trodden by the feet of the white man.

I could not bare for our friendship to end on a sour note and after making provisions with my neighbour to manage my fields and cattle I escorted Anna to her parent's cabin and then caught up with the Crockett's after only five days of slow travel. When I showed myself out from the swaying trees, the relief on Polly's face shamed me for already I could see that she and the children were suffering from the exertion of arduous travel. Mounted on her father's old horse she cradled baby William in her bosom whilst John Wesley sat on her front with his legs astride the horse's neck.

Leading the horses and walking at the front was Davy looking as energetic as ever and trailing far behind was old man Finley. He had generously offered to help his son-in-law through the arduous journey, but now it was plain to see his joints pained him and he had become a burden. Quickly I dismounted and relived his soreness by offering him my saddle, which he eventually accepted after his pride and stubbornness subsided into appreciation.

Unfortunately for me, he selfishly occupied my seat for the remainder of the remaining three hundred and twenty miles or so only touching the mud as the gloom of night descended to halt our travel. However, it was during the making of the camp we were glad to have him accompanying us, his skill with the axe equalled any man and by the time the sun had

The Life and Death of My Best Friend, Davy Crockett

displaced behind the huge mountain range and we had unpacked he had built a sturdy lean-to which could amply provide safe cover from the regular night storms and the spine chilling howls of the forest dwellers.

Onwards we continued the slow toil in the direction of the rising sun between tall barks where branches hung down to the surface, over damp root-infested spoors, across wide rivers, over vast endless prairies with knee-deep grass and up and down steep mountain ridges until we reached an area where fertile soil banked up against a fish abundant small stream and the surrounding trees were stocked with plentiful game of all types. If a man knew how to use a rifle and set a trap in this untouched wilderness, here no family would ever starve.

We rested for only one day and Davy selected the exact spot he wanted for his cabin, then over the next two months we chopped, cut and split tall straight timbers until by notching the corners together we constructed a sturdy fifteen and twenty-foot homely cabin. One door was cut to provide access and one small window for natural light. At the far end large stones were stacked to form a chimney and fireplace worthy for cooking, but also illuminating and warming the home through the long dark, and cold nights.

Over time sticks driven into auger holes provided a table, three-legged stools supplied seating and wooden pins bored into the log walls supported some shelving. A bedstead and frame soon followed and a tent sheltered the dry goods. By the time Mister Finley and I bid the Crockett's farewell to retrace our steps back to Greene County they were settled in their purposeful and comfortable small lodge.

The Life and Death of My Best Friend, Davy Crockett

Over the following two winters I heard very little from Davy, Polly sent word to Anna informing us only that they were all well and that Davy spent most of his days out in the woods or down by the river hunting for food. She informed us they ate very well and Davy was entirely charmed by the lavish forests and prosperous rivers. Unfortunately, he had neglected to make further improvements to their simple homestead. She lettered us that she was often very lonely in that Davy, being vagrant of spirit and imperturbable by the solitary too often assigned himself to the life of a frontiersman with great zeal and the nearest neighbor resided ten miles away.

Polly's last letter noted a new address, Bean Creek some ten miles distance their previous location, she did not mention the reason for the sudden move, but I figured it was due to Davy's restlessness.

It was around the time of the third spring when news reached us that there had been a terrible Indian uprising in the southern regions of Tennessee in which many white folks had been butchered and scalped.

For many years there had been relative peace with all the Indians who shared their regions with us, but in recent years immoral, lawless and vagabond traders had been unable to restrain their greed and thus they had set about plundering the small peaceful settlements of the natives causing unrest. The friendly Indians endured the provocation until finally, after slaughter was inflicted upon them many times they congregated into a menacing vast army determined to gain vengeance for the murders of their kin.

The Life and Death of My Best Friend, Davy Crockett

Gossip spread alarmingly that the Creek Indians were on the warpath and all pioneers, backwoodsmen and hunters who occupied the scattering of cabins throughout the region fled their homes and abandoned their corn fields to seek refuge and protection at Fort Mims. However their terror-stricken disposition did not have time to abate as hundreds of howling warriors surprisingly attacked the unprepared fort at midnight and no mercy was shown to the white-skinned families as in a wrathful demonic trance-like state the Indians indiscriminately butchered and scalped over five hundred men, women and children.

We were informed that only one survivor was reported to have escaped the massacre, after witnessing his father, four brothers, and four sisters slaughtered, a young boy leaped from the outer palisade and sped to the woods in a bid for survival. Hiding in the hallow of a fallen tree the young fella waited until the screams were silenced and darkness protected before he stealth fully crawled two miles to Fort Montgomery.

As a result of the barbaric bloodshed at Fort Mims the whole region answered the call of the bugle and picked up their arms to prepare for war and repel the vast army of approaching creeks who were advancing north towards Mississippi Territory.

The Life and Death of My Best Friend, Davy Crockett

Chapter 4 – The Indian war

Although I was not fond of brawls and fighting, I could not listen to the tales of the midnight conflagration without heartfelt despair for the Crockett's who were at threat of imminent peril and so without consideration for my jeopardy, I packed up my rifle, powder and led and joined a band of volunteers who assembled to venture out west knowing that if the savages were not quickly suppressed they would ravage the whole region and murder every pioneer and their innocent family's.

During the march through the majestic scenery, news reached us that a summons had been issued for every able bodied man in the county to gather his weapons and enroll for duty at Fort Winchester. At a suitable fork in the path I left my companions to search for my friend's cabin after assuring them I would happen up with them again at Winchester in a couple of days' time.

Eventually, after passing by a straggle of remote and empty cabins I was directed by a lone hunter to a shanty which was Davy's latest abode. To my surprise Davy had left Polly and the children to answer the call of duty, but not to my surprise, Polly was in a dire state. She nervously fretted for Davy's return and seeing me in her door frame she had presumed I was the bearer of terrible news.

After calming her spirits with make-believe assurances I managed to contain her anxiousness enough to cook me a hot supper and offer me some comfortable rest. We spoke at length to abate her fears of being attacked by Indians or dying from starvation should Davy perish in the fight. Tears flowed and her rapid nervous chatter was undoubtable, she was hundreds of miles away from her family and there were no neighbor's within a day's walk. She had no method of protection and she had two small boys to raise.

At sundown, she put out the fire and we huddled together, praying they would survive another night.

Davy had figured the best way to protect his family was by repelling the Indians. I could only repeat what my friend believed, that our countrymen, women and children had been murdered and the slaughter would continue until all the settlers had been scalped or the Indians had been exterminated. I tried hard to console her, but I wasn't very good with words of comfort or reassurance, indeed they were forlorn. I told her Davy had gone to do his duty as every other man had done in the region ad if they had not answered the call to arms they would be picked off one by one whilst hiding behind the walls of their log cabins, still she lamented.

Water globules still hung on the grass as I left early the following morning. My limbs were invigorated, but my feelings were sympathetic for leaving the vulnerable family and a worried mother in the wilderness where the presence of death threatened the fresh pine air.

Normally not a sensitive man, I sighed that morning and my heart ached for poor Polly and the boys. Several times as I turned my back on that lonely cabin I had to clamp hard my teeth to hold back tears of pity. Eventually, I concealed my shame with resolute determination, vowing to serve alongside the other family men who had wrestled with their conscience with the hope for a peaceful hereafter.

The Life and Death of My Best Friend, Davy Crockett

By the second nightfall I had reached the camp at Winchester, however I was informed that Davy had left camp with Captain James and a unit of one hundred men to rendezvous at a place called Beatty Springs. They had been given instructions to wait at the springs so that more backwoodsmen, armed with axes and rifles could mass and assemble to form an imposing army.

I stayed the night to rest my aching limbs and catch up with my travel companions before setting off again, this time for Beatty Springs. I arrived at the camp just before sundown to be aghast by the size of the gathering. As far as the eye could see men were purposefully busying themselves by cleaning their rifles and sharpening all kinds of cutting implements from knives and axes to pitchforks and scythes in preparation for the looming tempest. Still, I was unable to determine my friends location for quite some time and it was only when a Major named Gibson stood on a pile of logs to issue orders that I was able to confirm his presence in the camp.

Major Gibson stood tall, puffed out his chest and burst forth with lung-draining commands stating that he needed a dozen men to accompany him on a hazardous reconnoitering mission across and along the Tennessee River. He stated clearly to leave no doubts that he only wanted men of proven savvy and ruggedness. The tour would be conducted at pace with little rest so vigilance and guile must be equally fundamental as bravery and the ability to shoot and track. Were they to be captured certain doom would face all and there would be no doubting that their deaths would be administered by the most dreadful tortures imaginable. Although wide-eyed and alarmed, the stirred and restless gathering immediately held up their hands to volunteer once the bellowing appeal had silenced.

The Life and Death of My Best Friend, Davy Crockett

A clamorous frenzy surged forwards and Captain Jones put himself on a large boulder and signaling with his arms he urged for calmness. Eventually, he was able to speak, and he suggested that young Crockett was the most suitable for this enterprise. That's when I saw Davy's face in the fluky half-light. Without hesitation he stepped out from the crowd immediately consenting to go. This was followed with loud gahooting, whooping and pats on the back then there was another surge of raised hands, mine amongst them, but I could not get near to the front of the congestion for there was a barrier of older and larger brutes who were eager to seek out the adventure.

The Major selected his men and the clamor eventually calmed to apprehensive chit-chat as the men dispersed to idle around the camp. At this point, I managed to reach out and stretch my hand to Davy's shoulder enabling me to pull him about to face me. Immediately his jaw loosened and his mouth hung slack, overwhelmed to see me no words could be found and he reacted by embracing me in the tightest hug a man had ever given me, barring violence.

We quickly caught up around the hospitable flames of a raging fire and after stuffing my gut with roasted game Davy proposed that I should join the band of reconnoiters. Although jittery I sensed he wanted me by his side so I agreed and at once he led me to Major Gibson's tent. The Majors expression confirmed his doubts about my abilities and he rebutted the suggestion by stating 'I hadn't beard enough to be a man ……. I want men not boys.' I had not been in the presence of a Major before and, although nettled I failed to defend my honor due to my throat tightening and my tongue laying heavy. Davy however was wrathy and being confident with his wording he spoke direct without concern of any reprimand.

The Life and Death of My Best Friend, Davy Crockett

"You Sir are on the wrong scent for courage and you ought not to measure pluck by the length of a beard for if you continue to do so, I fear you will choose a goat above the preference of any man."

The rest of Davy's words I did not hear for my mind was lost with thoughts of raging repercussions which distracted my attention, that said to the Major's obvious consternation Davy continued with his persuasive tirade until shaking his head with almost disbelief the Major waved us away with a reluctant, but a agreeable nod.

Rest and sleep avoided me that night, my mind had become possessed with the nearing shadow of the death angel, yet Davy tucked up in a tight ball next to the fire slept without seemingly any such doubts or concerns.

As soon as the first vestiges of light cast a dull greyness upon the forests the thirteen of us gathered our horses and laden them with weapons and food in preparation for the perilous trek into the unknown. We headed south and crossed the Tennessee River at one of the few points where the water did not reach above the horses neck, then we continued forth deep into the thick forests which were totally uninhabited by the white man.

Any type of haste proved impossible, in most places there were no tracks and the trees and brush were so dense and overgrown that we had to axe our way through. So much was our progress hindered by the thick vegetation that by the end of the first day we had only advanced six or seven miles. Often my imagination shuddered my spine as looking though the shadows I sensed the hostiles watching us, waiting for us to become careless with our vigilance.

The Life and Death of My Best Friend, Davy Crockett

It was whilst we were making camp in a secluded hollow that Davy stopped what he was doing and arched low as if he were hunting prey, then he edged back into the shrubbery only to reappear later with his rifle, pressed hard against the back of a white man.

One of our group recognized the wanderer as a man called John Hayes and pledged that he was a good man who sought a living as an Indian trader. Hayes, standing perfectly still with hands obediently high said he was returning from a Cherokee camp when he heard our disturbance, and not knowing what to expect he was approaching with caution when he felt the steel of Davy's rifle press deep into his back. Upon our man's vow Davy lowered the shooter and welcomed the trader to rest and feed. During our nightly dialogue Hayes told us he had been trading in the region for the past decade and he was thoroughly acquainted with the landscape we endeavoured to traverse.

Major Gibson informed Hayes of the massacre at Fort Mims and that we were only scouting the region to gather information regarding the location of the Creek Indians. Hayes confirmed he had heard about the sickening slaughter from the Cherokee who he said were still at peace with the white man and wanted to distance themselves from the troubles of the Creeks.

He told the Major that two Cherokee lodges were only a couple of days travel and that if he approached them in a friendly manner they may be able to relay information regarding the whereabouts of the Creeks.

With everyone's approval, he consented to act as our guide promising he could navigate us through the obscure trails. The Major was pleased with the disclosure, however he did not want to exercise two days locating the camp, therefore he decided to split the search party into two groups, with Davy leading one and he the other.

Hayes explained in great detail the trails to be taken by the two leaders informing them once the information had been collected from the Cherokee, the first party should continue upon the same trail through the wilderness for about twenty miles where the small path would curve and rejoin the route taken by the second party. He confirmed a location of sanctuary where the two parties could safely wait a few days for the arrival of their comrades.

Murky light and long shadows were obscuring our vision when we reached the cluster of wigwams. We were greeted upon our arrival by a curious half-breed Cherokee by the name of Jack Thompson who stated his disgust and concerns regarding the attack by the Creeks. Although he could not offer us any news on the whereabouts of the murderers he said he could lead us to a larger Cherokee camp, where due to their numerous scouts and larger activities in the regions they should be able to offer our sought intelligence.

Thompson offered us shelter in one of his wigwams and insisted we should stay the night with him and his adopted family. He added that hating the Creeks he was eager to join our group.

Renewed optimism dispelled Davy's initial disappointment and, although he agreed to Thompson's suggestions he whispered to me that we should keep our weapons primed and concentrate with full alertness because he was not assured of Thompson's sincerity.

The Life and Death of My Best Friend, Davy Crockett

After breakfast we gathered foliage to brush away all evidence of our being in the area and we set along the track suggested by the half breed. By late afternoon some of the men started to get all antsy and fearing we had wandered too far into the ruthless slayer's domain without adequate numbers they wanted to turn around and not proceed any further. Davy urged them onwards, looking directly at Thompson for indications of betrayal all the time insisting we would not leave our fellow Tennesseans behind and that we should return to camp with the same number of men that we left with.

After about another twenty miles Davy's suspicions regarding Thompson's integrity could no longer be controlled and holding a knife to the scouts throat Davy pressed him for the truth. Thompson pleaded for calmness stating he must have taken the wrong track but, he knew there was another small and friendly Cherokee camp close by where we could rest and fill our water caskets. Knowing we were desperately short of water, Davy consulted the group, and noting our reluctance Thompson remonstrated vigorously that we would be greeted cordially and that we would benefit from the rest in a place of safety. Being in a region of utter solitude and carrying empty water canisters we dispelled our suspicions once again to nervously put our trust in the stranger.

Our arrival at the isolated homestead and greeting was not the one that Thompson promised. The door of the solitary cabin was pulled slightly ajar upon our approach and the steel of a rifle was pointed in our direction. Davy called out that our visitation was made with only peaceful intentions and he asked for the weapon to be lowered, however the quickly returned holler was one of cusses and blasphemous threats.

The Life and Death of My Best Friend, Davy Crockett

Bewildered by the hostile reception Davy enquired to the reasoning of the man's anger to which he admitted his hate for Thompson and if we did not immediately skedaddle he would split open our heads with his lead. A tirade of insults and death threats suddenly commenced between Thompson and the concealed man and it soon became evident to us all that grudges were held between the men of which we did not know and now it was obvious to us that Thompson had duped us into accompanying him to his enemies home in hope that with our support we would intervene and end the feud in his favor.

Angered by the betrayal Davy swung his rifle butt across the back of Thompson's head with so much violence that it thrust him out from the saddle and into the mud. Whilst Thompson moaned senselessly Davy explained to the hidden man that we had been misled and not wanting any involvement in their dispute he stated our situation emphasizing that any discharge of powder and lead would reverberate far and wide throughout the region signaling our whereabouts to the sharped eared warriors. Eventually, the iron was lowered and out stepped a white-bearded man who announced himself as Radcliff.

Davy dismounted and met Radcliff with a handshake on his small porch where they talked privately. After a short while a semi-naked Creek woman and two half-savage small boys appeared and offered us nourishments to which we dismounted and gratefully accepted.

As we made camp Radcliff described how he had married a Creek woman and that she had born him two half breeds. He insisted they were not barbarians and they were not involved in any part of the atrocities then he confirmed that being located in utter seclusion he had to stay at peace with the Cherokee, the white man and the Creeks to preserve their

The Life and Death of My Best Friend, Davy Crockett

existence. He said he had never been on friendly terms with Thompson due to his Cherokee prejudice and their feud had intensified after a dispute over hunting permissions. He confirmed he had lived a life full of abundance from his hunting and cultivation free from the cares which agitated civilization. He entreated that we should leave him as soon as possible because only one hour ago ten Creeks warriors all painted, armed and ready for war entered his land to feed their horses.

They harassed his family and interrogated him regarding rumors of white men's movements in the area and he confessed that he was nervous for if they spotted any horse trails that led them back to his cabin the Creeks would suspect that he had aided the white man and showed them sympathy then he and his family would quickly meet their demise as the tomahawk of the savage would cleave their skulls.

Davy, animated by the new intelligence astounded Radcliff with boldness by stating he could have no better luck than meeting these warriors for either a parley or a fight, however with the evening approaching and not wanting to bode ill upon our host he gave orders for us clear our tracks and move on using the brilliance of the full moon to aid us through the black and silver splendor of the uncharted forest.

We took Thompson along with us for a couple of hours, but fearing an Indian attack he cried for his release which Davy eventually granted after he promised he would never trouble Radciff again. We never heard of Thompsons or Radcliff's whereabouts ever again and their destiny to me is unknown.

The Life and Death of My Best Friend, Davy Crockett

None of us spoke a word after Thompson's release, we moved slowly and as noiselessly as possible through the darkness in fear of ambush and soon enough we had cause to reach for our rifles when we heard a disturbance. Davy signalled us to halt and with our rifles grasped tight we slid from our saddles to take cover against the hugest of trees until our concern was dispelled.

Heading straight in our direction and unaware of our presence were two dark-skinned fella's. Keeping silent and trying not to alarm the riders too much Davy stepped out from the cover and with his rifle leveled in their direction he ordered them to halt and dismount as quietly as possible. Obliging without any argument or resistance, with their eyes bulging wide and chests rising fast they reached their arms bolt upwards and offered their surrender.

Noting they were almost naked and carried no weapons Davy lowered his rifle to dispel their distress and then with his usual friendly chords he told the boys they had nothing to fear and that we sought them no harm. Emerging from the shadows we also questioned the fella's quietly about their circumstances and after explaining their ill fortune we encouraged them to ride along with us for a while.

The two brothers who were slaves had been captured by the Creeks when their owner's homestead had been attacked and all the white folks murdered. Bound and dragged into the wilderness by the Creeks for trade, they had worked loose their bindings and managed to escape their captors. As they endeavored to return to their former owner in Alabama they found themselves lost of all direction in this vast and dense woodland.

The Life and Death of My Best Friend, Davy Crockett

We welcomed our two new friends into our group and continued for another couple of miles until drifting cloud impeded the light and restricted our view so much that it made travel on horseback impossible. We took a short break to rest the horses, feed the new fella's, and get some shut eye when through the dense black trunks we glimpsed a distant flame. Davy eased our immediate doom by stating he thought it was the Cherokee camp that Thompson was leading us towards and that he would scout the perceived danger.

Volunteering to accompany him as quietly as possible we crawled our way through the undergrowth until a manifestation of beauty opened to our eyes. Sloping upon the banks of the mountain stream there was a plateau overlaid with ankle-deep dark grass as luxuriant and as soft as a mansions lawn. The only movement was the slight sway of the grass from the cool evening breeze.

Concealed beneath the dense and low-hanging canopy of branches and leaves, for a brief moment we were beholden to the charming view which would have treasured any artist with a canvas and brush. Intermittent argent moonshine pierced the slow-moving clouds to reveal eight Indian lodges and roaring in the center of the camp raged an immense fire of which its crackles and blaze threw a hue wide across the grassland and up to the barricade of the low-hanging canopy where we crouched.

We held our concealed positions and focused our attentions on the camp guards who loitered between the dwellings and occasionally looked out into the darkness, their probing eyes searching and inquisitive. We remained in the shadows not daring to move or announce our arrival until the morning sun could help us confirm the tribe.

The Life and Death of My Best Friend, Davy Crockett

Slowly the hours passed and eventually with the rise of new dawn men, women and children emerged to undertake various morning activities, their customary dress of bright colours, plumes and feathers revealing to our relief the identity of the Cherokee.

We agreed that Davy should approach the elders alone allowing me to alert our men of danger should he be met with peril, and so with arms held aloft signaling he was unarmed he stepped forth to meet with several peacock strutting warriors who wearily narrowed their eyes to the white stranger with the brave stride.

Engaging with them the best he could he soon returned with a relieved grin to tell me he had explained our position with the Creeks and that I was to bring the others into the camp.

The friendly Cherokee elders received us pleasantly and ordered their younger ones to feed and water our horses, then they gave orders to their squaws to offer us bowls of dried fish, maize and plentiful quantities of firewater to swill our dry throats.

The eating, drinking and general merriment continued until late in the afternoon, and then the elders invited us to test our accuracy with the arrow against the aim of their spawn, to which unsurprisingly they found great humor from our miserable failure and embarrassment. Eventually, as we fatigued from the excess of the mind muddling liquid we took to our bed rolls at the far edge of the camp where the silky grass thickened against the huge barks to make a comfortable mattress.

The Life and Death of My Best Friend, Davy Crockett

Bedding down with the sun dropping behind the towering trees I noticed Davy's attention was directed towards the camp and not the serene darkness which we all craved.

"Something's not right." He whispered noticing I too had become engaged with the affairs of the elders who shuffled uneasily around the dying embers with gesticulating arm waving and fingers pointing.

"You reckon." I replied watching one of the elderly warriors erect himself and set off walking in our direction.

As the long shadow of the lone warrior glided across the serene plateau, Davy hauled himself out of the darkness to meet the Indian halfway through his journey, and in barely understandable English the Indian explained with an accompaniment of hand gestures that the Cherokee were neutral in the war between the white man and the Creeks and being outnumbered by the Creeks it was very important for them to adhere to the impartiality so that they would not draw upon themselves vengeance from either faction. He explained the elders were feeling anxious for should the Creeks stumble upon them hosting their enemy they would inflict upon them indiscriminate misery and massacre all men, women and children.

In an act of bravado to demonstrate to the Indian that Davy wasn't scared of the Creeks he answered by stating that he would post scouts in the woods to look out for any approaching Creeks patrols and if any should they happen to come near to the camp he would slit their throats and take the skin from their heads to make a new pair of moccasins for his wife. The Indian laughed, shook his head and turned to return to the camp.

The Life and Death of My Best Friend, Davy Crockett

From the distance he watched the Indian report back to the elders who shook their heads in his direction, then probably with a great deal of anxiousness they slowly trudged away to disappear inside their wigwams.

Davy understood the Cherokee's concerns, their situation was similar to Radciff's, and not wanting to cause agitation or risk of ruining the kindness they had offered he ordered everyone to saddle up and prepare for a hasty exit whilst being sure to cover over any tracks.

After a couple of hours, we set down with our muskets by our side to rest our bleary eyes, but only minutes had passed when a distant rustle of branches silenced the forest night creatures and shook us from our doze. Davy nudged me with his rifle to signal approaching danger, I did the same to the fella next to me and within seconds were we all leveling our weapons in the direction of the disturbance.

Arching low, holding our breaths we trod forwards quietly towards the swaying branches which confirmed of an unidentified approach, then squinting hard in the darkness we sured our aim towards the foliage and prepared for the worst.

Fortunately, our distress was allayed when we realized the approach was too clumsy and without care for it to be a Creek snooper. In unison, we released our sweaty palms from around the trigger when no more than four strides in front of a blockade of rifle barrels emerged a solitary Indian youth. Immediately he ceased his progress and with rigidity he flung his arms into the air to offer his surrender. Even in the almost pure blackness, we could tell this boy's face was not daubed with charcoal or masked with the Creeks red berry extract.

The Life and Death of My Best Friend, Davy Crockett

Using his barrel Davy beckoned him forth, however he hesitated and remained stiff until realising his fear we fully lowered our weapons. Slowly nearing towards us he pointed to our rear and mouthed words we could not understand. Whilst still keeping his hands held on high again he pointed in the direction we had just travelled.

We smiled to ease his agitation and parted to allow him to walk between us, all the time he continued to speak with rapidity and incomprehensible words which baffled us. We followed him a while trying to understand his converse, all the time he kept his eyes forward and his arms stretched aloft.

Davy now understanding he was a returning Cherokee sensed alarm and he suggested, to which we unanimously agreed that we should follow the boy in a bid to gain more intelligence. For two hours the boy sped through the gloomy woods unconcerned about the noise and disruption he caused whilst we, wide-eyed and flicking glances in all directions trailed several paces behind him.

Upon reaching the edge of the forest and the grassy plateau where we had not so long ago left the youth launched into a sprint and released an ear-piercing shrill which alarmed the lookouts that leaped bolt upright and reached for their rifles. With fear dictating their reactions and clawing at their hearts they aimed at the mysterious sprinter.

The Life and Death of My Best Friend, Davy Crockett

Noting the danger Davy heeled his horse into an immediate gallop to put himself between the Indian and the line of fire, and whilst shouting commands not to shoot he waved his arms frantically and leaped from the saddle to tackle the boy to the ground and prevent his imminent demise.

Without a clear shot, the confused scouts hesitated from squeezing on their triggers long enough for the now disturbed elders to assess the tense situation. Seeing Davy waving his arm in their direction and noticing the rest of us stationed at the edge of the forest they chattered for a short while before holding out their stretched arms to signal the lowering of the weapons.

Davy hauled the stunned youth upright and released him to walk safely towards his camp. Watching from distance we saw the elders and the young Indian chatter with much animation and animal-like body movements.

Eventually, the elderly warrior who had conversed with Davy earlier strode out with urgency to cross the field. Davy brushed off dirt and met the elder, here the Indian explained in his best, but almost incomprehensible English that the boy brought the intelligence of which the white man searched.

He confirmed to Davy that over one thousand Creek warriors had earlier that day crossed the Coosa River at a place called Ten Islands and they were on the march readying to attack whilst the army of General Jackson was camped further north of the river banks.

The Life and Death of My Best Friend, Davy Crockett

Davy returned to the group forthwith with the news and within a few minutes we had again bade the Cherokee's farewell and about turned to make the sixty-mile journey without delay knowing to warn of the planned butchery we must make the three-day journey in no more than one day.

En route, we stopped to nourish at Radcliff's homestead, but finding the shelter forsaken of everything useful we figured the general alarm had pervaded quickly throughout the region and every man of peace, whether white or Indian had fled in fear of their lives.

Although hungry and nearing exhaustion we dare not venture to replenish the warm ash of the deserted fire and ignite the flames to warm our skin and boil our brew, instead we chose to proceed our return without delay.

Guided by intermittent moonlight along paths trodden smooth by the feet of countless generations of Indians we traveled in single file, every nerve strained to the extreme in fear of ambush and slaughter. However it wasn't too long before the hindrance of the night gloom began to brighten by the gradual morning splendor and being able to see where we were planting our feet we managed to increase our strenuous tempo.

After about thirty miles we chanced upon another uninhabited cabin, however this time the owner had fled with such haste they had left behind fresh corn, cured meats, ample fresh water and grazing for our horses to feed upon. Too fatigued to talk we ate, drank and rested until aided by the warm afternoon sun slumber unintentionally crept upon us.

The Life and Death of My Best Friend, Davy Crockett

After the briefest of rest Davy roused and rallied us from our imaginings to set us out again with invigorated determination stating the path we were to tread would also lead us to the rendezvous point with Major Gibson.

We rode then dismounted to walk, rode again, dismounted again and paced the path with good and undisturbed haste reaching the meeting point just as the sun began to sink over the darkening mountain range. To our disappointment, there was no sign of Major Gibson and our comrades, and there was no indication they had returned to the rendezvous point.

The shrubbery and spindly grass were undisturbed and free from horse or man trampling. After a lengthy wait, Davy decided we could not delay withholding our news and so urged on with the importance and urgency our news demanded we made good time enabling Davy to report the intelligence to Colonel Coffee at Fort Deposit before midnight. As most of us headed for the well to fill the dipper with cold and refreshing water Davy hurried over to Colonel Coffee to deliver the important information.

Expecting the news to be received with graciousness and trepidation, to our dismay we saw through the tent opening Davy's dander ignite and his face flush as the Colonel dismissed his evidence and waved him away from his desk. Returning with his temper hotter than a pepper pot, Davy told us he that the vainglorious Colonel paid very little respect to his report claiming he could not pay any reverence to it because Davy was not an officer.

Due to the lack of respect, we discussed immediately withdrawing our services. Unfortunately, due to our extreme fatigue we all voted in favor of staying to rest up for the night.

The Life and Death of My Best Friend, Davy Crockett

Although our minds were buzzing like bees in a honey pot we all soon relinquished our thoughts of anger as we soon expired into peaceful nothingness, however our sleeping was soon disturbed and we were awoken before the cockerel when hollering from the outer side of the palisade notified us of commotion in the distance.

Clamoring for our rifles whilst wiping the sleepiness from our eyes relief soon prevailed upon us as charging into our view was Major Gibson and not the Creeks we dreaded.

Assembling to greet Major Gibson we listened to him convey to the embarrassed and fidgety Colonel Coffee the same report which Davy's mouth relayed the previous night.

Accepting every said fact he immediately raised the alarm and issued orders to fortify the entire perimeter with a line of ramparts, for it was general knowledge the Creeks had in the past displayed military abilities far superior to other tribes and their savage combat methods frequently enabled them to laugh scorn in the faces of the inept, axe-wielding backwoodsmen.

By judging one man's word against his rank and position in life clearly rankled Davy, and as we primed our weapons he gazed at Colonel Coffee he vowed to me that he would never respect any man who led himself by the wicked ways of self-promotion and discrimination.

Express riders were sent to Fayette while fifty miles away in the opposite direction General Jackson was urged to assemble his army and summon forth to aid our rescue immediately. I hasten to say, that we stood with shaking legs and trembling hands squinting out towards the line of distant

The Life and Death of My Best Friend, Davy Crockett

trees with our rifles levelled ready all day and night, but we did not volunteer to expose ourselves as one of Coffee's couriers.

By mid-noon on the second day our uneasy frailty within the fort was relived as emerging out of the woodland and marching forward with his usual characteristic energy, General Jackson led out over two thousand of his blistered-footed men.

After due rest and sustenance and considering the intelligence, the decision was made by our leader to send out an expedition of nine hundred men to attack and destroy a nearby Creeks camp whilst their warriors were some distance away navigating their advance north through the vast forests.

To successfully complete this massacre the army was instructed to head forty miles north and double cross the meandering Tennessee River, then head west until they reached the expanding streams at a place called Muscle Shoals, thus by taking this indirect route they would safely circumnavigate the mass warrior army.

Eager to escape the fort and leave the service of Colonel Coffee, Davy and I ignorantly volunteered for this mission, and at a place called Muscle Shoals we encountered our first difficulties. Although the river could be forded our crossing was hindered by a mass of rocks and boulders that lay beneath the fast-flowing waters, leading many of our horses to get their hooves entangled in the crevices and trying with all our might we could not disengage them.

The Life and Death of My Best Friend, Davy Crockett

Even the best capable swimmers and men with huge chests could not hold their breath long enough to pull free the exhausted horses and save them from the terrible slow perishment.

We knew throughout the long, fast paced trek that Indian scouts and runners had been watching our every step and reporting back to the elders the advance of their foes so with nervous yet excitable eagerness the General urged us onto the camp with an unrelenting pace until we eventually we reached our destination in Alabama, Black Warrior Creek camp.

To my great relief, with the news of the advancement, and planned attack the remaining Creeks had fled their homes at the last moment, leaving smoldering fires and supplies untouched.

The camp's huge size and structures impressed all who gazed upon it for many of the lodges were far more luxuriant than our own homes back in Tennessee and it seemed almost a sin to torch to the ground such master craftsmanship, but destroy we must and all dwellings of much labor and stocks and all food which we could not ourselves carry were burnt, for we needed no reminding these tasteful abodes belong to the savages who unmercifully raped, mutilated and skinned our own kin folk.

With the task duly completed, upon our exit back into the cover of dense woodland we feasted ourselves on their corn, beans, bean pulp, and what remained of their game as our rations had all been exhausted the previous day. Once content we again returned to their camp to ignite and destroy their luxuriant corn fields.

The Life and Death of My Best Friend, Davy Crockett

Bellows of smoke rising high and spreading wide for all to see for miles around denoted our destruction and our successful departure, we cared little for thoughts of Creek retaliation, for our belief at that time was for the complete inhalation of this tribe. This was the only solution for a long-term peace.

That day we walked a further fifteen miles and no sooner had we traversed one endless landscape of forests, inclines, rivers and ridges then another one would open up before us until eventually the prevailing darkness enforced our rest. By dawn, we had packed up camp and we were on the march again, but by noon we had again exhausted all of our supplies. A unit of nine hundred marching men commanded a huge amount of food and the miserly rations of which we were supplied were inadequate for us to complete the journey and the food salvaged from the Indian camp had lasted us less than one full day.

Tightening stomachs and parched throats began to lead discontentment and before too long grumbles of disorder alerted the General to fear that his men would break from the ranks to seek game.

Knowing they would be easy prey for ambush by the shadowing Creeks he agreed with his men that only a renowned hunter should be granted approval to leave the body of the unit, and without traveling too far distant, hunt for game they desperately required.

Davy volunteered for the task and all the men accepted his nomination and so armed with steely resolution, without any doubts he silently entered the dense and dim wilderness with a vigilant gaze which pierced rapidly in all directions.

The Life and Death of My Best Friend, Davy Crockett

Less than one hour later Davy rode passed the company of marching with a slain deer folded over his horse's mane. Whoopees and cheers erupted and followed him as he made his way to the head of the line. Hankering, men offered their coins and trade for the beast, many of them besieging him with offers that any normal man could not refuse, but Davy declined them all to ensure the unfortunate creature was skewered and roasted, to be fairly, albeit scantly shared amongst the men for them to mix into their beans, corn, berries and roots.

After supper and when I finished licking the grease from my bowl I asked Davy how he could be so generous and refuse such rewards for the game and he simply replied, 'I'd rather be a poor man for the rest of my life than profit from a fellow man's suffering. I may have an empty purse, but my heart is full, full of consolation which money cannot buy.'

His generosity was unquestionable and those who sat beside him that night thanked him for it. As we took to our bedrolls that night Davy confessed to me that he had been lucky that day and that he had been taught a valuable lesson. He admitted it wasn't him who had killed the deer for he stumbled across it not too long after he had entered the woods. He told me the deer had been killed by a noiseless arrow and he found it still warm and almost skinned. He knew the deer had been killed by an Indian and at first thought the Indian had fled upon hearing the Tennessean's approach.

It was only after he had dismounted to inspect the dead animal did he consider at that very second that another arrow might be pointing with deliberate aim at his own heart from the concealed Indian.

The Life and Death of My Best Friend, Davy Crockett

Rapidly scanning in all directions he could not see or hear anything so with a pulsating rapidity he hauled up the deer and made his escape all the time praying that he had spooked the Indian with his sudden appearance so much that the Indian had fled with panic deep into the backwoods. He mused that next time he may have no such luck and he vowed never again would he be so reckless. How I wished that many years later he would have abided by his promise.

Finally, before clamping our eyelids tight he added that his conscience tormented him for stealing the game killed by another hunter, albeit an Indian.

The meager ration did not satisfy the hungered and early the next day we came across a drove of swine that belonged to a Cherokee farmer and cramping empty stomachs dictated the army paid no respect to the private property and without hesitation, respect, or sympathy rifles pointed and executed the Cherokees livelihood.

Later that day we came across another detachment of the army and together we marched to Ten Islands on the Coosa River, and now with us being exposed in the center of hostile territory we were ordered to establish another fort which was named Fort Strother after one of our Captains.

The Life and Death of My Best Friend, Davy Crockett

Chapter 5 – The Slaughter and the baby

Several parties reconnoitered the unknown region for food and one small group returned with two captured Creeks. With torture applied the Indians informed the General that about two hundred Creeks had formed a camp no more than eight miles north of the fort and so immediate orders were issued for a large detachment of soldiers to be dispatched for a surprise nighttime attack. Absorbed with words from the Lord's book 'Rescue those who are being taken away to death, hold back those who stumbling to the slaughter' and eager to serve our county with honor, without duly considering the intent Davy and I fronted the volunteers who lined up for the reckoning.

At the end of a gun, the two captured cowardly and immoral Creeks led the way soundlessly through the meandering trails until a distant blaze could be viewed in the darkness ahead.

Spreading out in double file, our fighting men encircled the camp to ensure any attempted escape to warn others would be impossible. With our positions accomplished without raising any suspicions and the camp secured, we knelt silently in the cover of the foliage until the dim morning dawn cleared the way ahead for our attack whereupon our leaders of the mission signaled to each other with wolf whistles that we must commence the final approach. In single unity, we raised up from the grass and began our deliberate slow-paced, and silent advance. Unfortunately, less than a dozen or so strides had been taken when an uncontrolled and almighty war whoop bellowed out which in turn ignited instantaneous ear-piercing and neck-tingling yells from every tongue in the camp.

The Life and Death of My Best Friend, Davy Crockett

At that point, bile rose in my throat and my legs jittered so much that I struggled to keep my legs balanced and my rifle straight. I flicked a gaze at my side and I saw that Davy was also ashen, but his eyes were determinedly fixed on the enemy ahead and his rifle was leveled impeccably. I returned my eyes in the direction of the camp to see demonic Indians raging with fury on a charge towards us. I bit down hard on my teeth, braced all my muscles, and sured up my nerves to ensure my shot was discharged true.

Thunder blasted, swirling smoke bellowed, and lead struck down the doomed Indians, halting their aggressive bounding leaps and throwing them high and backward into the air. Those who were not ripped apart by shot and dispatched to hell feared another assailment of deadly bullets and turning away from the storm of lead they fled at wild speed back towards camp.

The villainous fear had instantly eliminated my shakes and releasing my own frenzied battle cry I followed the rest of my countrymen and charged forwards to hack down the wounded and repel the few, brave or stupid who continued with the futile attack. Caught in a fever which eliminated any compassion and all godly reckoning, indiscriminate butchery raged from the north, south, east and west to prevent any runners from making an escape.

Within a few minutes the Creeks knew the fight was lost and many of them dropped to the floor and curled into a tight ball in despair, other men more defiant and proud threw away their weapons and with puffed out chests and chins held high offered their surrender. Children screamed and women bound with papooses clasped their arms tightly around the knees and coattails of our soldiers and begged for mercy.

The Life and Death of My Best Friend, Davy Crockett

Davy, I and a few others began to remove the weapons from around the feet of the surrendered fighters and, amiably marking respect of their bravery with subtle nods, for convenience we urged them to form a group, however what we witnessed next vexed us both for the rest of our lives.

A group of about forty men, women and children in fear for their lives broke away from the main group of prisoners and fled into one of the largest tents. Being unarmed I believed they could cause us no harm, but poisoned by the will of the appalling revenger, which could possess the will of the meekest man during the midst of battle the majority of our men began to circle the tent, and hollered out threats to the helplessly trapped.

Pausing in brief hesitation our boys halted their advance on the tent and waited for orders. Unfortunately their considerations were soon expelled when an Indian girl of no more than waist height appeared at the tent opening. Maybe anguished by her innocent beauty or the anguish from her tears which flowed from her tragic eyes our men failed to notice and react when she raised a bow and quickly fixed an arrow upon the string. None of her approaching foes paid any attention to taking cover or protecting themselves, probably thinking the delicate girls shot would drop short of any target and land in the mud, however she had a powerful arm, and the arrow was released with a deadly force. Lieutenant Moore was the unlucky recipient of her lethal aim and the arrow plunged deep into the center of his chest instantly crumpling him to the soil. As the Moore screamed and writhed in agony about twenty shots tore the girl open and plunged her soul into oblivion.

The Life and Death of My Best Friend, Davy Crockett

Still infuriated by the unexpected death their Lieutenant, our boys which I say with revulsion quickly reloaded to release another inexorable blast of thunder and hail which tore through the canvass, flesh and bone.

I palmed my ears to dull the screams all the time watching Davy as he scurried from one man to the next, forlornly pleading with them to cease the executions. Without success, he leaped in front of the killers and clamped his hands on their shoulders to beg and besiege the older shooters to relent only to be carelessly brushed aside without concern. The vengeful murders continued and blast after blast erupted until a few of the men took torches the sides of the tent. It mattered not that the flames consumed the flesh of young or old, innocent or sinful, living or dead.

Unable to prevent our stomachs from heaving we fell to our knees and dropped our heads into our hands. We were unable to block out the agonizing screams of death and the smell of burning flesh as the fire raged to slowly cease all life.

Yet still the suffering and agony continued, an Indian boy crawled out of the furnace and some of the men took aim, but laughing at the poor youngster's torture they stopped from wasting another shot and simply watched him slowly emerge from the flames. His arm hung loose having been shattered by a bullet and blood oozed from a hole in his thigh, and although one or two may have pitied his demise no one stepped forth to end his suffering. The intense heat blistered his naked body and he began to fry, yet still he tried to crawl away in vain and not once did he utter a groan of pain as roasting to charcoal he eventually slumped and ceased all controlled movements.

The Life and Death of My Best Friend, Davy Crockett

The slaughter was horrific. Only five of our men were killed, yet over one hundred Indians lay massacred in the soil. Our victory was not celebrated by many and mainly with muted tongues and regretful thoughts we returned to Fort Strother.

Still many years later, in the tranquility of my slumber, I am haunted and saddened with remorse by the events of that terrible day, and as for my youthful compatriots on that morning who were void of all conscience, I hope that their maturity has now aligned their sympathy's and considerations, and they now all reflect with great sadness and they pray every night for forgiveness.

The following day volunteers were required to return to the camp to forage for supplies, I did not raise my arm nor did Davy. We could not return to the scene of death where half burnt bodies and mutilations were scattered as if a demon had unleashed the full force of hell had scorched the earth and indiscriminately executed men, women and children.

When the soldiers returned with carts of food, weapons, and blankets they also delivered into camp a baby, not more than three months old. The braggarts told General Jackson they had found the infant boy lying in the bosom of his dead mother, her arm still clinging to him tight.

The General took the baby to a captive Creek woman and asked them to feed it, but in defiance they replied through the interpreter 'You killed the child's parents, now you kill the child.' With anger blazing red upon his cheek, the General withdrew his sword and held the baby at arm's length with the point of his steel creasing its soft flabby skin.

The Life and Death of My Best Friend, Davy Crockett

Still, the women refused his demands and so the General, hollering that the Indian women were heathens that deserved to die swung his sword wilding in front of their faces, and then retreated to his tent with the baby under his arm. A few minutes later he summoned for a pitcher of sugar and water.

I had heard tales of General Jackson having traits of heroism and being extremely brutal and pitiless towards his enemy, however at that time, I was humbled by his act of compassion and years later learned that the Indian child named Lyncoyer survived the ordeal and was adopted by the General and his wife.

Although our skirmishers had returned from the Indian camp with a substantial bounty of supplies, starvation soon began to threaten our existence. The sparse surrounding wilderness afforded us no scope for hunting and very little in terms of foraging for wholesome vegetation.

Our huge army had devoured everything they could to survive including roots, bark and now the hide of the slaughtered cattle. In a weakening and pitiful condition we guarded against a retaliatory attack and waited for supplies to be delivered.

One afternoon Davy and I ventured beyond the palisade to hunt for much-needed game. We had snared a few rabbits and squirrels and were in the position of leveling our rifles upon a large bird when a rustling disturbed our target and seized our attention. We swung our rifles sideways and watched anxiously in the direction of the disturbance and just as our fat bird flew to survival an Indian broke through the foliage with careless haste only to be stopped when the barrels of our rifles prevented his progress.

The Life and Death of My Best Friend, Davy Crockett

Throwing his hands immediately in the direction of the blue yonder, through panted breaths he told us in excellent English that without delay he needed to speak with General Andrew Jackson. We relieved him of his bow, arrows, knife and axe and curious to his urgency, he intrigued us and we began to interrogate him. Unfortunately, mostly keeping his lips sealed tight he said his words were for the ears of General Jackson only, and he stubbornly refused to change his notion. With no obvious alternative, we returned to the fort with our meager haul hanging from our waists and the Indian tight against the end of both our barrels.

In the fort a great snoopiness overwhelmed us and delivering our prisoner to the General's tent we tried hard, but unsuccessfully to listen to the discourse. Refusing to disclose the intelligence he had received the General stomped out from his tent, indignantly barged through the eager gathering of curious soldiers and ordered the drummers to beat a summons to arms.

Even though it was close to sunset, the General ordered an immediate evacuation of all twelve hundred soldiers and eight hundred horses, nothing was to be left behind.

We marched at an unrelenting pace in a southern direction guided only by the giant silvery ball which shimmered against the sheer pitch from on high and with no knowledge of our destination, hungry and cold, we miserably speculated our prospects.

At daybreak we crossed the icy Coosa River towards Talladega and during the permitted break in which we tried to warm and dry ourselves Davy confessed to me that he had heard some of the officers proffering around the flames of a campfire.

The Life and Death of My Best Friend, Davy Crockett

He disclosed to me very quietly that the Indian originated from the Crow tribe and securing a hollowed out of a pigs head to cover his face as a disguise, he had crawled on his hands and knees and had managed to escape from the Creeks to inform General Jackson that a friendly tribe of Crow's living in the fort at Talladega were currently surrounded by the army of the Creeks.

The Creeks who numbered over one thousand warriors warned their captives if they did not lower the barricade and join the Creek army in the war against the white man they would destroy the fort, take many lives and steal all their provisions which were stocked high and needed to see out the coming winter.

The hostage Crow's asked for a few days to consider the hostile proposition and as soon as the request was granted they sent several messengers to inform General Jackson of the situation and entreat him to come to their immediate aid. I wasn't too sure which nerved me more, knowing we were marching out to battle or trudging on the secret mission with assumptions based on an Indian testimony.

By the time we reached the stronghold at Talladega we were exhausted, bone weary, blistered and mighty relieved to see no waiting Creeks intent on war. However cautiously, General Jackson divided his army into two units with orders for us to separate and circle in two groups around the Crow fort and rejoin around the blindside of the timber walls.

We were met with raucous cheers of joy from the friendly Crow's who patrolled along the parapets of the tall timbers, but their calls of elation in broken English failed to penetrate our cold ears.

The Life and Death of My Best Friend, Davy Crockett

Then to our dismay, we marched on beyond the fort to bunk up on the other side several hundred yards distance. No Creek warriors were to be seen, only dense surrounding woodland and a small meandering stream ahead of us.

The General ordered Major Russel to cautiously lead a small unit of men toward the stream and survey what lay in the wilderness beyond our view. Watching our maneuvers with careful dismay the Crow's still yelled and hollered, but now with the distance and our lack of understanding for the native tongue, we failed to comprehend their messages and it was only when a few of their braves scaled down the fort wall and threw themselves in front of the General did we finally figure their urgency for halting us from progressing any further towards the stream.

From a distance we watched the Indians remonstrate with General Jackson and it gave us a dilemma, whether to proceed and obey the orders or turn about to see what all the fuss was about. Whilst we debated our course of action with the Major a demonic scream from a hidden dip just a few rods from our position fixed our deliberations. Screaming with rage a huge force of Creeks sped forth without fear of injury or death and reacting almost as one we turned and ran as fast as we could to rejoin the main group of soldiers who, after the initial shock from the spine-chilling scream, now raised and fixed their rifles in our direction.

As the warriors continued in an unbridled sprint we dived into the dirt allowing our boys to release a volley of skull splitting and rib-cracking lead. Many of the leading assailants were felled instantly and the momentum of the charge was lost as the mass of slumped bodies at the feet of the swarming warriors hindered the speed at which they traveled.

The Life and Death of My Best Friend, Davy Crockett

We drew breath and sprung up from the ground to launch ourselves towards our main body of men, but again seeing a second line of troopers taking aim once more we again hit the ground to allow the projected missiles to whistle over our heads.

Now our view was blocked by eye-stinging powder smog and all we could do was withdraw our long blades and hold them rigidly in the direction of the on rushing devils. We did not have time to offer a prayer or ponder our future as within an instant, undeterred by their significant losses the axe-wielding maniacs burst through the smog to weld their fury upon us.

The hand-to-hand combat with axe, knives, clubs, pitch forks and rifle butts, lasted for only a few minutes because our troopers quickly encircled the hysterical Creeks to attack them from the rear with unchallenged repeated shots until they were almost annihilated, unfortunately our line that consisted of novice militia, scared youths and weak men who lacked the furiousness and energy to prevent some of the Indians from breaking free and making their escape in the woods.

The barbaric slaughter lasted but a few minutes and during the combat I received a long gash across the side of my neck which required a tincture and packing, but I do not recall how this injury was inflicted upon me nor do I recall my actions in the midst of the fury. My instincts ensured my survival, but my eyes and memory retained little visions of the hand-to-hand bloodshed.

I was not alone, Davy admitted to me whilst he was having a hand injury stitched and strapped the fighting also passed him by in a blur and he told me all he could remember was swinging his axe deep into an Indian's shoulder so hard that he could not pull it free from the bone.

The Life and Death of My Best Friend, Davy Crockett

In desperation, he was forced to hit the Indian so hard on the nose that he felt his knuckles implode and his skin split.

Luckily the Indian crumpled and Davy's stomping foot incapacitated him.

Our army was too big to rest in the small fort so we made camp against the northern palisade. Whilst we were fed and our wounds tended to, the Crow's delighted in removing their dead enemy from the field of terror.

Rations at Talladega were equally as scarce as at Fort Strother, and although we were fed generously with what the Crows could afford us we could not be issued with additional supplies to ensure our return.

The Life and Death of My Best Friend, Davy Crockett

Chapter 6 - Deserters

By the time we had Fort Strother in our sights, the hunger pangs had been dictating our thoughts for some time. Although the mission had been enormously successful in the destruction of the Creek army, we had consumed almost all our rations and we could not be afforded any additional provisions. Our clothes were worn thin and unsuitable for the cold harsh winter, our horses were now emancipated and feeble. We desperately suffered from malnutrition and again we faced death, although not from the weapons of our enemies, but from starvation and exposure to the freezing temperatures.

Discontentment and insubordination set, and talk of mutiny spread around the nightly campfire parleys. However, we were not traitors or cowards. Our unit of volunteers had served well over the sixty days for which we were enlisted to serve and so with the agreement of the whole unit, we decided it was time to leave the fort and return home for a short period to obtain much-needed sustenance, fresh horses and re-clad in more suitable winter wear.

Word of our planned departure soon spread and our leaders, furiously fearing a mass evacuation, forbid us to leave the camp. The General addressed us stating that when the news spread of our departure then many of the conscripted soldiers, who had also served their enlisted period, may choose to disband the fort endangering the lives of the remaining soldiers who would be exposed to the still huge Creek army.

The Life and Death of My Best Friend, Davy Crockett

He was an unyielding leader who would not consider our appeal, he made it clear his will must be obeyed at all times and being the most profane of all men he announced to all and swore to everything he held sacred that he would prevent the departure of even a single man.

We resented his uncompromising demands and considered ourselves enslaved, being driven like cattle until we were no longer useful. We had faithfully served out our term of service and we deserved to be discharged with honor.

The uneasy discontent and suspicion continued throughout the night and long heartfelt persuasions were debated around the camp until a huge division of different opinions existed. At first light the majority of Tennessee volunteers had decided resolutely they would leave camp and return home to revitalize, while the dejected conscripts confirmed there would be no mutiny and they had no option, but to stay and obey the General.

The news of our departure again soon spread to the General and within a few minutes he dispatched a sizable troop of his most entrusted men, armed with artillery, to block the bridge over the river preventing our crossing on the only homeward route.

With our appearance at the bridge the soldiers, who stood upon the exit of the crossing, and who only a few days earlier had fought alongside us cocked their rifles and fixed them aim in our direction whilst others hurriedly positioned and prepared the cannon for discharge. Standing defiantly, we swung our rifles from our shoulders, and showing the same determination, we flicked alarmed glances between our former allies and the cannon.

The Life and Death of My Best Friend, Davy Crockett

It was the first time that I'd ever seen a cannon and I had little to no knowledge of its dangers. If I had, I fear I would have turned and run.

The General stood on the back of a cart and used it as a platform to address the discontented malcontents, his demeanor, and haughtiness confirming to us that he considered us less than equal to his enlisted veterans. His eyes flickered spitefully along our frontages, hoping he could catch our eye to evince his unfaltering stance. However, most of us ignored his bait and focused our attention on the shooters who surrounded him. Silently we held firm, staring at the countenances of some fifty yards away and trying to judge if our white brethren would bring death upon their own kinfolk and neighbors. We knew in these times of danger the General had no alternative other than to retain his numbers of fighting men, but his outright refusal of our offer still niggled us, and our desperation for food directed us to this point of no return.

At length, with calm bellows of authoritative deliberation, he reiterated his persuasions, stating we must at once return to the camp and serve alongside the enlisted men until they exterminated the Creeks. He tried appealing to the blank and disillusioned assembly, stating no action would be taken against any man who about-faced and returned to camp. After a while, his face began to redden, his eyes bulged and tones of anger became evident as he realized his message had failed to invoke a change in our attitude.

Some of the men to our rear called for him to stand down and let us pass, then others began to heckle, which prompted him to react by hailing a tirade of threats associated normally with traitors which began to silence our friend's disgruntled moans.

The Life and Death of My Best Friend, Davy Crockett

Finally, he turned to soldiers about him and told them to load the cannon with grape for he would aim its muzzle upon the traitors and bring down any man, red or white who stepped forth upon the bridge.

Hesitant glances and worried concerns regarding the development were muttered, but an old timer with a semblance of death stepped forward and shouted. "We ain't your darn slaves!"

Davy, shoulder to shoulder with the silver bearded man then declared loudly. "We are coming through or we are going to hell, but either way we are not going back to that fort to wither and die!"

Unrest quickly spread and dispelled any doubts or considerations for remaining, so hauling up our meager belongings and draping our rifles over our shoulders to eliminate perceptive hostilities or agitation we stretched our necks, held our heads high, and with our chests expanded we followed Davy and the old fellow's lead to step upon the wooden planks of the bridge. Together we strutted like peacocks, for we were no cowards who sought organized disruption and desertion. We merely desired to collect our winter garments, fill our bellies, and exchange our horses before they died from malnutrition.

The line of rifles before us remained level and the General who stood behind the cannon shouted. "Return to the fort boys!"

We ignored his order and continued forward with stern resilience towards the foreboding grimaces until our chests met the steel barrier of obedient muskets. Eyes flickered nervously from face to face and sweat from fear trickled down foreheads and legs. Fingers and legs trembled, yet no one spoke and no one moved.

The Life and Death of My Best Friend, Davy Crockett

Davy leaned into the barrel which prevented his advance and we did the same, all pressing forwards and stoically holding our position even though the steel hurt our chests.

"Can you live with the ghosts of this night?" Davy said to his opposite, who only days earlier had been standing by his side as together they fought against the hellish savages.

There was no reply, just fixed stares and rigidity.

"Will you look your sons in the eye when you tell them you murdered brothers?" Davy slowly pressed his hand on the soldier's barrel.

"Let us pass friend." He applied pressure, and the rifle slanted towards the floor.

"We are not your enemy." He added.

Without waiting for the General's intervention, the soldier lowered his weapon and slightly tilting his head to acknowledge his gratitude Davy walked between the line of soldiers and the cannon.

Only footsteps and the gushing water below our feet could be heard as compassion spread and one by one the enlisted men lowered their arms and stepped aside to allow us to pass.

With shaky legs, jaws quivering, and some leaky bladders, we marched with haste passed the silent, but appalled General, his deliberate gaze penetrating deep into the inner consciousness of those who were unlucky enough to pass close him by.

The Life and Death of My Best Friend, Davy Crockett

With sighs of relief and expelled breaths of sorrow we ignored the curious temptation to glance back and marched at a pace without falter until we reached and entered the concealment of dense trees.

The extreme hunger and exhaustion continued as we trudged home It was so cold that our teeth no longer chattered and our faces reddened and wizened from the icy endless breeze. Although in fear of being ambushed we no longer held our rifles in readiness, our hands and toes were numb and useless due to the lack of suitable protection.

Along the way near Albertville, we encountered a reinforcement of sixty men who were enthusiastically traveling in the opposite direction. To our great relief, they had no knowledge of our reluctant disobedience and they fed us with a plentiful hot meal before waving farewell to meet their fates.

We were not hindered by any further struggles nor jeopardized by any of the Creek scouts and within a further few days we had arrived at Madison County where our unit could disband to travel their final few miles to their cabins around Huntsville, should they not be charcoal ruins by the bloody hands of the violating Creeks.

Earlier Davy had suggested that I should convalesce with him for a few days at Bean Creek due to my lodgings still being well over another week distant. Without any convincing, I accepted the offer and before the darkness closed, our fifth day of travel we were warming our extremities around the comfort of Polly's hot stove.

The Life and Death of My Best Friend, Davy Crockett

With much relief and tenderness, Davy was greeted at the doorway by clasping arms, tight long hugs, and joyous tears. For that juncture my heart and thoughts were hundreds of miles away for I imagined my lonely wife peering out day after day, longing for my return. Yearning to hold my dear Annabella, Polly noticed my melancholy, and she kindly enticed me into the family embrace which momentarily eased my pain and welcomed me generously back into the Crockett household.

We ate, slept, rested, and warmed repeatedly for the next few days, all the time our minds occupied with the promised return to the fort at Ten Islands.

Polly took our considerations badly, and she collapsed fever-like needing full bed rest until she managed to reconcile herself with the despairing prospect of loneliness once more. Whilst Davy tendered to her needs and comforts trying to strengthen her resolve, I labored on the duties which had been neglected whilst Davy had been away.

The usefulness pleased me and the work distracted my loneliness and yearnings for home. I sent a composition of words explaining to Anna I was of good sense and well, but with us planning only a brief respite I was unable to return home until the winter had thawed or the destruction of the Creeks had been successfully completed, whichever came the soonest.

With fat in our bellies, our aching limbs rested and blistered feet healed news began to reach the settlements that still many homes were being flamed and families massacred by the relentless and uncontrollable Creeks.

The Life and Death of My Best Friend, Davy Crockett

A meeting to plan our return was arranged near Huntsville, but many of the volunteers became angered when a declaration was read out upon the orders of General Jackson. His message was clear, enlistment for merely sixty days was considered insufficient for him to plan a comprehensive campaign to thoroughly eradicate the Creeks. Justly he demanded should volunteers engage to serve alongside him and his regulars then the minimum term for enlistments would now be for no less than six months.

Throughout the night a great debate ensued between those opposed and those agreeable to the new demands. At length, the disagreements were debated and by sunrise, no agreement or compromise had been reached, and so many of the men decided to permanently withdraw from active service and return home to defend their property in solitude if necessary.

Davy, I, and about twenty other of the locals concurred that if we returned home we would risk eventually being at the mercy of savages and we may forever regret not performing our duty when the balance of the war was in our favor.

I knew as I gathered, pelts, blankets, cured meats, dried fruit, and berries that the screams and wails from Polly as she faced the perilous prospect of facing a long and lonely winter with her youngsters would water my eyes and so as quickly as I could I departed to the barn to load up provisions suitable for the cold season on our pack horse and leave Davy with the privacy he required for such a distressing departure. Although the pleas from Polly wrenched deep within my chest my conscience and thoughts were occupied with the trauma my woman also faced alone and over two hundred miles away.

The Life and Death of My Best Friend, Davy Crockett

With a sigh and a wipe of the eyes I waited for Davy to appear in the doorway. With detaining arms still locked about his neck and tears dripping onto his buck skin jackets he gently tried to release Polly's grip. However, all his tender efforts failed and Polly still pleading and screaming for him to remain was dragged across the muddy coloured snow to his mount. He did not use brute force nor violence to detach his pitiful wife, stern words and patience followed by tender promises led to her eventual submission and obedience.

Without a word, I heeled away to offer my fractured friend and his inconsolable wife one last private moment before the withdrawal, but a glance over my shoulder struck me with a lasting picture of heartbroken desperation when I saw Davy turn his back on the cabin and Polly crumple into the snow at the feet of his horse with her two small boys on their knees at her side.

As the fresh snow crunched under our departing hooves Polly screamed. "Go with god my husband. Go with god and I'll pray for your safe return."

I didn't need to look at Davy to know he was bleary-eyed and pained deep within, and so ahead I kept my eyes knowing the sacrifice had to be made if the territory was to be rid of senseless pillaging and death.

The Life and Death of My Best Friend, Davy Crockett

Chapter 7 – The Journey South

Silence often set between us for long periods and we spoke very little on the return to camp, even when we joined the rest of the volunteers at the fork in the path all congenial words were absent as all the men in the group had made the same difficult decision and all their minds were still occupied with the raw and tender farewells instead of a fanfare of music, cheers and a flag waving as it should be on such occasions.

When we reached Fort Strother, our brothers who greeted us had little enough energy to raise their heads and force a smile. Almost unrecognizable skeletons, dressed in rags and starved almost to death, leaned spiritless against their lookout posts whilst others slumbered exposed to the deathly freezing blizzards in a semi-conscious stupor.

We soon discovered the supply boats had failed to deliver provisions and as conditions worsened some of the regular troops escaped the fort in an effort to follow us however, they were soon captured and to prevent further desertions orders were issued by General Jackson for them to be executed. Just beyond the walls and below the frozen surface, their bodies had been laid alongside another seventy who had starved to death or met their demise at the end of a sneaky coward's arrow.

Still, obliging by our bond we signed up for the required six months and we were immediately assigned to a group of scouts with orders to ride out and join up with General Jackson, who had a few days earlier set out with over one thousand men on an expedition in a south-westerly direction.

The Life and Death of My Best Friend, Davy Crockett

And so, after leaving behind what supplies we could afford to offer, we rode with great speed in fear of being bushwhacked by a large party of Creeks through the silent and snowy mudded trails that threaded the vast solitudes of woodlands and by late January we reported into the General at a place on the Tallapoosa River called Horse Shoe Bend.

Although we saw many hoof prints in the snow and we rode through areas with evidence of Creek activity we had nothing to report to the General, which irritated his already unwelcoming demeanor.

That night we camped in a large dip which surrounded by dense trunks provided us protection from the continuous icy gusts for the first time in over two weeks. Campfires were quickly ignited and supper prepared whilst patrols were positioned carefully around the perimeter and within the forest to warn us of any cowardly attacks.

Wrapping ourselves in blankets and bedding down within a pile of withered leaves we dozed for the first time in many weeks with the security of armed numbers about us. We were well accustomed to resting whilst subconsciously listening to the often alarming nightly critters, however on this our first evening within a huge camp our confidence was misguided and it was not the screams of the wildlife which startled us, but the flash and thunder of shot. Noiselessly some Indians had crept upon us from behind the cover of the wide trunks and having slashed the throats of our sentinels and being protected by the impregnable darkness, unchallenged they released volley after volley of destruction in our direction.

The Life and Death of My Best Friend, Davy Crockett

A couple of our fellas scrambled to douse the fires, but exposed by their silhouettes Indian lead immediately tore them down. With no warriors to be seen, only the flash of their rifles, and surrounded with all routes of escape blocked, we had no option than to stay down low and return fire the best we could in the direction of the momentary flashes. In the distance, we heard the doomed screams of some of our lookouts who were trying to flee to save themselves from their certain death. Some of them had returned to fight only to find themselves being not only attacked by the Creeks but also by ourselves, as in the chaos and confusion we mistakenly fired upon them.

Thuds, splatters, and screams erupted all around us as projectiles of lead and arrow penetrated deep into trees, mud, bone, and flesh. The deathly hail continued for several hours until the early daylight began to illuminate our foe in the final vestiges of the darkness.

Aware their advantage was slowly decreasing, they strategically dispersed deep into the shadows cast by the sky reaching timber shafts and slowly the attack ceased and our retaliatory fire proved useless.

Being careful not to raise our heads too fast we stretched up with considerable stiffness and soreness of our backs, necks, and fingers to check upon the condition of our comrades. Many were injured, a dozen lay dead, and three more slowly exhaled their final breaths.

We traced trails of blood in the snow hoping to find the bodies of our foes, but we only found shattered wood and the scalped heads of our lookouts.

The Life and Death of My Best Friend, Davy Crockett

General Jackson ordered a funeral pyre and we said goodbye to our brothers as they perished in the flames preventing the Indians from returning to collect war trophies such as teeth, scalps, and fingers, we constructed several sleighs to drag our incapacitated braves who suffered intolerably from the cowardly attack over the rough and narrow snowy trails.

During this period, in which we endeavored to track the Indians, Davy became hugely popular with the troops as a result of his natural optimism and humorous nature which raised the moral of the sullen and the injured. His instinctive tongue for providing analogies often resulted in unexpected and much-needed humor.

He was warmly greeted by whomever he rubbed shoulders with and come nightfall everyone knew which campfire he was squatted around because of the bursts of laughter and the merriment. His joviality was equaled by his good nature, thoughtfulness, and kindness of heart, and he was often sought out for his opinion in all matters. He was blessed with a strong memory that never seemed to fail him and during the small talk, he could enquire to the wellbeing of the soldier's wives and children by reciting their names.

He had an inexhaustible consideration for others and he would often go hungry by feeding the more needy and he would gladly shiver at night because without hesitation he had wrapped his own blanket around the shoulders of the vulnerable. Vanity did not appeal to him and he did not take merit or later take rewards for his oblations as within his characteristics he was gifted with the rarest of all qualities, for he did not judge, and although he never considered anyone as his superior he did not deem himself to be better than anyone else.

The Life and Death of My Best Friend, Davy Crockett

He considered all men equal and he would not allow any kind of violation to alter his principles or morals.

Although of an equal build to most men he stood out from the ever-present crowd who trailed his every step. His character and language was crude and colorful, he was bright and bold as is black to white and day to night, yet he was so humble that he would never swank or look down on anyone with condescension.

Often our leaders including the General would seek him out for accompaniment, share their considerations, and listen to his point of view for his knowledge of the lands, the natives, and his survival skills which exceeded any other man within the army.

He became noted for his courage only a few days after the attack when it was necessary for us to cross a wide and exposed creek. Unbeknown to us, our scout's vigilance had failed them and they did not identify the enemy that lay in wait for us behind in a line of trees which grew on a steep ridge on the opposite side of the river. When approximately half of our men were waist-deep in the midst of the water, the Creeks exposed themselves just enough to open up an unopposed assault of rapid rifle and bow fire upon the powerless men below.

Bullets and arrowheads rained down on the defenseless troops who, with panicky splashing had no alternative, but to wade onwards towards the bank knowing they would still find no protection from the torrent of deadly missiles.

The Life and Death of My Best Friend, Davy Crockett

The water turned purple and death wails and the screams of wounded men and horses reverberated far and wide over the winter wonderland that only minutes earlier was perceived as a tranquil and peaceful utopia far from the gates of hell.

The soldiers who frantically made the crossing found no mercy from their assailants positioned on the high bank. Stranded on the slippery steep bank of the wide river without weapons or weapons rendered useless by the icy water, they scrambled as low as they could in the snow-laden long grass. Those in distress in the middle of the flowing water found themselves easy targets, too far traveled to return, they bobbed and ducked hopelessly as about them unbaiting missiles of slaughter took lives with adroitness.

Davy led our group to the bank without losing many casualties, but it was obvious even in this darkest of times that there would be no relenting from the slaughter. So pulling free his axe he expelled a mighty war cry and without any consideration for danger, sped out from the blooded snow to charge toward the enemy on the slope.

With our desperation and survival instincts overpowering our fears, doubts, and hesitations, our entire unit followed Davy's lead and clambered the bank with reckless and desperate speed until we were charging directly toward the hostiles. Many others who now also made it across the river to our rear soon followed us and before we had reached the edge of the trees the cowardly Indians turned and fled into the labyrinth of protective timber.

The Life and Death of My Best Friend, Davy Crockett

The interruption and distraction of the charge enabled General Jackson to quickly get the remainder of his men over the river and set up a defense should any of the Creeks decide to return and engage in further warfare, as for Davy and the other brave Indian repellers, once the frantic beat of desperation calmed and the realization of the danger they had exposed themselves took set in their bodies quickly fatigued and they crumples at the edge for the forest, breathless and senseless with their hearts pounding and their limbs quivering from the impulsive charge.

Panting heavily we concentrated deep into the forest searching for signs of movement, but the odd swaying branch did not tempt us into stepping towards our suicide. Instead, we calmly held the post whilst behind us a defensive position was set up.

After a short while of calm, carefully our soldiers hauled the bleeding and the grave out of the snow and waded back into the icy waters to drag some of the lifeless out from the water, sadly many who perished in the icy flow could not be retrieved as in their final moment of decline the strong currents had dragged them away with as much ease as the Indians had taken their lives.

We lost many friends that afternoon, and the ambush was a huge embarrassment for the General. With his tail whipped and raging from humiliation, our advance was over and as soon as the funeral pyres had finished their business we departed the blood-stained slope and sought refuge in the nearest camp, Fort Williams at Cedar Creek.

The Life and Death of My Best Friend, Davy Crockett

Our next few months of enlistment dragged by with tedious routines of hunting, scouting, and keeping watch over the woodlands that surrounded our small fort. Frustrated and incensed by his failure, General Jackson's irritable mood was evident for all who served under him to witness as he impatiently waited for an opportunity for retribution.

The windy days and ice-cold nights passed exasperatingly slow as we waited for detachments to bring us favored news of intelligence regarding the happenstance of the devilish Creek army. Unfortunately, we were out hunting and two days solid walk from the fort when the news finally arrived in March, and by the time we returned to the fort our irked leader had ordered a hasty dispatch, calling all able men to arms and leaving the fort almost dissolute. We were informed that our scouts had informed the General that the vast Creek army had been located on the banks of the Tallapoosa River at Tehopeka and unable to contain his wrath, and with revenge preceding any strategy or reasoning he had immediately ordered the withdrawal of everyman who could walk and carry a gun.

Forbidden to leave and catch up with our advancing army, our small party of hunters were not allowed to travel and we were given strict orders to defend the walls against any stray hostiles who saw the easy opportunity for a raid. Dejectedly we loitered on the walls and stared hour after hour at uninhabited surrounding forests.

Monotony greeted us daily and so dull was our occupation we wasted days upon days just cowering under tarpaulins and skins to protect our inactive bodies from the constant rain and chilling wind. Occasionally we studied old news pamphlets which had been left behind to scatter in the wind. These reports detailed the aggression being applied by Britain and the violations of American rights.

The Life and Death of My Best Friend, Davy Crockett

Davy considered the dispute a matter of honor and he stated if called upon he would volunteer to uphold our American rights as his father had years earlier.

On a rotation basis we paired up to hunt for game, but whilst the exercise rid us of boredom in the damp and muddy wilds our long hours of stalking and tracking provided us with scant rewards.

It was two weeks or so later that a dispatch rider brought us the comforting news we had been nervously waiting to hear. He confirmed that the sudden appearance of Jackson's army had surprised and panicked the savages, and unprepared for a sudden attack they retreated hastily to a Creek village on Horse Shoe Bend. The lay of the land and loop of the river gave our General the advantage and an opportunity to trap the Creeks for to their sides and rear was the Tallapoosa River and to their front was an unprotected incline of grass. Quickly the General split his troops to form a line along the banks of the river to surround the village and prevent any attempt of escape. The thought of exterminating the fleeing Creeks whilst stranded in deep fast-flowing water seemed fitting and ironic the General had mused to his officers.

The chiefs tried to negotiate a peaceful surrender, but unyielding and unwilling to listen to compromise or terms for peace, General Jackson ordered with devilish amusement a barrage of cannon blasts upon their wooden erected fortifications stating that justice must and will be served.

The destructive cannonade continued for over two hours and the annihilation exposed the remaining and overwhelmed Indians to frontal attack. Over one thousand men with bayonets fixed charged down the slope and into the camp to slaughter indiscriminately all living beings.

The Life and Death of My Best Friend, Davy Crockett

Across the river, the soldiers heard the excited screams of their comrades and they saw the attack and unable to contain their lust for Indian blood they lunged into the water and crossed quickly to cut down any escapees. The awful massacre continued for over another two hours until almost every Indian had perished and the few wounded who remained were utterly dispirited and void of all threat.

When the General returned to the fort almost unscathed we joyously thought our conscript would be terminated and we would be relived our of duties enabling us to return home to our lonely loved ones, however our illusionary dreams were soon shattered and we were disheartened once more when news reached the camp that a substantial force of Creeks had not been in the camp at Horse Shoe Bend and they had fled to Florida to be protected, fed and armed by an invading British army which had landed at Apalachicola with a force of over three hundred men.

During this unexpected period of inactivity, we listened to first-hand accounts of the slaughter at Horse Shoe Bend by veterans of the battle. With queasy stomachs, we sat around the campfires with sickening astonishment as tales were passed from lips to ears detailing and glorifying the barbarity we had previously thought only existed within the behaviors of the red man. Souvenirs of ears, fingers, scalps, and skin were produced and gloated over as if the soldiers had been rewarded with precious treasures, we learnt that the General ordered for the noses to be cut from the dead so at a later opportunity they could count the number of Creek casualties.

The Life and Death of My Best Friend, Davy Crockett

Davy asked one of the old timers why he had performed such an abhorrent act on the dead and without a care for his judgment he replied, "Fracture for fracture, eye for an eye, tooth for a tooth, whatever injury the red skin have given to a person it shall be given back to them."

Another soldier added. "The butcherers slayed my brother, his wife, and their two little boys. I was poisoned by battle blood and the devil within me asserted a retribution that could not be stopped."

After that, we distanced ourselves from many of the soldiers and we waited for our orders. Several days later General Jackson quelled the uneasy restlessness by electing to make a rousing speech explaining the situation and promising to descend upon Florida with force and full intentions of terminating all the remaining savages and end the war by beating the British army at the same time. He announced that he was awaiting approval for the mission from the President in Washington which he expected would take a couple of weeks, therefore all volunteers could return home for respite until the call of war against the Creeks and their British allies warranted them once more.

The Life and Death of My Best Friend, Davy Crockett

Chapter 8- Death and Cowardice

Whilst Davy faced another tearful remonstration from Polly, due to the news of another impending departure I returned home to Greene County to unexpectedly find my cabin empty and homestead in ruin. Upon visiting my neighbor I was given the terrible news that Anna had been taken away from this world by God's angels after she contracted bilious fever. Consumed by grief for the loss of the woman I should have never left, a sense of failure, regret, and self-incrimination flooded my thoughts. 'I should have been kinder to her. I ought to have treated her with more respect and not left her for so long' Guilt overwhelmed and dictated my every thought. 'I should never have left her. I should have been at home to care for her throughout the cruel hours of her lonely misery.' I could do nothing, but repeat my regretful sorrow and blame myself for her premature demise whilst I had abandoned her to selfishly seek glory. I tried words of consolation, repeating that I was obliging my duties, but they all failed to relieve my guilt. I tried justifying my actions with selfish persuasion, 'I needed to protect my wife and property from the terror of the forest devils.' It was everyone's fault except my own, I cursed the Lord, the Devil, the Creeks, General Jackson, and Davy Crockett.'

No matter what antidote I administered nothing eased my selfishness and every night in my brief periods of slumber I was tormented by my despondent conscious reminding me of my deplorable failure.

Three weeks later I received the departure call, but there was one last farewell I could not let pass. I rode down the spruce-splitting path that led to the graveyard at the edge of town and slid down from leather to kneel beside the new marker less grave.

The Life and Death of My Best Friend, Davy Crockett

With my eyes filling with the sting of tears, I kissed the cold sodden grass and whispered, "Forgive me. Forgive me for failing you."

I rendezvoused with Davy and a handful of volunteers at Peaks Cave and we fixed a plan to head south and intersect with General Jackson's army at Walnut as they marched south towards Florida.

He profoundly offered his consolations regarding the passing of Anna, but my tale of woe did not seem to increase his conscience or concern regarding the welfare of Polly and his children, for all the considerations and the kindness he often granted to others he seemed to contain a darker impassive sense of indifference towards the affection he placed upon his own family. This flaw would never leave him.

As with his nature and statute, often without any violation, his redress for occupying any doubts or concerns for leaving his family in awful solitude in the deep wilderness was to rouse himself with the fascination and chivalry of fighting and his overriding pursuit and love for pure adventure, this time his lure was for fighting the British.

Without respite we trekked towards the northern frontiers of Alabama where we were disappointedly informed the army of General Jackson's two thousand men was two days ride ahead of us. Without rest or nourishment, we urged on and eventually, we happened upon Major Russel and his band of two hundred veterans who had been assigned to muster reinforcements.

The Life and Death of My Best Friend, Davy Crockett

Together we did our uppermost to catch up with the prodigious army and we moved forth through Chickasaw and Choctaw nations without hindrance or molestation, but our rapidity across the various and vast landscapes did not reward us with the anticipated fight.

Jackson's army reached its destination unhindered only a few hours ahead of us, but seeing they were vastly outnumbered the British wisely fled to their ships and quickly spread their sails to safety, whilst the Creeks avoided Jackson's fury by slipping away under the cover of darkness.

Failure to gain further revenge on the Creeks for the river massacre still irritated the General and so when we arrived with Major Russel he spilt the army into two detachments, he was to lead an attack on the British at Mobile where he anticipated their ships would dock for supplies and we were to accompany Major Russel and pursue the Creeks until we had annihilated them completely.

Upon our return through Indian territories, approximately one hundred and eighty Chickasaw and Choctaw paid an unexpected visit to us to proclaim their hatred of the Creeks and to request permission to join us in the pursuit of their enemy. With their offer for support applauded and granted for the next two weeks we continued on the trail of the Creeks, who being fleet of foot always managed to keep two days ahead of our relentless pace, and so when we neared Fort Strother it was agreed that we should dispatched eight miles north to the Creek camp we had attacked a few months earlier with the objective of hunting down any stray cattle which may have returned to the area after the slaughter.

The Life and Death of My Best Friend, Davy Crockett

The sorrow that beset my upon eyes from the charcoaled ruins, remnants of clothing, and scattered bones were soon lifted when a hollering from the distance confirmed the cattle which had been spooked and fled when the firing erupted had indeed returned to graze. We gave chase and a few bullets ensured that evening there would much-needed feasting, and after convalescing for a short while and rummaging through the rotting destruction we moved on with our haul, and by dusk we reached Fort Strother where we found our luck had not yet expired. A barge laden with supplies of coffee, sugar, and the finest of everything or the worst, depending upon your scruples, had docked only a short while ago.

The spectacle that presented itself that night was unrestrained and spectacular. After months of living on scraps, berries, roots, and river water around illuminating campfires soldiers, scouts, Chickasaw and Choctaw feasted on roasted quarters of beef that turned on enormous spits and they drank concoctions of mind-poisoning spirits.

Davy and I ate and drank until our insides hurt and our eyes blurred, but mainly we laid with our backs well-padded and feet raised as near to the flames as we could withstand, all the time watching the exhibition of hilarity and frivolity. As the liquor's potency began to dictate the activities, fiddlers played, soldiers stuttered and stamped on duckboards, and the naked, but magnificently painted warriors performed trance-inducing chants equaled with convulsive dances around the high-reaching flames.

Never before had our eyes witnessed, nor could we have ever imagined such a sight. Colorful feathered plumes and fringed leggings swaying as the carousing of echoing drunk chants and delirious cries blended into the perplexing clamor of unrefined festivities.

The Life and Death of My Best Friend, Davy Crockett

Even now, I believe this almost uninhabited expanse of woodlands on the banks of the Alabama had never and will never again reverberate with such a vibrant cacophony as executed by this great carousal.

That night I observed a change in Davy, a glint shone bright in his pupils and an incarnation emerged which confirmed to me that his soul could only be satisfied by the adventures born out of the savage wilderness and that life at home would seem in comparison too spiritless and simple to be endured.

He spoke at length of perilous adventures which rewarded with a bounty of satisfaction that money and wealth could not provide. I knew it there and then for Davy, there would be no long-term return and faithfulness to the life of a cultivator and an animal breeder.

The following morning after shaking off a cloudy mind and a drum-beating brain with several mugs of steaming hot coffee, along with fourteen others we were given orders to accompany Major Russel, and the buzzed friendly Indians across the Alabama currents to scout the whereabouts of the disbanded Creeks.

The Chickasaw pressed opinions that the Creeks would have by now split into several smaller groups and chasing them with a huge unit of men across hundreds of acres of swampy forests would be ineffective and they volunteered to leave the force of the army to conduct their own pursuit.

Passing judgment begrudgingly through gritted teeth, no doubt fearing the Chickasaw sought out the glory for eliminating the remainder of the Creeks, the Major approved the Indian's request under the condition that a unit of Tennesseans accompanied them.

The Life and Death of My Best Friend, Davy Crockett

Not far into the expedition, we came upon a spot where the winding river had burst over its banks and flooded the plain. The vastness of the overflow spread as far as we could see across the undulating meadows and woodlands. After testing the depth for several yards against protruding trees the notion was agreed for us to wade through the cold expanse rather than wasting days on a detour circumnavigating flood.

Hours passed slowly as armpit deep with numbed legs and feet we waded through the swirling and exhausting currents. Twelve monotonous and grueling hours had passed by before we finally gained solid ground where we hastily erected huge fires to dry our clothes, equipment, and thoroughly warm our crinkled blanched skin and marrow.

The following morning we traversed very cautiously approximately another six miles alongside the river only halting when we saw a small plume of smoke. Ensuring we were not detected we concealed ourselves within the thicket to watch from distance the source of the smoke. To our disappointment on a small island in the center of the swollen river were just two wigwams, three Creek men, two squaws, and four small children. Unable and unwilling to risk crossing the river we watched the Creeks conduct their affairs, the children played with beads, the women ground roots and the men smoked and chattered around the fire.

After several minutes of watching this tedium two of the Creek men dragged a canoe to the edge of the water and armed with only bows and arrows, they paddled out yonder in the opposite direction of our squat.

The Chickasaw chief, his interpreter, and the Major debated at length our next course of action. My understandings convinced me the Major wanted to abandon our position and move onward leaving the family at peace.

The Life and Death of My Best Friend, Davy Crockett

He believed these Creeks, being bereft of numbers and only armed with bow and spear could not have been a part of or involved in the tribal wars. The Chickasaw Chief however, remonstrated these Creeks were still the enemy and it was against all the principles they held close to their hearts not to attack. Never fully trusting the Chickasaw Chief, fearing treachery and being vastly outnumbered by the natives the Major yielded to the Chief demands that the two men should be captured and interrogated under the condition the Chickasaw warriors must cause the two Creek hunters any harm.

An assembly of twenty Chickasaw and four soldiers which included Davy and I were painted with striking war paint and dispatched to track and capture for questioning the huntsmen.

After a couple of hours of careful searching, crunching ahead in the foliage confirmed we had successfully crept up on the two redskin's whilst their minds concentrated on their hunt for food. With fleeting light steps and speed the Chickasaw warriors had rounded the two hunters and cut them down in a hail of arrows which fleetingly hissed through the silence. Being unprepared for the merciless attack we could not intervene nor divert our rigid eyes from the sickening butchery which occurred next.

Without indecision, a couple of the savages next lunged forth to beat the skulls of the dead with the butts of their rifles. The thud of wood cracking against bone rasped in my ears and my stomach heaved. Such was the relentless force of the savagery that the crazed blows broke and split open one of the rifle butts. I tried to divert my eyes, but a firm hand gripped the back of my neck and held my face forward.

The Life and Death of My Best Friend, Davy Crockett

I flicked my eyes sideways and saw my three soldier colleagues also being held by two Chickasaw, their skin ashen, eyes bulging wide and every muscle perfectly rigid both with fear and disgust.

After the barbarism had finished with the beheading and scalping of the limp and bloodied bodies we were released to drop down on our knees, then trembling with disbelief we watched as one of the Chickasaw attached a rope to each of the heads and swung them from an overhanging branch. Once the heads were swinging the Chief took a loose branch and, using it as a baton, he lunged forward to whack the heads as hard as he could. Then, grinning with satisfaction, he passed on the wood and each Indian took it in turns to inflict more violence on their dead enemy. With the heads still swinging and blood spraying far to splatter the barks and grass crimson, the Chief and his interpreter approached us nervous gathered white folk. He held out the baton and through singular words of English, he informed us we should also beat the mutilated heads with a severe blow because if we did not, it would bring dishonor upon his brave men.

The Chief sensed our revulsion and silent objections and he signaled a knowing glance to his assassins, who drew their blades and closed in tight around us. Davy sprang forward and pushed one of the outstretched blades aside, then without hesitation, he reached out for the baton. Pushing the Chief aside with the flat of his palm, with speed he swung the wood and cracked it against the pulpy head. Once the act was done to the Chief's satisfaction he wiped a spray of blood from his face and turning towards us he held out the club. To live we knew that we must reluctantly all complete the vile ritual.

The Life and Death of My Best Friend, Davy Crockett

In a sickening trancelike state, we returned to camp in half the time of the outward journey, no words were spoken and no comradery executed. We distanced ourselves from the brutes keeping alert as we moved fast.

Another heated debate ensued between the Major and Chickasaw leader. Our formidable and unfearing Major accused the Chief of betrayal for disobeying orders which resulted in another standoff and difference of opinions.

 The Major wanted to leave the small camp, without warriors, they were not a threat he argued, but the Chief remained stubborn stating that walking away from any enemy was a sign of unacceptable cowardice and it dishonored the souls in the sky who had sacrificed their lives to the hands their foe.

The Chief's irritation at the Major's attitude and disapproval was obvious to all, tension and agitation nerved us all and slowly the Chickasaw warriors gathered about us with axes and spears gripped tight.

The Major remonstrated again that this Creek family were not warriors and they had been camped here for a while therefore they could not be part of the attacks on either their white or red neighbor.

Beads of sweat on the Major's brow eventually betrayed his resolute notion and with a doleful conceding nod he turned away from the fierce glare of the Chief to end his objections and pleas for humanity.

The uncomfortable enclosure of bodies around us drew back and fragrant fresh pine replaced the fetid stink of the unkempt warriors. Then with a hearty sigh, we watched from a distance the Chief and a dozen of his murderers take the Creeks canoe and paddle across to the small camp.

The Life and Death of My Best Friend, Davy Crockett

At first, the tragic family in the peaceful camp had no concept of what had happened to their men and it was only when the canoe near the island edge did they became aware of the Chickasaw. The squaws immediately gathered their children and with their arms locked tight around them, they fled inside the wigwams.

The solitary male, knowing his end was approaching fast stood erect with his arms defiantly folded across his chest and his eyes held unnervingly on the approaching enemy. He lifted his face towards the sky, stretched both hands upwards, and released a call to his gods in the clouds, then without resistance, he was escorted at the end of a spear towards the canoe.

Walking tall and proud he accepted his fate, unlike the screaming women and children who were violently hauled and dragged frantically by their pigtails to the water's edge.

Helpless and sickened we stood and regretfully watched the families of the Creek cross the water and disappear into the forest. Torturous and slowly we listened to their pleas and screams dim until finally silence peacefully beset.

Although concealed from the brightness by the tall overhanging trees, our weather-beaten faces paled and our hearts pounded knowing the family's fate consisted of an inhumane ceremony of evil barbarism, but unable to intervene for fear of our own demise we walked dejected on. None of us spoke, our eyes fixed only on the path at our feet knowing how it felt to be a coward.

The Life and Death of My Best Friend, Davy Crockett

Concerned by the events and conscious of deceit and treachery Major Russel did not wait for the Chief to return and instead of permitting the scouts to lead the advance, he purposefully led the way for another thirty miles until he found a suitable spot to make camp on the bank of the River Conecuh. We knew it wouldn't be long before our satanic allies settled beside us and as the darkness began to shroud and restrict our view the Chickasaw Chief entered our camp to demand the attention of our Major.

The Chief claimed one of the Creek women in her weakness pleaded for her baby to be spared from death and she had information regarding the location of a Creek warrior settlement. With our food almost exhausted and scarce game to be hunted Major Russel informed the Chief it would not be prudent to attack the camp until the soldiers and his warriors had been invigorated with fresh supplies. With a disgruntled agreement, the Chief agreed to the Major's plan of deploying Davy to paddle downstream twenty miles or so in the canoe until he reached the supply camp which was commanded by Colonel Blue.

Davy was to inform the Colonel of Major Russel's intention to ascend the Conecuh and attack the large army of Creek warriors. Davy was to request that Colonel Blue should dispatch river boats immediately with reinforcements and supplies.

Davy wasted no time navigating his route along the wild and windy swells and he completed his journey in just over six hours without incident, but the following evening he returned to camp with just a stern rebuttal. Colonel Blue's objection stated there was evidence that the Creeks encampment consisted of only a few none hostile and inoffensive families who were no threat.

The Life and Death of My Best Friend, Davy Crockett

The Colonel's scouts had informed him there were only half a dozen wigwams providing shelter for half-starved women, children and old men. He deemed it unwise to send reinforcements and valuable supplies just to enable an attack of desolation and woe to such a few humble homes and he counteracted the request with orders of his own.

Now fearing starvation and betrayal by the Chickasaw, Major Russel reluctantly conceded the mission's objectives and at first light issued orders for our detachment to march along the banks to join the main body of Colonel Blue's troops at a rendezvous point called Millers Landing.

That night Davy told me he was relieved, and glad Major Russel gave him orders to leave camp. He said he shivered now knowing that he did not originally perceive danger from the Chickasaw and he warned that whilst ever we were within their presence we faced peril of the most hyenas type. In full agreement with his view, I asked him why he had returned to face the danger. He did not reply.

On route to the meeting point we lost two men when a small party of Creeks intermittently fired upon us with arrows from the opposite side of the river, but a mounted dispatch of troopers and a dozen Chickasaw swam the river with their horse and forced the cowards to flee. There were no further encounters with the enemy and to our relief we reached the huge camp of white soldiers without further incident.

Noting our exhaustion and condition of frailty we were granted two days rest before being issued with orders to pack up rations for a twenty-eight-day expedition. Later we learnt that Indian scouts had reported the Creeks had settled to form a huge camp on the banks of the Chattahoochee River, over three hundred miles away.

The Life and Death of My Best Friend, Davy Crockett

Here out of the reach of the white man's army, they planned to stay and gain strength by increasing the size of their numbers, stocks and ammunition.

The opportunity to launch a surprise attack and finally decimate the Creeks was a challenge our commander could not resist and so the entire twelve hundred men were ordered to commence upon the toilsome march across the territory towards the Chattahoochee River.

Progress was slower than anticipated and the journey was troublesome. The route taken led through waist-deep mud banks and pathless overgrowth where vast numbers of soldiers could not pass without hacking and sawing their way through the vegetation. Progress was exhausting and when the planned twenty-eight days expired we were only three-quarters way through the journey. Hunting expeditions for food failed to provide the mass of emancipated skeletons with the nourishment they required to keep mobile however, regardless of our miserable condition we were urged on, and by the thirty-fourth day we finally came upon the camp.

Situated in an open sloping meadow roughly one hundred strides from the cover of the forest a small cluster of wigwams were in a perfect position for a surprise attack, and so with rifle loaded and blades sharpened we wasted no time and valiantly advanced into a charge to deliver our tempest of wrath only to find to our vexation that there was not one left savage. The camp was deserted and every single article of value, including food and livestock had been taken.

The Life and Death of My Best Friend, Davy Crockett

In hindsight, with our despairing situation, we had become careless in our advance and it would not have been difficult for the Creek scouts to determine our intentions and flee deeper into the uncharted regions where it was beyond the capabilities of our famishing army to follow.

After the failure and disappointment, our commander of the mission deemed the army should be split again into another two units. One-half of the troopers were to retrace its steps, and then head towards Baton Rouge to rejoin General Jackson who was anticipated to be traversing back north from New Orleans.

The other division, under the command of Major Russel, was to continue advancing north until they reached Fort Decatur where it was expected they would find much-needed provision and shelter.

Having traveled forth into regions beyond our ableness, the Chickasaw contingent was also spilt into groups, this being due to the implications of the treacherous wildlife. For our survival, our entire confidence and trust had to be placed upon the guidance of their skilled scouts to lead the way through the perilous entanglement of thorn, brush, and branch.

Our band of volunteers were assigned to accompany Major Russel and natural hunters like Davy and I were afforded liberty to leave the main body of our army to hunt for raccoons, squirrels, birds and forage for edible berries and roots, any other means of support was nonexistent. At first darkness, all the hunters would rejoin the rest of the fighting men to cook their scavenging's and divide amongst the masses as equally as possible.

The Life and Death of My Best Friend, Davy Crockett

As the march continued and hopes of survival diminishing, in an act of desperation Major Russel divided his unit again into several smaller units hoping the healthier men could advance faster without the delay of helping the weak stragglers. It was hoped the lead party of spirited men could reach the fort and send back aides to assist the feeble and needy stragglers who were slowing our progress.

Davy led the first group of men behind the pacey Chickasaw scouts, but soon a distance of several hours developed between us and the lead party of fleet-footed Indians, and in turn we were several hours in front of Major Russel's men.

Without food, we weakened quickly and fear and agitation intensified. Some of the men wanted to slaughter our horses for food, but Davy resolutely argued against the execution knowing without them we would never survive.

One of our men, Ginty Malloon got bit by a snake. Felled instantly by paralysis he writhed and screamed in agony pleading for someone to cut off his leg. The flesh around his bony leg immediately swelled and his veins blackened and bulged up from his white skin, we knew he was going to die and so we thought it reasonable to leave him with a loaded charge and comfortable bed against a fallen tree. However, we never did hear the blast of his shot so we presumed the poison took him before the lead and furthermore, being distracted and attentive to the dying man we carelessly allowed the varmint to get away before we could skin and eat it, how we rued our carelessness.

The Life and Death of My Best Friend, Davy Crockett

As we suffered in our toil through the vast realms of damp forest gloom, deep marshes, unknown rivers, and wide spread prairies of desolation we happened upon a group of butchered Indians. Friendly or foe we could not determine for all that remained was scattered bones, shredded flesh, and strewn bowels. The circumstances of their demise we could only guess, but as one we believed our allies, the Chickasaw had hunted, killed, and feasted upon the dead as though they were deer or goose.

None of us spoke much as we investigated the devastation, our narrowed darting eyes and probing fingers searching the soil desperately hoping to find some discarded scraps. Being almost starved to death and nearing god's gate the devil descended upon me and instead of bearing thoughts of revulsion envy conquered the aghast acts performed by the savages and I could find no compassion for the tortured souls who's bones were scattered around our feet.

Without any success we sat a while, exhausted, fraught, and despondent, with little hope of any salvation and knowing in our desperation we would have reduced ourselves to the principles of the savage. I rested my back against the damp spongy earth and closed my eyes to the nullity of silence and the blackness of creeping expiration.

Her sweat calling mutated into a dry rasp and then gradually into a tone of much deeper anguish until her softness had been fully displaced with the resonating chords of Davy. Her reaching hand pulled away into the pitch and I flicked my eyelids against the brilliance of the sunlight. Shading my eyes with my hand, Anna's luring eyes and pure white smiling face vanished and Davy was knelt beside me using his rifle as a rest.

The Life and Death of My Best Friend, Davy Crockett

I shook my head several times, he was shouting something at me, but my senses had not been restored, he shook me to rouse me from my daze, and grabbing my shirt he hauled me upright.

"Get Up!" He shouted excitedly, "Get up!" He repeated continually and beckoning with his hand he urged me to follow him. I rolled over onto my side and with exhaustive effort I raised to me knees and lifted my head. Davy had dashed about ten yards, but seeing my lethargy he sprang back to cup his hand under my shoulder and haul me up onto my unsteady feet.

"Grab your rifle and follow me …… come on Leander, Come on and follow me."

He led me through the unconscious and weak, who like me had given up, and succumbed to meet their god with thoughts of reuniting with their departed ancestors.

"This way. This way." He urged me on all the time supporting and dragging my weak body.

For a distance of what seemed about half a mile, he pulled me through tall untouched grass and wildflowers until we came across a trail that had only ever been touched by the feet of wild life. The narrow path entwined across the peaceful landscape and led to another forest in the far distance. We wandered for some time with our rifles gripped tight and ready, but again disappointedly we found nothing. By now the trail had entered the forest and we weaved around the wide undisturbed trunks without entering the semi-darkness.

The Life and Death of My Best Friend, Davy Crockett

Looking both high and low eventually Davy spotted a squirrel on the limb of a huge tree and he leveled his rifle to release thunder and bring the poor rodent down from the branch. As the rifle roared to our rear a large flock of turkeys, disturbed by the blast, rose from the marshy tall grass and flew in a curve above our heads. Instantly I swiveled my rifle skywards and angled by sights upon the fat gobblers. My eruption of lead was successful, and I caused the fleeing turkeys to panic and turn back in front of us. Their change in direction gave Davy time to reload and without delay another turkey thudded into the soft soil near our feet.

Believing we had stumbled into a haven of food we continued on for a while, however after searching for over two hours, and only adding two further squirrels we returned to the group for we feared if we ventured too far into the maze of barks alone we would find ourselves detached from the rest of the troopers.

That night we rejoiced, filled with renewed optimism and buoyed by the feasting we slept well. Early the next morning whilst the dew still sparkled and the water droplets arched over the tall grass, Davy, I and another proven shot called Ty Van Zandt entered the nearby gigantic forest again to explore its luxuriance and hunt some of its hidden riches. We had not traveled too far into the shadows of the tall shafts when we spotted a fine gallant buck that appeared to be on the lookout for its foe whilst the rest of the herd in the far distance chewed on findings that covered their lowered heads. Daring not to move for fear of spooking the alerting and beautiful creature we held our breaths whilst Davy squinted along his barrel to take aim, from this considerable distance only the truest of shooters had the confidence to dare take aim and not jeopardize the target with further encroachment.

The Life and Death of My Best Friend, Davy Crockett

Davy's bullet hit the antlered beast, but it did not immediately fell him, and as frantic birds flapped in alarm from their nests high above both the injured deer and the herd fled into the mass of timbers. At speed, we pursued after the limping animal following its trail of blood until we had to pause for breath and rest upon a fallen tree, which being colossal in size practically blocked the way ahead and obstructed our view.

As we panted to regain our breath and listened to the sound of the forest for disturbance suddenly a growling roar shivered our spines and buckled our legs. Fear rooted us still as in front of our ridged bodies and gaping eyes emerged an immense grizzly bear that had been idling on the other side of the tree. Useless to react and unable to flee we could do nothing except watch as the mammoth bulk snarled at us, showed its great teeth, and erupted hot air into our faces, then uninterested it simply turned to plunge and hide itself again in the dull green and browns.

With our hearts beating fast and without a word, we launched ourselves in the opposite direction at full speed, snapping branches and plowing with haste through dense skin-tearing foliage. After we tore our way through a couple of hundred strides of vegetation, we paused to control our gitters and wipe away the brute's saliva from our faces. Nervously we laughed about the encounter, still with our eyes and ears alert to signs of movement. Then once again, too desperate to give up the chase, we recommenced on the trail of the wounded buck. Without further incident, we found the dying animal and ended its suffering very quickly, and then with the feast hanging limp around our shoulders, we returned to camp. By this time Major Russel and the main body of our army had caught us up and so our salivation for the abundant feast was immediately repressed and only one mouthful of meat was afforded to us.

The Life and Death of My Best Friend, Davy Crockett

Before our departure, the forest was searched again for game, but with nothing hunted and no ammunition left to shoot down birds, the army trudged forward another twenty miles until we reached the Coosa River. Apart from a little corn which was offered to us by some friendly Indians all we found to eat were shrubs and berries and the entire unit was now in a deplorable condition of starvation and weakness. Still, we strained onwards to our destination, incentivized knowing a gut full of food was now within our grasp. However, upon reaching Fort Decatur to our consternation our prospects of survival could not be bolstered.

The small stockade could not offer shelter from the elements for such a large force nor provide the urgently needed rations we desperately sought. The commander of the garrison afforded us only punitive supplies and one very small meal per man, which did little to ease our bloated stomachs, moderate our weight loss, and alleviate the extreme tiredness. With no gains to be had in the ill-stocked camp the following morning we departed to follow the banks of the Coosa once more, our objective of now being Fort Strother at least some fifty miles distant across stony and hilly fragmented country. Slowly we led our skeletal horses wearily over the harsh terrain surviving once more on only a handful of parch corn and berries until we found rest at a newly established small garrison called Fort William.

Yet again rations were scant, and our serving consisted of one piece of pork fat and one scoop of flour for each man. Without subsistence nor adequate rest we once again took upon the route towards Fort Strother, for to delay any further would have resulted in starvation.

The Life and Death of My Best Friend, Davy Crockett

Sadly now the famishment and the strain began to induce unmerciful sufferings upon our brave and trusty four-legged friends. Exhausted to beyond the point of any preservation, one by one their last remnants of strength and strong will began to fail them and distressingly they crumped at our sides. With a heavy heart many of us had no option, but to leave our brave companions, still saddled and bridled, to the horrors of the vultures and wolves for we lacked both shot and energy to end their sufferings quickly.

Mid passage we staggered across the battlefield at Talladega where a year previous, under the command of General Jackson we had slaughtered over three hundred Creeks. Ghoulish memories of that terrible day muted me and caused a trembling in my hands and my legs which I could not hide. Scattered all about us was the appalling sight of the slain whose violated bodies had been left unburied to decompose or be devoured by wild beasts. Some skeletons still lay as they fell, all skin and clothing perished, their final dying brace still evident in the arrangement of the white fragments.

There was nothing to be salvaged that would aid our survival and worryingly Davy found fresh moccasin footprints. Unbeknown to any of us, as our eyes were entranced upon the harrowing scene and our minds still recollecting the manic carnage, Davy followed the meandering trail of footprints along a winding path for about four miles until he spied upon a cluster of wigwams. Entirely alone he boldly strode into the village, for now he feared death from starvation more than the threat of the tomahawk.

The Life and Death of My Best Friend, Davy Crockett

Without us having any knowledge of his presence he put himself entirely at the mercy of the savages, if he was to be murdered we would have never known how he met his fate, assuming only he must have dropped to the dirt and perished along with the many other by our side who did not possess the composition of inner strength required to withhold the call from the angels of death.

However fortune shone upon my friend that day and by dark he had caught us up, his hat and shirt tied and balled to hold a supply of fresh corn which he readily shared with those fortunate to greet him on his return.

Mid-morning the following day our luck and prospects for survival increased dramatically when we were fortunate to encountered a detachment of US troopers who were on the march to Mobile, Alabama.

This division, having just set upon their journey was well supplied with food, footwear, lead, and shot of which, noting our perilous condition they freely shared and liberally distributed amongst us. Equally heartwarming with the encounter and by coincidence amongst the soldiers was a unit of men from Morristown which included Davy's younger brother, John, and several of our old friends and neighbors.

The only progress made that day consisted of rejuvenation and a good catch-up as we mainly hunkered around the campfires eating, drinking, and conversing about all things pertinent. The fresh, ignorant recruits and their assertive commanders found themselves aghast by the senseless, cruel blundering, and disastrous orders to which we remained faithful, and they confidently vowed not to repeat our failures.

The Life and Death of My Best Friend, Davy Crockett

With our vitals refreshed we proceeded the following day towards Fort Strother with our conviction and our fortitude for survival reinvigorated. By dusk we finally entered the gates of the small fortified garrison, and yet after only a few days, due to the overcrowding and the strain weighted upon the resources our leaders issued orders to stand down about half of the army with instructions they must return to camp and serve out the rest of their service once a new strategy had been obtained from the hierarchy in Washington.

Rising to the dawn chorus Davy along with a dozen Tennesseans from Franklin County eagerly packed up their remnants and walked freely out of the stockade towards home for their deserved respite and recuperation.

The whole group urged me to join them, Davy was vocal and forceful and it took several hours of stubborn persuasion to decline his persistence with offers of honest Tennessean hospitality and the promise of a roof covering and plentiful food. However, without the warm welcome of women awaiting for me, I held my position and decided to stay within the fort to serve my final month with the undertaking I would pay my respects to Davy and his family at the soonest opportunity.

My friends from Franklin County did not return to complete their service and with no calling to beckon me home, I extended my enlisted for another two years which advanced mostly dire boredom as mainly my days were mostly occupied with tedious boundary patrols along the Black Warrior and Cahaula Rivers.

The Life and Death of My Best Friend, Davy Crockett

The hardships which we endured during our service bittered my allegiance to those I served and often I brooded for a wholesome occupation, so finally upon my discharge I again welcomed the idea of investing in my own land and working diligently in the fields until I was prosperous enough to attract a new wife. Although I missed Anna with every heartbeat, and I looked for her face every day in the clouds, a little of my inner soul envied Davy's success and I knew my loneliness would not end until I found an endearing companion.

The Life and Death of My Best Friend, Davy Crockett

Chapter 9 – Death of Polly and Davy's resurrection

One month later I found Davy facing the hardest trial of his life. Without invitation, that cruel annihilator which is oblivious to all prayers, tears, and the needs of helpless infants had entered his cottage only two weeks previous to my arrival to snatch away his loving tender wife, and affectionate good mother. The duty of the almighty raked deep within Davy's soul and devoured his heart banishing from within all the remnants of his motivation and desires. Out of necessity only he ensured his children's survival by intermittently tearing himself away from the listless torment to hunt for food.

I lived in Davy's barn to help guide him through the long and painful passage of grief to which I had slowly accustomed however, his suffering reverberated within my consolations as during the worst of my pain I found relieving distractions from my occupation at Fort Strother, as for Davy there was no distraction, he was surrounded by Polly's reminiscents, everything in the homestead she had nurtured and nothing had been untouched by her grace. I considered my situation marginally more favorable.

A few weeks after my arrival his brother John and his sister-in-law arrived for a long and helpful visitation, neither of us could replace the natural capabilities and guidance only a loving mother could provide. After a while, during the long dark nights we discussed at length the requirements the family needed which Davy, no matter how determined or how hard he tried, he would never be able to provide without the natural instincts of a woman.

The Life and Death of My Best Friend, Davy Crockett

Davy considered that his only option was to split the family up, he knew his siblings would kindly provide the orphans a loving home with the staples needed to see them flourish.

With a great affliction upon his heart, he made the decision and he began to make the arrangements to disband the family when a passing neighbor mentioned there was a lonely and suffering widow of Davy's age, with two young children who needed the accompaniment of a strong new husband to ensure her and her children would not perish in the approaching winter.

At first, Davy was reluctant to meet the women and he avoided attempts of introduction stating it was not God's will or fate that he should form an alliance with the women, but the harassment from busybodies, including myself who thought they knew best continued until eventually after much persuasion and convincing eventually got their way and Davy conceded under the condition that I would chaperone him throughout the duration of the visit to the women's deteriorating homestead.

From the first introduction, Davy and Elizabeth Patton found mutual respect and fondness for each other. Both spoke with honest sincerity not hiding their grief nor equally their desires for supplementing the needs of their families. Widow Patton found common ground with Davy explaining her husband had perished in the same Indian war in which he had fought and although she was a capable woman, she could not raise her children on the homestead without the strength and skills of a good man. Davy reciprocated his tale of woe admitting that he needed a stepmother to help raise his children and comfort his needs as and when the time was right.

The Life and Death of My Best Friend, Davy Crockett

The lonely couple chattered along quite comfortably for several hours and upon their genial parting, they agreed to meet again in private.

Davy's gloom and the affliction which pained his heart was momentarily lifted and upon our journey home he confessed to me that he had been surprisingly pleased with the widow's attractiveness, elegance, and benevolent nature. Several times he justified his sudden optimism for life and he spoke about how the almighty who is always right had taken his wife, then just as he felt that his situation was the worst in the whole world the Lord had once again shone a light upon his path by introducing him to Elizabeth. Finally, he admitted he could not bear the thought of scattering his children and he thought he would make the widow a good husband and be a good step father to her two children.

During their second convergence, they agreed to undertake a formal courtship until the amiable marriage could be arranged and conducted.

Only a few weeks had passed by when the two mourners harmoniously came together to wed. Leaving the couple to enjoy their newfound affection and contentment I left the Crockett homestead with my own ambitions to find courtship, close down and sell off my neglected business affairs, and together with my earnings from the war use the wealth to purchase another homestead which would more than equal the best of Tennessee's ambitious farmers.

Only six months had passed by when I received a harrowing message from a local trapper informing me Davy had died. At once I again left my affairs and hired a laborer to head up to Bean Creek without delay and all haste to ascertain a factual account and help Elizabeth and the children in their moment of despair.

The Life and Death of My Best Friend, Davy Crockett

Upon my arrival at the Crockett's humble cabin, it was strikingly evident neglect and ruin had set. Starving animals foraged wild, discarded corn and vegetation had withered and flies feasted on rotten game which swung on hooks, its stench fouling the swirling breeze to create the most undesirable welcome.

Elizabeth did not respond to my gentle taps on the door, she simply sat unresponsive, her eyes staring blankly at the cold charcoals where once the fire warmed the damp cabin. The children lay together in a silent slumber under pelts which provided a comfortable warmth, but they all were thin, pale, and lethargic.

I called out several more times and eventually Elizabeth roused just enough to acknowledge that she recognized a familiar face, but tightening her fingers to clench around a wet handkerchief she still said nothing.

With great urgency, I ignited the fire and scavenged through the house and grounds seeking nourishments of which to make a broth. Within the hour warmth again filled the room and the odor of root and vegetable pottage replaced the stench of rotten decay. Gently I coaxed the children out from under their covers and slowly I encouraged them to swill their throats with the hot liquid until eventually, they began to cast off their lethargy and gulp down the nourishment with unrepressed fervency.

Spoon by spoon I pressed Elizabeth to open her mouth and take the offerings and slowly, very slowly she too regained her courage and the dim grey sullenness in her eyes began to lift away revealing signs of revitalization and a glimmer of hope.

The Life and Death of My Best Friend, Davy Crockett

By now the sun had set and little could be done except keep the cabin warm, bring to boil some coffee and encourage everyone to rest, and allow the sustenance to develop.

The next morning I collected enough fresh eggs and milk to provide an ample breakfast then I dealt with the immediate emergencies of the animals. Later I rode a short distance visiting upon several neighbors until I found a man named Clancy Bird who sought paid work.

With an agreement in place for Clancy to tender to the needs of the farm for the season I returned to the cabin to find Elizabeth had strengthened and had grit enough to contain her grief just enough to explain to me what had happened to Davy.

In detail, but with eruptions of tears and cycles of silent pauses Elizabeth told me that Davy had stated he was concerned with the lack of prosperity that the farm provided for the increased family, he had harbored ambitious ideas of establishing a new enterprise on fertile land he had seen whilst serving with the army in Alabama.

Davy said he was going to cross the Tennessee River and continue south for two hundred miles until he neared Tuscaloosa. He enthused the land here was in a region of unbroken wilderness of fertility in which ample supplies could be easily hunted and farmed. Joining him on the expedition were two locals called Robinson and Rich who had also expressed a desire to seek a new adventure.

With an accompaniment of flowing tears she said that about three months after they had departed, she watched Robinson and Rich dejectedly trudge with their heads hung low along the muddy path to her door.

The Life and Death of My Best Friend, Davy Crockett

Instantly she knew they were about to deliver the feared words she dreaded to hear. With sincerity and remorse, they told her that one night during their rest something spooked their horses and they fled. Although all three men gave chase Robinson and Rich soon became exhausted and gave up the pursuit, but Davy still being vigorous continued to press on until eventually they became detached. They expressed in vain that they searched the thick bogs, ravines, and dense woodlands without any success until they came across four Indians who told them they had stumbled across a severely ill man who matched Davy's description. The Indians said the man was very weak, suffering from fever and very close to death, but rather than leaving the man to be devoured by the wild beast of the forest and being kind-hearted by nature they carried the man to a trapper's cabin where they hoped he could be treated.

The kindly Indians left with directions for the lonely cabin, but upon their arrival, they noticed a fresh rise of soil which denoted a new grave. The hunter in the cabin sorrowfully explained his wife had tried desperately hard to cure the suffering man's illness with her remedies and curatives, but he was too delusional and too weak for salvation and he passed over during the first night. Robinson said they purchased two new horses and left with a prayer for their friend to return home.

Elizabeth disclosed the thought of Davy lying in soil far from home tortured her every minute, and she begged me to return him home to his family. Repeatedly I objected to the plea, stating many reasons for my disinclination of transporting a carcass two hundred miles across wilderness where already slow travel is hampered by the lack of any tracks and savage Indians who roam freely to attack the vulnerable.

The Life and Death of My Best Friend, Davy Crockett

Relentless was Elizabeth's soul probing pleas and over and over she continued to cry that the process of mourning could not commence nor could her pain ever diminish whilst Davy lay far away in some stranger's field. Eventually, due to the consistent bleary remonstrations my conscience would not allow my mind to rest, and against my better judgment, I relented from my objections. I told Elizabeth that I would find Robinson and Rich and ask them to accompany me back to the hunter's remote lodgings.

Her relief equaled, but contrast to my grimness, I knew the mission was likely to fail for if Robinson and Rich, who were considered Davy's friends, had decided not to return home Davy's dead body they must have good reason. Also, I doubted they would be able to recall their journey to the isolated, faraway cabin.

After stocking the Crockett's homestead with ample supplies of wood, and food and attending to the animal's needs, I left Elizabeth and the children in the willing, but inexperienced hands of Clancy and departed the short fifteen miles to find Robinson and Rich.

After first welcoming me with a dense and hot goulash, their demeanor suddenly transformed into one of surprising concern when I disclosed my intentions and the reason for my calling. Both men outright rejected my appeal for a guide and both tried desperately hard to convince me to abandon my considerations. They stated clearly that I was wasting my time and I would put my life at risk by venturing into extremely dangerous regions alone.

The Life and Death of My Best Friend, Davy Crockett

Regardless of their expected negativity, I left the two men muttering their disapproval and dismissal behind the closed door and I ventured once more into the wilderness which I still hated, this time without the surety of an army and only the accompaniment of my two horses.

Guided by the position of the sun, I followed the vague instructions given by Robinson, crossing the Ten River and striking the upper waters of the Black Warrior, then I followed a stream for a distance of nearly one hundred miles until I found an isolated cabin near Tuscaloosa, reclaimed by nature, covered in ivy and creepers with tall shrubs growing out of the door and window. Here, where the grass was tall I rested for a week and nourished myself and my companions on the bounty of wild game and rye.

Soon after my recommencement I found myself alerted. As I exited foliage, I came face to face with an Indian hunter. After a long skeptical pause, each of us waiting to see if there was to be any hostility, with broken English and many hand gestures the Indian told me he did not know of any trapper in the region, but he knew another Indian settlement ten miles north who may offer the knowledge I sought. I thanked him for the information with the offering of a rabbit from my haul, but with my thoughts agitated with suspicion, I moved slowly and stealth fully, concealing my frame as much as possible between the wide trunks to avoid an arrow in the back.

That night I did not light a comforting fire nor did I sleep and after a short rest I journeyed forth to the edge of the advised camp, for in this vast unknown region I knew without guidance I would never locate the trapper's homestead.

The Life and Death of My Best Friend, Davy Crockett

No relief eased my anxiety as my eyes gazed upon the half dozen wigwams and a raging fire around which naked children played, women cooked, and three elders squatted and smoked.

For a long while, I secretly studied the tribe and the serene activities before me for I could not recognize the tribe, however nor did I see any warriors. Assuming the younger men were away hunting I secured my horses to a branch and walked into the camp holding my arms upwards to clearly display my weapon-free hands to the elders who arose to meet me. To my relief, the Indians were not hostile towards the white man and one of the wizened old natives spoke a few words of English. He offered me a seat by the fire, a smoke of his pipe, and a fill of their root broth, but fearing my welcome may not be so well received should the warriors return I politely declined all offers and directly asked if he knew any white skinned trappers or traders who lived in this region. Displaying a toothless grin which identified his great pleasure at being useful he drew in the soil a map of the woodlands and dissected it with meandering channels to display several streams. Near a bend on one of the streams he fingered into the soil a drawing of a cabin, and then he drew a large sphere above the symbol and with his fingers mimicking steps he marked two lines. I understood his depiction to mean the cabin would be found on a bend after a further two days of walking in the direction of the sunrise. I bowed my head and placed the flat of my hands together to thank the Indian for the knowledge and I smiled and nodded to the gathering children and women who curiously peeked from behind his back, then memorizing the drawing with all the concentration I could muster I walked backward, to avoid turning my back out of the camp. As quickly as possible I collected my horses and sped away from the camp caring little for the resulting noise and disturbance.

The Life and Death of My Best Friend, Davy Crockett

Mercifully the old man's intelligence proved to be accurate and two days later I saw in the distance a smoke plume rising out from a canopy of leaves and branches. Unfortunately, the dwellers in the cabin were not the ones I searched for, but the wily seasoned trapper knew of traders in the region who may be able to help. After an ample belly fill of scrumptious hot meats he set me on my way with fresh provisions and detailed knowledge for a safe progression without chancing any contact with Indians.

By late afternoon the following day, another pillar of smoke led me to a shock that dazed my head and defied belief, as no more than ten strides away from me turning over soil with a spade was my best friend. Noticing my stunned hesitancy at the boundary of the homestead, Davy dropped the tool, and beaming a huge grin he sprang to greet me with a breath-shackling hug. Hollering with an excited flurry he asked me what the hell I was doing this far west.

Davy was ashen-faced, emancipated, and saggy-eyed, but he certainly was not the corpse I was expecting to find. My legs weakened and my body arched, then my stomach heaved and I stuttered out my disbelief with nonsensical words.

A squaw woman appeared at Davy's side and resting her hand on his shoulder she expressed to him her concern for him being excitable. She warned him to calm down stating he wasn't yet recuperated enough for such exertions.

The Life and Death of My Best Friend, Davy Crockett

Hearing the disturbance a long-bearded man cracked open the cabin door and displayed his rifle. After a cautious stare, the bearded looking brute left his station, and hauling me upright he asked if I would like a mug of his corn liquor which I was mighty quick to accept, then he stated that I should rest my weary limbs and aching bones.

Resting on a crude stool and sipping gently on the throat burner Davy formally introduced me to the kind couple, Jesse Jones and Sweetgum, and then he asked me again what I was doing this far out in the wilds. He was equally amused and angered when I explained my reasoning for venturing alone into the depths of hostile territory. He cussed at Robinson and Rich, then apologized to Jones and his wife for using such profane language within the boundary of their grounds. He bemoaned the two men were not his friends and they could not be trusted. He lambasted their cowardice and their lack of loyalty or scruples.

Shaking his head probably at his own foolhardiness he told me about the chase with the horses and that in the moment of utter desperation and panic, he could not find his way out of the thick maze of trees to locate his two associates. Without food, water or weapons he searched until finally thoroughly exhausted and with every joint and limb hurting beyond his pain threshold he collapsed on a bed of damp leaves and foliage. He had nothing except roots, barks, and dew. Expecting to rest a while and regain enough energy to continue his search he began to realize that his body had objected not just to the toil, but now also a fever took advantage of his weakness and began to spread through his veins. With no known whereabouts of any habitation, he sensed the cloak of death enclose around him as all his hopes of survival were disappearing fast.

The Life and Death of My Best Friend, Davy Crockett

Lying prostrate with all his sensibilities befuddled he lingered in pain and delirium until the dark angel raised him up from the ground and lifted him on high for the journey into the clouds.

Davy's recollections corresponded to the two Tennesseans up to where they stated they found his freshly covered grave. At this juncture, Sweetgum spoke, and in perfect English she explained whilst Jesse was out hunting he happened upon the explorer who he found slumped at the base of a tree. Unconscious and close to death, Jesse found it beyond his moralities to leave the young man to die alone therefore he hauled his skeletal body over his horse and led him home to die with as much care and comfort as we could afford.

Immediately recognizing the telling signs of malaria Sweetgum, explained how slowly she administered Davy with sips of an herbal remedy that she had learned from the elders of her tribe. At first, his stomach rejected the potion and it seemed that soon he would be free from the burden of life, however unperturbed she persisted with her attentive care, cooling his burning skin with cold compresses and dispensing the traditional tonic drip by drip.

She paused, purposely and Jesse cut in to explain, that it was during this period two strangers called at the cabin begging to buy supplies and horses. Initially, he refused their trade, but they persevered and increased their tender for the horses until, finally, their offer was too good to refuse.

Once the deals were complete and we had exchanged notes for the horses they insisted that I should offer them a hospitality beverage and they forced their way inside without being offered a welcome, then it happens that as soon as their studious eyes fell upon our patient, and

The Life and Death of My Best Friend, Davy Crockett

Sweetgum told them that he had malaria, they skedaddled without taking any food or drink. Jesse added that without introductions he never got to know the fiend's names.

Sweetgum, then continued, telling me that for over a week Davy was unconscious, and then for another two weeks he had a high temperature and suffered from extreme delirium. Finally, when the signs of recovery became evident she could fortify his weakness with liquid curatives and after a month or so he was almost recovered. Bearing a righteous smile the squaw finished by saying instead of parting ways to return home Davy insisted he wanted to thank and repay the Jones's for their spirit and acts of kindness by working free of charge on their homestead.

Davy added that he had hoped to send news home with a passing traveler, but the homestead was so isolated only Indians wanting to trade passed by their door.

Admiring Davy's dexterity around the farm and his expertise for hunting Jesse admitted he was jubilant when Davy insisted he was going to stay on until he had repaid their kindness.

For the next few days I convalesced in Jesse's corn store, often helping Davy as he tendered to the vegetation patch, fed the animals and hunted for meat, but all the while we were occupied with the Jones's, Elizabeth and the children despaired and needlessly suffered. This irked me badly and urged me daily to reunite Davy with his wife at the soonest and so once Davy's earnest efforts had established with abundant stocks and flourishing vegetation we packed up our own provisions and bid Jesse and Sweetgum a fond goodbye.

The Life and Death of My Best Friend, Davy Crockett

The return journey to Bean Creek, although dire and tedious was accomplished without reportable incident, the only note worth recalling was the many unusual stops we had to make due to Davy's lack of stamina.

Great astonishment greeted Davy upon his return home. Instantly he was enveloped in a rush of overjoyed limbs as loving hugs from his children prevented him from stepping beyond the doorway. However following her children out of the cabin, Elizabeth paled and fainted so quickly her fall gave us brief concern.

After the short draw back Davy once again, over a bowl of steaming goodness recollected the tale of woe and subsequent kindness given to him by Jesse and Sweetgum to the intrigued and silent listeners who sat motionless around the huge log table. Finishing the venture it came as no surprise when he told Elizabeth quietly that he intended to visit Robinson and Rich at the first opportunity.

As was Davy's way, he did not rush to seek retribution, instead he spent time with his family, eating, resting, playing, and enjoying being the head of the family and a father once again. By the time he ventured across the meadows to demand an explanation and to seek justice, the cowards had excused themselves from the region and scarpered like mice. We later found out they sent word back home to their loved ones stating they had enlisted in the Army of the Tennessee to fight against the Indians, we did not hear of their whereabouts until some years later when a friend told us they had deserted the army and fled to Florida. We never knew whatever became of them after that.

The Life and Death of My Best Friend, Davy Crockett

Chapter 10 – Colonel Crockett

Still, the near-death experience had not dispelled from Davy's bosom his desire to seek out a new venture and relocate his family to a territory with increased fertility and an abundant supply of timber, fresh fish, and bountiful game. His appetite was further stoked when news reached the region that the government had purchased a new territory from the Chickasaws and, although it was not yet adopted with any legal statutes or law control settlers were promised free land if they relocated within the current year.

Against Elizabeth's wishes, Davy insisted this time, here in this region of unsurveyed solitude in South Tennessee, that he would find his paradise. Davy was convinced he would locate the perfect spot and so, only two months after his recovery I helped him pack up all his worldly belongings onto the back of his horses and oxen to accompany the Crockett's the two hundred-mile trek southwestwards to a lawless and ungoverned spot called Shoal Creek.

Along the route, we soon came into contact with several other families who had heard of the land purchase and also aspired to the same ambitions as Davy, so it came as no surprise when we finally reached our destination, log cabins not separated by a mile apart were rising in all directions. Although disappointed, with plenty of neighbors to aid us a cabin was soon erected on the banks of a crystal clear stream, and with our basic tools and a hatchet, beds, tables, and chairs were soon assembled.

The Life and Death of My Best Friend, Davy Crockett

With my finances concluded in Greene County I also decided to stay in the 'new purchase' territory and build myself a home on the fertile land alongside the other pioneers who were rapidly rising cabins in their quest to build a new existence. With my finances slightly advantageous over my fellow unmarried rivals I considered my prosperity would soon lead me to find new companion however, the pioneers who crowded the 'New Purchase' seeking their fortune consisted of only a few desperate families who fled impoverishment and a multitude of young men you sought their fate through adventure. In addition, this land of new opportunity attracted the villainous and vile who fled their homelands to escape the laws of criminality that they had violated.

These reckless vagabonds cared little for right or wrong, they stole and abused without constraint or conscience. They shot down Indians at first sight without giving prior consideration to their threat or allegiances and they raped and killed squaws, tortured children, burnt down wigwams, and stole from them whatever they could carry without a care. Around the settlements of their white-skinned countrymen, they drank wildly and outrageously teased the women and threatened and insulted their daughters. The news of the territory which existed without the regulation of US laws spread fast and attracted only more undesirables who did whatever they pleased without giving any consideration to their neighbors. There was no control for collecting debts, no rectification for violence, and no punishment for theft or murder.

For many settlers the land of promise suddenly soured and with their endeavors for a prosperous and peaceful future appearing to be futile the honest and hardworking families began to move out leaving my prospects of finding a suitable bride invalid.

The Life and Death of My Best Friend, Davy Crockett

Finally, a gathering was organized by the still ardent pioneers to discuss methods for mutual protection. Davy with his natural instincts for volubility, reasoning, and debate led the discussions with good sense, and before the night was concluded the assembly had agreed to appoint their own justices of the peace to execute recriminatory commands against any wrongdoers and assign constables to execute the decisions issued by the newly elected officials. Overwhelmingly Davy was nominated as the senior Justice of the Peace.

At first, he declined the proposal admitting he knew nothing of regulations and peacekeeping, but the council trusted and respected him, and being resolute with their conclusion they stated there was no better man in the region for the daunting task which lay ahead. They pressed he was a man with a good sense of what was right and wrong in all things of significance and his honesty could not be challenged. Being pleased by the nature of the esteem placed upon him by his respectable neighbour's he eventually accepted the post.

Within weeks his actions supported by the constables began to lift the gloom and the hopelessness around the supper tables and instead of the talk being dominated by theft and violence, it now embodied glad tidings of recrimination and retribution. Soon men who owed money without intentions of paying their debts were arrested and brought before Davy to be judged.

Often the offender would suddenly find ways to clear his liabilities by either miraculously finding money or agreeing to a period of free labour. If no recompense or agreement could be found Davy would issue orders for the guilty party's possessions to be seized and sold to pay off the debt.

The Life and Death of My Best Friend, Davy Crockett

Occasionally and especially in the first few weeks, challenging resistance faced Davy by the scoundrels who had plagued their torment upon the honest folk, and Davy often had to meet the dissenters with bravery and boldness. In the street, he was attacked from behind by a coward with a knife, but his alertness to danger and his swift reaction saved his life and ended the one of his attacker. His notoriety for divisive honest actions vexed the troublemakers which resulted in further agitation for a while, but also it encouraged the hardworking and fearing homesteaders to raise complaints and at last seek out justice.

Whilst some sentences resulted in bloodshed many were petty and resolved amicably, but one of the most vile and harmful crimes which was committed by the villains was the theft of livestock. Stealing the settler's most valuable assets irked Davy so much that from day one of taking up the position he informed everyone that he was determined to stop this wicked act by authorizing the most severe punishment to those who were proven guilty of the charge.

In the first hearing, nonconformists tried to harass Davy and a large skeptical crowd formed to block the meeting house doorway and windows as the attention intensified with many wondering if the new Justice of the Peace would stand resolutely against the villains and deliver on his promise to deliver righteousness. A rise of vehement cheers of whoopees of approval and relief sounded loud as Davy's first verdict reached their ears. A wiry deceitful chancer called Abel Turley had been found guilty of swine theft and Davy's sentence was that he should be stripped naked and dragged through the streets where at a suitable station he should be strapped to a tree and flogged until almost at the point of death.

The Life and Death of My Best Friend, Davy Crockett

If he should somehow survive the beating he would then be forced to watch his cabin be burnt to the ground after which he was to be horse dragged out of the territory and left in the wilderness where God would decide his final fate.

For the next two years Davy's deliberations ruled and I along with several other trusted men worked as a constable, gladly performing the acts of his will. Crime declined, the undesirables moved out and the settlement prospered growing daily in size and prosperity. Eventually, the Legislation of Alabama annexed our region to Giles County and brought us finally under the domain of US law. Under the conditions of the law, the Justice of the Peace faced re-elections and because Davy had performed his duties to the entire satisfaction of the community he was duly re-elected and legally appointed with the official title Esquire, although as with most people who received the fancy named title everyone referred to him as Colonel out of courtesy, a term that would stay with him for the rest of his life.

Under the new jurisdiction, our roles remained the same, albeit we had to attend more reading and writing classes to ensure all of our warrants and affairs were legally documented, recorded by our own hand, and witnessed with a signature by a fellow justice of the peace or constable.

Davy's popularity within the community remained fully respected even if it was at the envy of all men. He became well known throughout the state for his impenetrable sense of justice, knowing how to judge right from wrong, and those more local to him knew he had a memory for all things important, or equally for delicate matters such as remembering family names and politely thanking people for their efforts.

The Life and Death of My Best Friend, Davy Crockett

He developed an astonishing command for conversation often using slang which he was never embarrassed to use regardless of whom he addressed. He never dallied, hesitated or neglected to act when called upon to do his duty, even when the decisions were difficult and tested his own principles and resolve.

As the settlement developed and its populace increased it was deemed a regiment of militia would be assembled and Davy was petitioned to be selected as the Major of the regiment. To my surprise and the consternation of the locals who knew him Davy made it known that he was finished with army life and he respectfully declined the position adding he had no desire for such esteemed honors.

Captain Mathews, a wealthy settler new to the region sought to elevate his status and his standing within the community and so he badgered Davy relentlessly citing that if Davy supported his claim for the Colonelship he would in turn support Davy's application to be elected Major. Again Davy refused the approach and repeated he was not interested in the role, however Mathews was intent on gaining the position and he knew with Davy's backing he would have a serious advantage over the other candidates so the harassing continued and he lured Davy by stating they would both gain further respect and influence from the citizens if Davy held the newly created position and he took the vacant role of Colonel. Eventually, Davy conceded to the barracking and consented to give the Captain his support. With the change of view he took a deep interest in the enterprise and the new role of which he had previously distanced himself from.

The Life and Death of My Best Friend, Davy Crockett

A huge frolic was organised and everyone in the region clad their best attire and gathered to feast, drink, and dance and once the fiddlers had stopped playing, cast their vote to select a new Major and Colonel.

During the festivities, I was made aware that Captain Mathews had betrayed Davy, and whilst my friend boisterously praised the Captain's credentials to all his associates the Captain had secretly only lobbied the townsfolk to vote for his son and boasting his son's appropriateness for the role he slandered Davy behind his back.

I informed Davy of the skullduggery, informing him that when the festivities had stopped, and Davy had promoted himself for the position of the Major, and vocally offered his support for the Captain with his usual idioms, the Caption intended to take to the stump and double cross him. Instead of offering his support for Davy as he had promised, he would invite his son to stand for the position and take the stump to transmit a prolific speech with prejudice tones of refined phases that were sure to appeal to the common voter. Combined with the Captains shenanigans the young man's masterful lecture would win the father and son the vote for both positions.

The unworthy treatment roused Davy's indignation and being fearless by nature and never having conducted or even considered such a vile act as betrayal he immediately confronted the Captain.

The cowardly and embarrassed Captain denied any wrong doing claiming he did not know his son was preparing to stand for election and he tried desperately to persuade Davy to continue with the plan. Feigning his disgust, Davy acted as though he believed the Captain and even apologized for the misunderstanding.

The Life and Death of My Best Friend, Davy Crockett

He then confirmed he would still offer his full support when the exchanges recommenced, but on shaking hands to depart Davy nerved the Captain by admonishing. "Often a tongue can break a bone."

Half a dozen candidates stepped on the ceremonial trunk as per the custom to loudly and boastfully proclaim why they should be elected to the positions including Captain Mathews and his son. After almost two hours the last contender to mount the stump to persuade the voters of his credentials arose to an immediate cheer and a prolonged ovation. Davy's reputation as an able leader had already appealed to the gathering, but to everyone's surprise including myself Davy's address did not proclaim why he should be elected, instead without nerve or embarrassment he delivered an amusing oration of why he, Captain Mathews, and his son should not be elected due to their total inability to be a commander of a regiment where lives would be risked.

To roars of belly laughter, applause, and a great deal of head scratching Davy kept the whole assembly entranced with his peculiar, but enthralling performance for over thirty minutes. When convinced his objective was achieved he shouted. "Do not let us meddle in what we cannot mend." Then he bowed and stood down to rapturous cheers, pats on the back, and two unamused scowls from distance.

When the election came several hours later Davy's ambition proved to be correct, none of the three men were elected and whilst he was surrounded by confused supporters who pestered him for an explanation for his behavior a couple of fancy-dressed businessmen from out of town managed to pull Davy out from the melee to solicit him with ideas of standing as a candidate to represent the county of Lawrence and Hickman as State Legislator.

The Life and Death of My Best Friend, Davy Crockett

So convinced by the honest reputation he had acquired and by his natural ability for performing with gusto in front of a large scrutinizing crowd the men told Davy they would back his election campaign all the way to the White House.

Although he was ignorant of government affairs, Davy agreed to meet them for further discussions the following day. Elizabeth Crockett gasped a sigh of relief upon hearing the businessmen's aspirations. Although she knew the change of profession would take him away from home for long periods, she had sensed restlessness within him, indicating that once more he was considering uprooting the family again to locate and farm in new pastures far away. He had already concerned her by agreeing to take a drove of horses from Tennessee to North Carolina, a venture that was planned to take almost three months.

The following day Davy asked me to accompany him to the meeting where around a table with the two businessmen men we shared roast game, tankards of cider, and discussions detailing their proposal. Eventually, to their disappointment, Davy informed the men he would like to stand for the election, but it would be impossible because he had an obligation to deliver horses to North Carolina. The men informed Davy they would hire another drover and I offered to take on the task, but shaking his head, he stated that he had given his word, and that under no circumstances would he relent from the arrangement.

Also, he honestly concerned to the gentlemen he knew nothing about government affairs, most laws, or bureaucracy. With his natural jovial spirit, he admitted that he had never even seen a government document and until he saw a poster at the fete yesterday he did not know that Quincey Adams had been elected as president.

The Life and Death of My Best Friend, Davy Crockett

The gentlemen told Davy they were not concerned, they expected nothing less than his pure honesty and his concern for his poor education did not deter them from giving him their support and the finances required to conduct a successful campaign, for whilst all other candidates could talk politics and recite legislature references all night long, none of them could hold the attention of an audience like he could. They confirmed all he was expected to do was to just continue being Davy Crockett, the humble and trustworthy frontiersman from Tennessee.

Davy demanded to know what gains benefitted the intellectuals who sported expensive attire and in the spirit of openness and trust, they earnestly admitted that they required his backing to support their campaign for relocating their resource-exhausted town to the center of the state where natural and abundant resources would benefit all, not just the ambitious and money motivated businessmen. They expanded a little further and after a few moments of consideration and deliberation they shook hands to form a pact under the condition, they loaned him a substantial advance of funds.

In the weeks prior to the election, Davy's fortunes had begun to increase, and he saw an opportunity to diverse his interests and invest in a small gist, powder mill, and distillery however, he needed to borrow heavily and the funding from the businessmen enabled him to hire employees and make the enterprise functional.

Three months later I joined up with Davy in Hickman County as he directed his first steps on the electoral campaign as a candidate for the Legislator. His new business associates had arranged a squirrel hunt on the banks of the Duck River as a public event and carefully prepared, the event was organized to introduce Davy to the locals of Hickman who

The Life and Death of My Best Friend, Davy Crockett

carried the bulk of the votes. Mostly being humble backwoodsmen the businessmen thought a man of their equal standing would appeal to their rational and encourage them to take time out to vote, rather than the usual dull legates who tried to dictate to them with intellectual words they lacked any belonging to.

The hunt lasted for two days then a huge barbecue and frolic was arranged where all the hunted scalps were counted. It came as no surprise to me when Davy was announced as the easy winner. Enjoying the food, drinks, music, and general chatter with those all about, the plan prevailed and when Davy delivered his first speech which was plied with his customary cheerfulness and analogies the receptive crowd cheered for more words and refused to let him step down from the decking, their eyes excitedly watching every entertaining gesture and their heads angled so their ears captured every word.

Finally, with the assembly roaring with laughter, Davy bid them good afternoon by stating his oration had to be completed due to his throat being dryer than his powder horn and he needed to wet his whistle. To more raucous cheers, cap waving, and pats on the back Davy hustled his way through the crowd to the drinks tent knowing he would not have to pay for any drinks that afternoon.

I accompanied Davy on the campaign route through several towns witnessing the same responsive reception and outcome at each event until we arrived in Vernon for a huge gathering which included all of the other candidates who were running for the position. These men, highly educated in law and politics with exceptional fluency skills scorned and dismissed the backwoodsman as an ignorant exhibitionist who merely amused the equally uneducated and impoverished.

The Life and Death of My Best Friend, Davy Crockett

For once Davy was nervous upon seeing the many dapper-clad city candidates. He feared his rude command of inferior language would now lead to his embarrassment after following the displays of these free-flowing speechmakers. With increased anxiety, we stood at the rear of the candidates allowing them to hustle amongst themselves to mount the stump and begin their lengthy and self-proclaiming parables of stretched ambitions.

The candidates, in turn all spoke at length each trying to outdo each other with baffling statements and words ignorant to many of the assembled. By the time it was Davy's turn to make his stand the crowd was restless and fatigued by the lengthy procedures.

Noting the opportunity Davy sprang forth with his usual buoyancy to immediately capture the attentions of the voters by remarking how each of the candidates had bored everyone with prolonged sermons of politics which found no common ground with the contingent. In contrast to his opponents, Davy's speech was short and direct without fancy words and fake promises. He spoke only of what he knew to be fair and right and how he would represent his equals from the wildest regions and fight for the entitlements of the impoverished settlers. Everyone looked at the backwoodsman who stood proud on high, they gawked as if entirely captivated by the man with the face and voice of some glad diviner. Again his closure was met with rapturous cheers, applause, and a long night supplied with free drinks, and then just one week later the voting was conducted and Davy was overwhelmingly elected.

The Life and Death of My Best Friend, Davy Crockett

Chapter 11 – Back to the Wilderness

Once in Nashville, with a deal of apprehension due to his ignorance with a quill and having little capacity for acquiring knowledge from the pages of books, Davy thought it wise to submit himself to studying by earnestly listening and questioning his following legislators on all things legal and political.

Unfortunately, less than two weeks into the new role, disaster struck Davy's life again when the great flood of the Tennessee River destroyed his entire mill and distillery. With huge loans to pay back, no substantial income, and no friends to offer financial help because the violent storm destroyed their own homesteads, the Legislator for Tennessee was a broken man. He had debts he could not repay and, adding to his worries, his conscience burdened him because he could not pay his employees and friends for their labors.

I had seen very little of Davy while he was attending to his duties in Nashville, when I presented myself to help him salvage what we could from the destruction of the flood, I noted there was a change within him. He was dour and his personage displayed all the agitations of a troubled man however, I knew the disorder was not entirely because of his debts and tragedy, his angst and abjectness clouded him due to the political assignment he had undertaken. He had nothing in common with the suited men in Nashville who found amusement with his attire and speeches. He did not trust them and he was offended by their scruples, believing many had sought their position only to increase their personal wealth, and so he considered them shamefully disloyal to the people and the nation they represented.

The Life and Death of My Best Friend, Davy Crockett

At the point of despair and whilst Davy was at his lowest ebb, another man's ill fortune resulted in being Davy's savior. His father-in-law, Robert Patton died and Davy inherited eight hundred acres of valuable farming land and a substantial stone-built property. With Elizabeth's agreement, Davy sold half the land off to clear his debts and moved his family into the empty homestead.

I assisted Elizabeth with the relocation and concluded Davy's affairs in Bean Creek, then upon the adjournment of the Legislation and after only being home for a few days, without motive other than pure boredom, Davy told me that he intended to take his eldest son, John Wesley on an exploring tour of the wilderness. He later admitted he had again found himself restless on the family homestead and he hoped to find another region with abundant vegetation and game suitable to build a new home.

Also growing tired of the mundane repetition, I invited myself along on the adventure and so without any objections, we laden our horses with provisions and blankets, and along with eight-year-old Henry, we plunged deep into the backwoods. Once more, day after day we waded through streams, clambered hills, lumbered through marshes and trudged through dense dark forests, and huge ravines. Resting occasionally and stopping only when darkness prevented our safe travel, each night we constructed a frail shelter to protect our backs from the frequent downpours and we lit roaring fires to roast our hunt and boil our water.

Happily, without concern, incident, or regret, we traversed the pathless lands for over one hundred and fifty miles until our eyes beset upon the perfect patch of luxuriant soil near to the Obion River.

The Life and Death of My Best Friend, Davy Crockett

The surrounding area was entirely uninhabited by man, either white or native, and lavish game roamed at will. The nearest cabin at our rear was over fifteen miles distant and the friendly settlers who dwelled there confirmed their cabin was the only one in the entire region.

However, this region, chosen by Davy because of its solitude had, in its recent past, been convulsed by several terrible hurricanes which had prostrated huge areas of woodlands scattering huge trees in every direction as far as the eye could see leaving dreadful indications which proved the force exerted by this tremendous force of nature. Hundreds of trunks were flung and piled high and enormous roots were exposed on deep fractures of land. Looking in from the edge of the devastated forest and towards the tangled abyss of wood, dense underbrush and foliage had risen wild to cover the high piled trunks and render many areas impenetrable by man creating a perfect hunting ground. The fear of any desolating storms had prevented any settlers or Indians from raising their wigwams in this mistrusted region and so without reason to flee from hunters the surrounding area was bounteous with elks, deer, beavers, rabbits, and squirrels, but also wolves, panthers and bears.

Unconcerned with nature's wrath, Davy insisted this was the perfect area for his new cabin and selecting a position near a see-through stream, but this time on higher ground well above flood ground we took to collecting and assembling fallen timbers.

Again, Davy seemed the happiest of men. To the side of the cabin he talked about planting corn in the wide expansive meadow, and just beyond the grass a short walk led him to the inexhaustible supply of fuel and food.

The Life and Death of My Best Friend, Davy Crockett

After only a few hours of hard work a basic settlement was created and furnished with animal skins for comfort. By the end of the week, a meadow had been turned and corn seed planted with the assurance of knowing it would return its yield several hundredfold.

With no plans to return and collect Elizabeth yet, the three of us set out to backtrack on our steps to associate and trade with our nearest neighbor of some fifteen miles away, a man called Owen Flatt whose pleasant introduction we had made on our journey several weeks earlier. By the end of the day Davy had cleverly negotiated and bartered exchanges of pelts for flour and so friendly were the negotiations that Owen approached Davy to transport trade provisions to Mc Lemones Bluff, thirty miles downriver. In return for the labor we were to receive four barrels of dry meal, one barrel of salt, and ten gallons of whiskey. Without delay, we joined several other pioneers to pile the barge high with whiskey, flour, sugar, and furs and depart down the meandering river to complete the trade at our destination some thirty miles away with the local Indians.

As expected the journey was difficult as navigating the homemade vessel through the winding bends whilst avoiding huge boulders on the rapid currents was toilsome and often we had to plunge into the icy flow to release gigantic fallen trees that encumbered the river and blocked our progress.

Several days later, with the undertaking complete, along with our fellow traders from the riverboat we returned to Owen's and stayed the night. Drinking our host's whiskey and relaxing for the first time in over a week, loose tongues gossiped between the consumption of hot food and the tunes of the fiddle, and humor provided a carousel of cheerfulness that liberated our fatigue.

The Life and Death of My Best Friend, Davy Crockett

Davy was once again in his element, free from the shackles of politics and the congestion of the city. He kept the whole company entertained with unabated amusement. Constant roars of laughter echoed out through the gaps in the ill-fitting log walls and bacchanal bursts of parodies and songs penetrated deep into the blackness and painfully into the ears of the alert and cautious nocturnal creatures.

By the end of the evening, everyone's steam had been driven out of them, and with full stomachs and whiskey-poisoned blood the only sound resonating beyond the cabin walls was the contented rasps and snores of the deep sleepers.

For a few months, we again lived the indolent life, seeds had been planted, the cabin weatherproofed and furniture constructed. Most days we lounged in the sun and went hunting or fishing. Never did we return without a generous haul weighing heavy across our shoulders.

Barren of anxiety and little consideration given to our futures we loitered languidly through the warm hours of the long summer and if rain dared to ruin our relaxation we took to cover from the elements to cut and sow our tanned malleable deer skins into shirts, leggings and moccasins.

Occasionally we were visited by Indians who wanted to trade and unfearing of the Indian, Davy believed that if you gave them an honest welcome they would respect his valuables. When needing company we would visit Owen and his good wife to enjoy their hospitality and several times they made the reciprocated journey however, one late summer evening just as we bade Owen and his wife goodbye a raging bear leaped out from the edge of the forest to cut down Owen with one quick powerful swing of its paw.

The Life and Death of My Best Friend, Davy Crockett

Whilst I ran back inside the cabin for my rifle Davy reacted by pulling free his knife and charging towards the huge grizzly beast, and then at full speed, he leaped upon its back as it tore apart the screaming man. Repeatedly Davy stabbed down hard his knife into the bear's neck, however incensed it continued unmercifully to rip apart Owen with its huge snarling teeth until eventually, the holes in the bears necked pained it so much that it rose up and swung its back ferociously until Davy was tossed high into the air and into the foliage.

Rearing high and turning its attentions towards Davy I managed to perfectly discharge my lead into its expanded chest causing it to shriek loudly and scurry back from where it came, unfortunately not before it stretched out a claw in the numbed woman's direction.

I reached the blooded scene just as Davy emerged from the thicket, and together without words we gazed down upon the dead couple. Owen lay on his back with his lungs and innards exposed while his wife was slumped limp on her side with her head hanging loose and only remaining attached to her neck by a thin strand of flesh. For a short while we remained perfectly still listening for rustling movements within the forest and imploring god to forbid the bears return.

Quickly, then we returned to the cottage. I reloaded and Davy collected his rifle and then, checking upon the welfare of young John we gave chase to the bear.

Following a path of destruction and splattering's of blood within the hour, we had the huge beast within our sights however, gratefully no further lead was required. We covered the bear with loose branches, planning to return for its pickings after we laid Owen and his wife in the dirt.

The Life and Death of My Best Friend, Davy Crockett

The tragic incident did not deter Davy's ambition to establish a permanent home in the region and in early autumn he returned to Elizabeth to collect his family and belongings. I stayed behind with John Wesley and in Davy's absence together we constructed an eight by ten-foot shelter for myself just a short walks distance to give the family some privacy for once the Crockett's had returned and settled. Although small and dreary, the cover was adequate as it still was my desire to return to my homestead to manage my own affairs.

In late November, whilst I was out hunting, I spotted Davy in the far distance leading his family towards their new home. Walking in front with his rifle held over his shoulder, he led his two pack horses which conveyed all the Crockett's household belongings. Elizabeth and the children, all also leading horses and hounds, followed on behind in single file along the narrow path.

Slowly nearing into clear view I could clearly see their poverty was in the extreme as gaunt and skeletal the perilous journey had wreaked its toil the settlers and animals alike.

After a few minutes, I was greeted with a welcoming embrace that I had never experienced before and it pained me to see such relief permute on their ashen faces. We rested a short while, but the family was eager to complete the final mile or so of the journey and finally reunite with John. Spirited by the thought, and the promise of a green harvest which awaited them the pace increased and was pleasantly accompanied by merry singing.

The Life and Death of My Best Friend, Davy Crockett

After a brief recuperation period Davy, John Wesley, and I took to harvesting the greens and with plenty of wood stored, game in abundance, the larder full of bread, corn flour, and the most delicious meats anyone could crave, the Crockett's were prepared for the approaching harsh winter months.

Boredom beset upon us all in these short days where the light barely penetrated the dense grey clouds to illuminate the small cabin. Endless large snowflakes fell softly feathering the cabin and piling up against the timber walls to muffle any sound of the outside world and so with the onset of the early winter, my planned departure was delayed until the thaw was established. Although I was another mouth to feed both Elizabeth and Davy seemed relieved I would be staying throughout their first winter.

The Life and Death of My Best Friend, Davy Crockett

Chapter 12 - Christmas

As Christmas drew near apprehension emerged when we discovered our supply of powder lacked its worth making hunting for game impossible. With strict meat rationing, Elizabeth confirmed there would be enough to last us until the thaw, but every Christmas since the arrival of John Wesley Davy celebrated the holy morning by discharging salvos with his rifle.Ignorant to most matters of religion, he ensured on Jesus' birthday he would gather his family to celebrate by indulging in excess whiskey and entertaining with amusing stories and buoyant songs. Without the early morning salute, the day's events would not be the same, and not wanting to break from tradition, he told Elizabeth that he was going to walk across the white blanket of virgin immensity to Owen's untouched cabin where he could salvage some powder.

By now most of the region was covered with knee-deep snow and where the snow had not settled, streams had swollen to flood the vast lowlands which were between the two cabins. Elizabeth and I remonstrated the journey was foolhardy and that he should not risk his life traveling waste deep in icy waters just to uphold a tradition.

My considerations favored waiting for a break in the weather and I too pleaded with him not to make the dangerous journey, but never a man to change his mind, Davy laughed away our concerns and with his rifle over his shoulder, knife tucked in his belt and a spare set of cloths balled on the end of a timber shaft, without concern he ventured out into the cold, alone.

The Life and Death of My Best Friend, Davy Crockett

I knew we needed the powder. Without it we would not be able to hunt sufficiently to feed a family, the stock would only last another month or so and snared rabbits and slender fish would not sustain the family through the long harsh winter.

Elizabeth had deliberately exaggerated the stock to prevent Davy from taking any desperate action, but purposefully Davy used the traditional morning gun fire as an excuse, for he too did not want to cause alarm in front of the children.

For a few minutes I watched his footsteps begin to cover in the snow and then donned my thick skins and followed his trail. With my head down against the chilling wind, I urged forward crunching through the sinking deep snow with haste to catch the lonely trekker within the hour only to find his resolute stance had not weakened.

He urged me to return and upon my defiance, he finally admitted his true concern. He told me that a few days earlier he had found footprints in the snow around the boundary of the homestead. He was sure Indians had been watching the activities around the homestead and evaluating the value of the stock. Although he hoped they would just want to trade, he could not rule out that the harsh winter may have increased their desperation for satisfactory gain, and without the deterrent of shot he knew his bargaining power would be relying purely on their goodwill. He begged me to return forthwith and remain vigilant and active displaying open courage which may concern the Indians and prevent an approach until he returned with the dry powder.

The Life and Death of My Best Friend, Davy Crockett

On the second day of Davy's absence, a side-blowing gale set in with a fresh covering of heavy snow which drifted high and covered all familiarities of the surrounding landscape making it devoid of any landmarks. On the third day, the blizzard eased, so I explored the periphery of the homestead in search of footprints. I found nothing, but a few animal tracks. By the fifth day, the snow blasts had returned and the family was frantic with fear, so laden with a supply of additional clothing and donned in several thick skins, with no sign of any Indian trespassers, I ventured out into the blinding whiteness to search for my friend.

For four hours in blinding icy gusts, I trudged through the knee-deep snow with my extremities numb and my face burnt. Often and intensely I considered turning round wondering how far could I travel in these conditions before I reached the point of no return.

My legs ached from pushing them through the drifts and I cussed Davy for his stubbornness, confidence, and his lack of appreciating danger, but I continued onwards with my head arched low and my eyes peering over my raised hand which I used as a protective shield.

An eerie darkness loomed as the short day ended, but the surrounding blanket of brilliance ensured I could see even in the depths of the night. I planned to rest in the next forest where I hoped to find shelter and protection using a fallen tree to protect my back from the continual horizontal gusts that swept across the open fields and swirled around the deep meadows stinging my face and freezing my eyes.

The conditions in the forest were only marginally better. In the semi-darkness and being void of any paths, walking proved to be just as difficult and several times I tripped over snow-covered stumps and rocks.

The Life and Death of My Best Friend, Davy Crockett

Eventually, I rested against a pile of wrecked trees, and without too much effort I was able to prop above my head several branches to provide a little cover from the unrelenting white droplets.

Although my body was accustomed to hardship, never before had I encountered pain and exhaustion from such shivering. I curled up and breathed into my clothing to warm my body, then I cupped my hand over my face until they were warm enough to tuck under my furs without adding further to my distress. Having only made the journey to Owen's cabin on a few occasions, I was not familiar with the route and now with all landmarks covered in a thick blanket of white my uncertainty of finding Davy alive troubled me. Nothing was to be gained by sitting too long and once my lungs and legs were rested, I once more despondently straightened myself to continue forwards without the confidence I was heading in the right direction.

At the exit of the forest was a wide river which called to mind some resemblances to me and this encouraged my determination to continue with the search. The wide river was still flowing and on its surface were large blocks of ice which were being dragged quickly by strong currents. I scanned for a means of crossing and dropped into the water a branch of about eight feet in length, but it disappeared under the depth of the water and was immediately dragged away.

This was the point of no return and I shook my head reluctantly acknowledging my failure. Still, I looked all around considering my options, and not wanting to give in battling against the elements I blinked hard against the chilling wind to scan along the banks of the river, and the steep slope which was met by the forest.

The Life and Death of My Best Friend, Davy Crockett

Fallen trees and uprooted stumps lined the edge of the waterside, some had toppled into the water and lay on top of each other to form a natural dam and I considered crafting a small raft to traverse the sixty feet of freezing water. I dragged a couple of large logs to the water's edge, then lining them alongside each other I dug into the snow to gather damp foliage which I used as twine. I was just about to wipe off the canopy of snow from a nearby bush when suddenly something peculiar caused me to look again onto the opposite side of the river close to where I was now standing.

A large tree with exposed roots rising up to chest height was half covered in snow and attached in such a way it could not have blown there by the gusts was a distinct tarpaulin. With great optimism, I hollered repeatedly across the river. There was no reply and no movement and so I shouted again as loud as I could above the constant swoosh of howling gusts. I picked up some small pieces of wood and threw them close to the cover, still there was no response and no sign of movement.

With an unexpected sudden burst of invigorated hopefulness and energy, I dropped my supplies and I grabbed one of my carefully placed trunks, and ran towards the partial wood dam further along the bank, then without delay, I stepped onto the flotilla of logs and being careful to balancing the trunk across my arms I positioned my feet from one log to the next until I was about twenty feet across the river. At this point being driven totally by desperation I threw the trunk into the water and plunged in behind it resting my arms over the log so that I could kick out my legs and swim as fast as I could for the remaining forty feet or so to the bank.

The Life and Death of My Best Friend, Davy Crockett

Void of all breath and with no feeling in my arms and no control over my legs I had just enough vitality to reach the bank and to grab a solid boulder which I used to haul myself out of the freezing water. Panting repeatedly to regain my breath and composure I braced my arms about me and patted vigorously every part of my body to keep my blood flowing, and then unable to control my euphoria I crawled through the snow towards the cover calling out Davy's name.

Shouting out again I pulled back the canvas to reveal only an empty hollow, shock contort me and within an instant, my vision blurred, and a swirling blackness replaced the brightness, my final recall was my cheek thudding into swampy cold mud.

I do not recollect what happened to me whilst I was unconscious nor do I have any notion of how long I lay asleep, but eventually, a familiar calling roused me from certain death. Slowly opening my eyes to the caller who was shaking my shoulders finally his words reached into my soul and the face of Davy replaced the dull blur.

Asking many questions that I was not able to understand or answer, with his uppermost exertions he dragged me into the shelter of the woods where he forcefully and quickly stripped off my wet clothing and redressed me with dry skins and furs. With great and painful effort, I gradually recovered the use of my limbs and my relieved body began to warm enough to allow me to wave my arms and increase my warmth with the circulation of my blood.

After resting for a long while Davy told me the way back to Owen's cabin was also perilous so whilst we both still had our faculties and vigor we should continue to make haste and return home.

The Life and Death of My Best Friend, Davy Crockett

From his bounty of supplies which he had collected from Owens's house, Davy uncorked a bottle of whiskey and, after a huge gulp to vitalize our innards, we exited the forest to once more expose ourselves in the unendurable blasts of windy gusts.

Upon the bank of the river, we searched again for safe passage across the river, but once again a solution could not be found. Davy told me when he crossed the river he had straddled a wide log and paddled across, but not in sight anywhere that log must have been dragged away by the strong current. Davy made two tripods to attach the bundle of supplies to and the precious keg of gunpowder, and then as quickly as possible we stripped from our clothes and replaced them with cold wet ones. Securing our dry clothes on one of the tripods and holding them high to keep above the water we waded into the freezing water to wrap one arm each around a large floating log.

Immediately our bodies numbed and our legs had scarcely any feeling in them, but frantically with all the effort we could muster, we flicked our legs rapidly to cross us over the river whilst we were hung over that huge trunk. Davy painfully maintained aloft the powder whilst I desperately held high the branch with our clothing, knowing that if I failed to keep the clothes dry we would soon perish.

Reaching the soggy bank again we stripped as quickly as possible and redressed in the dry skins, and then with our teeth chattering, brains thumping and our bodies stricken with uncontrollable shivers we sped to the nearest cluster of trees and found refuge from the freezing tempest.

The Life and Death of My Best Friend, Davy Crockett

Our rest was deliberately brief and several hours later, leaning on each other for support we were cheered and immensely relieved when through our frosted eyes lashes we sighted a column of smoke and then the gradual emergence of Davy's cabin.

Both the warmth from our welcome and the heat from inside the cabin, I cannot find the words to illustrate my utter relief and gratitude. For at that moment, again I realised that I had been very close to death.

The Crockett family immediately rushed to the door and momentary gasps of shock were replaced with tears of exultation and tight binding hugs.Within minutes we had replaced our clothes and our stomachs stocked with hot tasty stew and fresh warm bread. Unable to finish the meal, with the warmth spreading through our veins we both drifted into a welcomed slumber and settled into comfort with our exposed feet throbbing near the stove.

Resting as peacefully as I have ever slept before, I was finally awoken by the nose relish and mouth salvia caused by fried bacon and baked biscuits. I rallied to my senses in no time and joined the family around the table to listen to Davy's tale of peril and survival. He explained to alert ears that when he first set off upon the journey the wind was a mere breeze and the snow only a few inches deep, but after reaching the midway point the wind increased and blizzard conditions set, depositing snow knee-deep in no matter of time.

Whilst the children listened with consuming enthusiasm, Elizabeth tutted and bemoaned his foolhardiness, stating he had responsibilities at home he should not jeopardize for such unimportant gains.

The Life and Death of My Best Friend, Davy Crockett

Davy flicked a knowing look in my direction, but deciding not to cause alarm by admitting how desperate their situation would be without the powder and ignoring her remonstrations much to the pleasure of the wide-eyed youngsters he continued by stating to cross the river he first boarded a huge chunk of ice and that he used a log to paddle and float across the raging icy currents.

Walking without rest through day and night he reached Owens's spiritless cabin by midday and lit a fire, warmed, and ate, but feeling no bad hardship he gathered the supplies he needed and set off for an immediate return. Unfortunately, the snow gales had intensified and after a couple of hours, he was forced to return to the safety of the lonely cabin. Through the night the freezing gusts continued to blow fiercely and the following morning after an inspection he was induced to stay a while longer by the warmth of the fireside.

By the fourth morning, fidgety with restless energy and with an irresistible urge to get home he once more ventured out into the thick snow to begin the homebound trek only to find the severe conditions hampered his progress to such an extent that after a few hours he again turned back to find protection in the cabin.

That night he didn't sleep, he admitted that he was agitated by his failure and dejected by not paying attention to Elizabeth's warning, and knowing his family would be in a state of great anxiety he strengthened his convictions to shoulder the musket and provisions, this time knowing it was Christmas eve he was determined not to turn back.

The Life and Death of My Best Friend, Davy Crockett

He hoped the thick snowfall and icy gales would have iced over the river enabling him to make the crossing without submerging himself into the bitterly cold current however, he had only traveled three hours when he trod on a sheet of ice which spread in all directions as far as the naked eye could see, the river had burst its banks and the overflow had flooded the lowlands with waist deep water which had gradually iced over.

Carefully Davy placed one foot upon the ice and tentatively raised his body slowly, he then raised his other foot from the snow and gently nestled it on the ice until gradually he allowed all of his entire body weight to settle on the glacial sheet. Tediously slow he moved forth treading as carefully and delicately as possible across the creaking shield, however after only five hundred yards the ice suddenly cracked again to drop his body waist-deep into the freezing slush.

With panic-driven urgency he reached out for his axe and swinging wildly to break the ice before him, he waded determinedly to a trapped log in the distance. Laying over the log for support he again took the axe and broke the ice around it until it gradually drifted along in the current for a few miles or so until a rise near a clump of trees provided solid ground.

Avoiding rest due to the bitterness he continued walking and several hours later he reached the banks of the wide river where his curiosity led him towards a snow-covered canvass shelter.

The silent audience was left with no doubts that both of us were extremely lucky to be alive and any normal human being with less tolerance for suffering and tough convictions for endurance would have perished in the snow to become animal fodder.

The Life and Death of My Best Friend, Davy Crockett

Now with one duty, and the most important one to Davy, he grabbed his musket and powder with juvenile enthusiasm and joviality then he palmed the exited family out of the door to instruct each one of them how to fire off the gun into the air for the traditional Christmas morning salute.

The Life and Death of My Best Friend, Davy Crockett

Chapter 13 – Old Rattler

After a couple of days of rest with nothing to do, but watch the snow fall, then rain, then snow again, Davy's restlessness once more became obvious. He walked in circles around the table, he peered out, and sighed at the snow-bearing clouds, he dried wood and stoked the fire, all the time yearning to get out into the forests to fire off his newly acquired powder. Our meat supply was not yet exhausted, but we were on rations until the conditions eased enough to permit a bountiful hunt. Finally, after two tiresome days, a cast of sunlight broke through the clouds and illumination lifted the gloom. Davy did not wait for the sleet to stop, with exhilaration he tossed in my direction a fur and within minutes we had unshackled the hounds and we were following their lead through the knee-deep white and cold slush.

Keeping up with their pace we raced alongside an overflowing stream, through a dense forest, leaped prostrate trees, and hacked our way through almost impenetrable thickets until finally together the three dogs raged with uncontrollable barking and burst forth into a sprint. Onwards they sped at full speed with Davy and I struggling behind them the best we could, half blinded by sleet, impaired by our heavy and bulky coverings onwards we ran through the gloomy dreariness, swerving passed the storm-desolated wreaked trees, and ripping through the icy-covered briers and thorns in pursuit of our crazed seekers. For miles, we continued with our search knowing the scent trail would lead the reliable hounds to a sizable reward.

The Life and Death of My Best Friend, Davy Crockett

Davy's optimism regarding the improvement in the weather now seemed premature, the low dull clouds had returned and blocked out the brief radiance of the sun beam and once again a gathering storm began to unleash it wrath upon the already frozen wilderness. Violent sheets of icy rain battered pitiless against our unprotected faces and the returning gusts stung our skin and numbed our knuckles and fingers which were closed tight around our rifles ready to fire in anticipation.

Davy cussed at his lead hound, Old Rattler and he stated when he caught up with him that he was going to shoot him. He was convinced the dog's usefulness had expired and he was not contributing. He claimed he was going senile and leading the others, Soundwell and Tiger on a wild goose chases. He bemoaned that Old Rattler had just become a food eater and nothing, but a burden. I felt sorry for that old saggy-eyed companion who had served Davy well over the years, but I understood if he did not contribute then he was of no use.

Branches and bushes were bent over with the heavy ice making it impossible for us to penetrate whilst at the same time providing safe cover for our pray, but finally, upon a break between the trees and on an exposed slope we were able to take aim upon two fat and exhausted geese and dispatch them to heaven. It was whilst we were stringing together their legs that Rattler raised a tremendous howl and ferocious barks which indicted to Davy we could be onto hunting something much more rewarding and substantial than gander.

"A bear." He mouthed watching old Rattler's telling signs, fervent saltation's, exposed salivating teeth, bulging nostrils, and alert eyes. Davy nodded and confidently repeated. "A bear." Then he shouted, "Go get 'em boys. Let's make war!"

The Life and Death of My Best Friend, Davy Crockett

Immediately upon the command they sped as one, swerving their nimble bodies around the obstructing foliage and lunging high over fallen trees. With Davy cleverly hacking a marker at each passing tree with his axe, as fast as we could whilst gulping in lung-bursting mouthfuls of cold air we tried in vain to tail our servants, but soon exhausted of all energy we were about to give up the chase when we rounded a huge spruce to set our watery eyes upon such a wild beast that it stopped us immediately in our tracks.

With our equilibrium all in a spin due to exhaustion now our legs and fingers began to shake, for before us and not more than twenty yards away roared a beast as high as a cabin. The hairs on my neck spiked as I watched Davy's three hounds move slowly around their prey, barking and growling, their excitable eyes flicking between the formidable grizzly and Davy intuitively summoning their master for aid.

Davy dropped the axe and replaced it with his rifle. 'Old Betsy' was greased and rubbed for the ready, and although she was a rough old piece he had looked after her and she had seen plenty of hard times. He boasted that she never told him a lie, and that when he caressed her in the right way she always discharged the ball right where he told her to.

"Go get him boys!" Davy yelled as he leveled the rifle toward the trapped animal. To his command, all three fearless hounds leaped into instant motion and assailed the huge beast. With an ear-bursting roar the brute reared up on his hind legs and sprung high with disbelieving agility to grab a large branch and raise himself up a tree leaving the snarling dogs to leap hopelessly into the air, their snapping teeth clamping on nothing, but pine air and drool.

The Life and Death of My Best Friend, Davy Crockett

A shot bellowed out from Davy's rifle and smog briefly clouded my vision, but through the grey haze I saw the bear wave his arm and roar as though he was fanning away a wasp from the fur-concealed bullet hole. Without pity or remorse, I took aim and successfully discharged my lead too whilst Davy quickly reloaded. Again the bear roared and this time shuddered, but rolling his head to search for an escape route he defiantly remained in the tree. Another blast from Davy's rifle resulted in the brute throwing back his head and screaming loudly into the air then with bulging frantic eyes he tumbled head first to the icy ground.

Before the huge thud of his landing had reached our ears the dogs had sprung upon his injured body to gore deep their teeth through the thick fur. The howling bear lashed out fiercely with its huge claws and reared up on its hind legs to shake off the dogs. Soundwell and Tiger whirled through the air crashing hard against trees and the frozen foliage which momentarily knocked the fight out of them, but Old Rattler's jaw was locked and his teeth embedded deep enough that his flapping body would not capitulate to the violent shakes.

Blood sprayed in all directions, dousing bright red to vividly taint nature's pure white. Without consideration for his own safety Davy composed his shaking limbs and withdrew his hunting knife, then as I had witnessed before he hastened to the aid of his old companion by springing high and landing the tip of the blade into the neck of his superior foe.

With quivering fingers, I tried to reload, but in my panic I dropped my lead ball into the snow. As I fumbled in my squirrel bag for another bullet my eyes fixed upon Davy who again and again withdrew and slammed deep the knife into the back of the raging animal's neck until finally the struggle waned and a throat rattling glug of blooded air signaled the fight was

The Life and Death of My Best Friend, Davy Crockett

over. With one final gasp, the bear slumped with limp limbs and rolled onto its side. I dropped to my knees and gipped out my breakfast and then wiped the water from my eyes.

Davy panting heavily collapsed and leaned against the dead animal with his arm caressing Old Rattler who had exhaustedly flopped across his master's knee. Tiger and Soundwell sniffed and pined, but wearily keeping their distance they circled the blood-drenched area of death and destruction.

"Knew the old fella would never let me down." Davy wheezed, his arm patting the dogs quivering hind.

With the beast being the size of twenty men we decided that we needed to split up. I agreed to stay with the carcass, warn off predators, and begin the boning out and skinning whilst Davy would return home to collect the travois and the eldest boys to help us haul back our valuable meat and hide.

Davy followed his axe marks in the trees until he was out of the forest and with urgency and without rest he paced home.

I had not prepared for a cold night out with only the canopy of branches providing any cover, however to keep myself from freezing I occupied myself with the butchery of the beast and once completed I warmed myself in his tepid huge fur.

It was nightfall when the Crockett's arrived and supplied with canvasses, additional skins, and dry wood we made a large fire and made camp for the night cheerfully knowing the bear meat compensated the ordeal suffered collecting the gunpowder.

The Life and Death of My Best Friend, Davy Crockett

As customary Davy amused us all and yet terrified the boys with his account of the hunt and capture, and hugging Old Rattler he laughed out 'The old fella might sometimes bark up the wrong tree but eventually, he always comes through with the tangibles.' I'm sure that wily old hound played Davy, as licking his wounds and gnarling on a deserved bone he never once took his eyes away from his master.

The Life and Death of My Best Friend, Davy Crockett

Chapter 14 – Politics

When the new shoots of spring appeared and the weather appeased us we gathered all the animal skins we had collected through the winter and we trekked down to Maddison County, stopping on the way to recuperate in a thriving settlement called Jackson. We bartered our valuable pelts for rarities, such as sugar, coffee, and salt. We also restocked our lifesavers with lead and powder.

It was whilst we were refreshing ourselves in a local tavern that some of the drinkers recognized Davy. Joining us in the conversations and revelry were some fellow soldiers from the Creek war and holding fond memories of their former colleague, they reminisced over a few drams recalling his heroics and considerations for helping the less fortunate who suffered from malnutrition in the needless campaigns. Listening in and observing how Davy was venerated in the region a group of strangers became impressed by his popularity and after a while the men, who introduced themselves and investors approached the backwoodsman to convince him to stand for the nomination as State Legislator for the region.

Immediately Davy declined their attempts to lure him back into politics. He had tried it once and the role did not appeal to him. He stated he lived forty miles from the nearest white settlement and he enjoyed his life too much, being a simple hunter and forager out in the wilderness to be tempted back into the deceitful complexity of political lampooning.

We returned to our cabins with our horses laden with our new valuables and the subject was not given any further thoughts or converse until two weeks later when another gentleman searched out Davy's cabin and told him that since his visit to Jackson, his appearance had roused the locals

The Life and Death of My Best Friend, Davy Crockett

into such fervor that he had been pressed into taking the long trek with the obligations of convincing Davy he was the right man to represent the citizens of Maddison County.

The gentleman produced several news documents and articles from Jackson, which confirmed his claim and referred to Davy's popular nomination. Davy's interest was once again roused and opening a keg of red eye with great zest the men discussed electioneering plans and opposition threats. I knew at once that my plans to return home were to be forsaken yet again.

Throughout the beer-drinking evening, Davy learned that his closest rival was Doctor Butler, the nephew of the former General Jackson, now current president. Davy's companion told him that Butler was a man of significant pretensions, and along with his friends, he had he had heard him publically slander the backwoodsman as for being merely an uneducated bear hunter, then he had insulted him by calling him 'a gentleman of the cane' an insult designed to emphasize and belittle Davy's impoverished existence whilst he, was man cut from finer cloth who suited the role of public representation.

As with a few years earlier in Lawrence County, a great gathering was called in Maddison for the electioneers to deliver their customary biased speeches to proclaim why they should win the votes and be elected as the State Legislator. The large assembly consisted of the most voluble men in the community and a variety of backwoodsmen, who clad with coonskin caps and stitched deerskin two pieces had traveled far with interest.

The Life and Death of My Best Friend, Davy Crockett

The electioneering speeches began with the usual political braggarting and demeaning ripostes as one by one the candidates took to the traditional stump.

Aspiring to convince and influence the bored crowd to gain an advantage Butler opened his speech by offering everyman in attendance free and copious amounts of flowing whiskey and considering his astuteness a success when he stepped down from his deliverance he bore a mouth-stretching grin which reached from ear to ear. Davy however, noticed an opportunity, the whiskey had poisoned the stomach-hungry audience and he jumped onto the stump to shout out and amuse the drunken onlookers attentions with his usual satire and gusto which demanded an attentive ear. Doctor Butler did not recognised Davy and assuming he was one of the drunken backwoodsmen who was just engaging in fun he stepped in front of Davy and demanded he should resign from the stump.

Davy stood firm and introduced himself to enormous cheers and hat waving, then he apologized for being so humble that he could not afford to dress in an Eastern suit like all the other candidates. As Butler's face reddened he quaffed in a bid to hide his embarrassment and he feigned an apology for not recognizing the fabled hunter, but Davy quickly added to Butler's shame by stating that he had just crept out from under his cane, then he launched into a tirade stating he understood the gentleman's misjudgment because he was at a great disadvantage for being poor whilst he and the other candidates were rich. Davy's timing and judgment were perfect, for whilst Butler furnished the voters with free whiskey it was he, Davy who benefitted from their alcohol-driven cheerfulness.

The Life and Death of My Best Friend, Davy Crockett

Davy continued to enthrall the crowd with his amusing tales and his candor for hospitality stating that 'whilst he only owned just one coat, he would never leave a man worse off than when he first met him'. He answered shouts of laughter with bravado and with enthusiasm. He answered the calls of hecklers with quick homely wit whilst denouncing his challengers by stating their fancy flow of words were no proof of wisdom, because true wisdom is rare and their talk was cheap.

Whilst Davy toured the region citing rhetoricals interceded with amusing tales and anecdotes all of which as usual made him immensely popular with the locals who regarded him as one of their own, I once more returned to the Crockett homestead to ensure the prosperity continued.

The chatter around Lawrence County was that Davy had all the requirements and attributes needed to represent voters and sensing the electoral defeat Doctor Butler descended into unscrupulous acts of bribery and solicitation of the needy to boost his appeal however, his promises of coinage and furtherance failed to appeal and on election day Davy secured a huge majority and for the second time, he was selected to serve as a State Legislator.

Davy served for two years as a Legislator, but the dullness of routine and lack of adrenalin bored him, nevertheless he remained popular with his fellow legislators and when Colonel Alexander's position on the National Legislator was due for re-election Davy's colleagues persuaded him to oppose Alexander and challenge for his seat in Congress. At first, Davy declined the pressure applied on him from his supporters stating Congress was a step above his knowledge and that he knew nothing of affairs in Washington.

The Life and Death of My Best Friend, Davy Crockett

Still, Davy's lobbyists insisted he was the man for the post and they would not relent in their pursuit until eventually Davy's resistance waned and he declared his interest in the position.

At that time a tariff was proposed to be introduced on the profits of cotton, and although Davy knew by voting for the new legislation he would offend his constituents his integrity would not allow him to appease his people by opposing something in which he believed. He persisted with his loyalty stating once the tariff was introduced the price of cotton would fall to everyone's benefit, but unfortunately, his beliefs led to his failure of being elected as venting their disillusion his supporters denounced his actions and voted to re-elect Alexander. As a consequence of his sincerity, Davy lost his position as Legislator and returned home.

The Life and Death of My Best Friend, Davy Crockett

Chapter 15 – Devil's Elbow and Re-election

Upon his return to the banks of the Obion, he confessed he had no ambition for Congress and the back snarling of betrayal which ruled the way to success and progression amongst the elite who aspired to rule.

For the next two years we farmed, fished, and hunted the abundant stocks of elk, deer, and bears with determined ambition and success. By the second summer we had stocked fifteen bear skins and a valuable pile of pelts taller than the cabin so with the bounty idle we decided to hire a couple of fellas to help us build two flat-bottom boats in which we could sail down to New Orleans and sell our haul. Besides the surplus skins and furs, we had a huge collection of staves which we had purpose of selling to the barrel makers for a decent reward.

With our loads piled twenty feet high and secured, we embarked towards New Orleans by setting sail down the Obion until we joined the majestic Mississippi. Here, because of the strong current and the rough waves we needed to apply additional obstinacy to our crafts, and so to assist us we lashed the two boats together.

A couple of further challenges tested our abilities and strength to the full. Firstly, it soon became apparent that landing to set foot on dry land was impossible, then at a place called Devil's Elbow we engaged in the hardest trial I have performed to stay alive. Here the unruly currents prevented us from commanding the tug and we could not dock to rest, nor try as we might change direction from where the water wanted to take us. Totally exhausted from our efforts we collapsed and gave up trying to control the vessel allowing it to drift sideways at a frightening speed until we struck a large bolder which spun us violently into a protruding tree.

The Life and Death of My Best Friend, Davy Crockett

Angled downwards and beyond the flapping waves a thick lance-shaped trunk pierced the side of our boat to allow the fast-flowing muddy water to flood our vessel.

Davy leaped below deck to inspect the damage and I grabbed my axe to cut through the securing ropes and detach the two boats, however upon releasing the boat to quickly drift away the punctured vessel suddenly arced and I lost my footing and fell hard, cracking my skull against the deck. For a few moments, I lay in a silent blackness, not knowing where I was until I was able to shake away the black clouds from my vision and open my eyes.

My evenness still spun, but as my vision slowly cleared I heard the cracking of the staves and I despairingly saw the load unbound to fall against the hatchway blocking Davy's only exit. For a few seconds I had to squint and blink several times to clear my vision enough to see my fallen axe, then swinging furiously I took to chopping the bind which held the beveled pieces of heavy wood together. After a few savage swings with the blade the staves fell loose from the bail, but once again, with rapidity the boat turned steep forcing me this time to leap across to the banking.

Now the boat was sinking fast, and the tilt was so steep that the boat's only doorway was submerged. From the river bank I heard Davy hollering for help, and so I sprinted towards the hind of the vessel where I saw his hand waving through a small rope hole. I planted my feet solid and by stretching out, with fury I attacked the side of the boat with the axe to try and make an escape hole close by. I swung with furious speed and without pause, but the boat sank lower so quickly that three-quarters of the boat had disappeared under the waves and water began to pour through the rope hole.

The Life and Death of My Best Friend, Davy Crockett

Davy's hand had disappeared and his desperate calls for help were interrupted with his gasps for air. I chopped wildly and rapidly in desperation and soon a small hole was made, but now the river level had reached my small breach. I continued to hack around the hole under the water until I saw Davy stick out his arm and plead with me in desperation to drag him through it.

I seized his hand and pulled with all my might until his head and half of his shoulder jerked through, but plugging tight in the hole, the rest of his body would not move. The water flowed over his head and caught in his throat as he screamed and begged me to pull as hard as I could, even if it meant pulling off his arm.

I wedged my feet and leaned back to try again with one last mighty effort and just when it seemed all my exertions had been in vain, a passing stranger heard the pleas and mercifully ran to my aid. Together with fierce jerks, we stripped Davy's body of all his clothing as we finally dragged him free from the disappearing boat.

Breathless and gulping in mouthfuls of recuperating fresh air together, Davy almost naked and painfully skinned, the three of us watched one boat disappear under the water and the other float away, both taking with them our entire load of furs, food, and rifles. However, we were not despondent, the momentary distress was displaced by a painkilling-induced joy for simply being alive and surviving the ordeal. The kind hearted fella, seeing that were we totally destitute gave Davy his vest and bade us farewell, stating that if we managed to walk ten miles to Bracey Bridge, his wife would cook us a wholesome meal and supply us with a hearty pack up.

The Life and Death of My Best Friend, Davy Crockett

Ragged to the bone and soaking wet we sat upon the river boulders for a few hours nursing Davy's deep and long abrasions, his shoulders and hips were scared and his back shredded. Whilst we contemplated which direction to trudge a passing merchant tug appeared in the waters and we hailed to catch the crew's attention until finally they sent a skiff to collect us. The Captain was a gentile old fella loaded with plenty of garrulous prattle and after listening to our misfortune he took pity upon us and permitted us to stay on board until we reached Memphis.

In Memphis, Davy met up with an old friend who supplied us with additional clothing and money which we used as fare to Natchez. Here we hoped to locate our drifting boat, but we were informed although our boat had been seen about fifty miles south and although an attempt had been made to land it, all efforts failed, and so the unyielding boat continued upon its rogue journey unmanned.

The river disaster had drained our finances and almost taken Davy's life and upon the long trek home he confirmed the role of a Congressman suddenly appealed to him and we discussed again standing for election at the upcoming congressional elections.

With the price of cotton now substantially decreasing and Davy declaring it was due to the effects of the new tariff he once again found himself popular with the politically minded locals, unfortunately without wealth, Davy was unable to fund a serious campaign against his two rivals William Arnold, and his old foe Colonel Alexander. With his chances of being elected diminishing fast, I decided to sell off most of my stocks in order to loan him the financial backing he needed to compete on the campaign trail and expand his influence in the distant towns where the intelligent lawyers and intellectual business men were generally favored.

The Life and Death of My Best Friend, Davy Crockett

Once my saleables had been exchanged for cash, Davy was able to attend the final three rallies and address the voters alongside Alexander and Arnold. Once more knowing he would be unable to compete with his foes technical abilities, their free-flowing political grammar and academic discourse, Davy employed the old trick that was used against him several years earlier by Doctor Butler. Whilst Arnold took the stump and spoke at length discrediting Colonel Alexander's political credentials, Davy purchased several kegs of whiskey and issued them to the bored gathering with perfect timing so that the liberal stimulant began to bewitch the attendees just as he stepped up to the stump.

Davy again concentrated his rhetoric on non-committal jocosely which appealed to the now jovial spectators and when he stepped down to applause Colonel Alexander again rose and endeavored to preach on matters of finance, tariffs, political affairs, and the incompetency of Arnold. Finally red-cheeked and sweaty-browed, Colonel Alexander stepped down to hisses and heckles to allow Arnold to stand, and as usual, deliver an address that opposed everything the Colonel had proposed.

Neither man made any reference to the third candidate alluding they did not consider Davy as a threat and within minutes the restless crowd lost interest in Arnold's boisterous blabbering. Beginning to talk amongst themselves to great amusement many of them found entertainment from a large flock of Guinea foul which waddled towards the stump causing mayhem with their noisy hissing and clucking to the annoyance of Arnold, who kicked out his legs in their direction and angrily ordered for their removal to an eruption of laughter and ridicule.

The Life and Death of My Best Friend, Davy Crockett

Davy jumped to the stump to once more make a lasting favorable impression on the crowd. Turning to his left to face Arnold and Colonel Alexander, he announced that he was also annoyed, not from nature's interruption, but from the lack of respect shown to him by his rivals. He stated neither of the politicians had the manners or the decency to mention him as an opponent and they considered the interruption of the fouls more of a threat than himself, and although they had managed to drive away the nuisance of the fouls they would not rid themselves of this opponent.

Immediately the crowd responded to Davy's witticism and once again universal laughter broke out along with calls of 'Crockett' which repeated loudly throughout the town square. Glancing at each other, Alexander and Arnold feared Davy as a serious candidate, and their concerns were proven when on Election Day, Davy the ill-educated bear hunter won the vote to claim a seat in Congress to represent the Memphis constituency as National Legislator for over one hundred thousand people.

After stocking up the homestead with supplies for the oncoming winter of 1827, Davy emerged from his cabin in the wilderness to take up his seat in Congress. As he closed the door behind him to bid farewell to his family, dogs, and rifle he was in a pensive mood, yet he was looking forward to the adventures in Washington.

Against his command, I loaned him another one hundred and fifty dollars to help pay for his expenses, and then I accompanied him by horse for the first sixty miles until we reached a small juncture where he was able to purchase a carriage ride to Raleigh.

The Life and Death of My Best Friend, Davy Crockett

Neither the Crockett family nor I heard any news or received any correspondence from Davy until the New Year when a passing trader from the east told us he had acquired information that suggested Davy's rawness had caused quite a stir in Congress and he said the politicians at first hadn't taken too well to the deer skinned fighter.

During the first few weeks he had been regarded as a carnival act however, he added that his honesty and integrity had been well received by many in the building renowned for its muckraking and unable to get the better of him in the debates they found him to be a person of popularity and immense interest.

In spring I transported pelts by cart to Roanoke, Virginia, and upon my arrival, I immediately found Davy's notability in Washington had spread far and gained enough substantial interest that tales of his humorous rebuffs and anecdotes filled the front pages of the local news sheets and message boards, a few of which I purchased to take home to read out to Davy's practically illiterate family.

One article I read with hilarity described an account of Davy standing up to a gang of aggressors in one of the taverns he had stayed in while traveling to Washington. The author of the piece detailed that Davy, being cold, wet, and tired wanted to warm himself next to the warm flames in the tavern's hearth. However, a couple of local bruisers occupied the room and blocked out the heat from the furnace, and so Davy had to politely request for them to move a little so that he could feel the radiance and warm his bones. Unimpressed by the wild man's drawl and appearance the three men refused to cede their position and they took it upon themselves to intimidate the stranger who dared to entreat their habitation.

The Life and Death of My Best Friend, Davy Crockett

Challenging him to announce himself Davy wisely reacted by standing resolutely tall to boastfully entertain.

"I am Davy Crockett, fresh from the backwoods of Tennessee. Half horse and half alligator with a little touch of a snappy turtle."

The noisy revelers who crowded the small tavern silenced as they found their attentions seized by the calamity Davy was causing.

"I can wade the Mississippi, leap the mighty Ohio, and ride upon a bolt of lightning and dive without a scratch into a hornets nest." Shaking heads and mutterings of laughter began to arise, but undeterred Davy continued. "I can whip my weight in wildcats, and if any gentleman pleases for a ten-dollar bill I can roll and throw a panther and I can hug a bear too close for comfort."

Noting the establishment supported Quincy Adams by pinning propaganda behind the crude small bar Davy bravely chose to end the fun and state his political way of thinking. "And I'll eat any man opposed to General Jackson."

Instead of reacting with violence, the amused men admired his audacity and they moved aside to permit the spread of the warmth whilst others hurried to the bar intent on supplying the entertaining intruder with liquid goodwill.

Some pamphlets nicknamed him 'The Lion of the West' whilst others printed articles on more serious matters. One documented Davy being invited to dine with President Quincey Adams whilst other columns were filled with his many narratives which often accompanied his debates with his fellow politicians.

The Life and Death of My Best Friend, Davy Crockett

With my trade completed I returned to Lawrence County spreading the exploits of my friend to every stranger I became acquainted with on the journey and every neighbor whose lands I crossed.

For the next two years, Davy stayed in Washington, returning home when only Congress was in closure. In 1829 his reputation for integrity and incorruptible representation led to him being re-elected and later in the same year his endeavors rewarded him when his party leader, General Jackson was elected as President of the United States.

Although being a staunch supporter of Jackson, over the next few month's Davy found himself opposed to some of Jackson's proposals. He did not agree with his leader's views and ambitions and therefore Davy's conscience forced him to speak out the truth especially when President Jackson's new Indian bill was confirmed.

The newspapers raised a storm with a tirade of one-sided accounts of Davy's opposition to the new law which would remove the Indians from their homelands. Back home everyone knew Davy would not betray his honesty and turn his opinion at the expense of his conscience even though many who sat beside him in Congress advised that if he did not relent and give his backing to the bill he would be cold shouldered and alienated by those around him and by those he represented, and as everyone knew opposing President Jackson was considered an unpardonable sin.

Davy's views and arguments were not published and soon every article printed was designed to damage his integrity with invented misrepresentations and wild claims against the man who defended the rights of the natives.

The Life and Death of My Best Friend, Davy Crockett

The consequence of Davy standing firm for his convictions and his opposition to the bill was that he lost the next election and once more he returned to the life of a hunter.

As soon as Davy set foot on home soil I knew he was a changed man. The past pleasures of solitude and the peacefulness of the forests no longer taunted him. Hunting no longer appeased him and having simply enough food and warmth no longer satisfied his needs. He had sampled stature, endless handshakes, and pats on the back. He had dined with presidents and tasted the hospitality of well wishes who wanted to boast about meeting the famous backwoodsman, but now he was back amongst the rodents and wild animals who only recognized the threat of another faceless human.

The peaceful rambles in the woods with only the calls of wildlife echoing inside his ears had now lost its luring charm and the isolation away from the bustling excitement of supporters bored him and I knew at the first opportunity he would pursue re-election.

Often it appeared that he was trying to convince himself that he was a better person away from politics and he would justify his actions by exclaiming 'Better alone than in bad company' and with a sad disconsolate emphasis he would quietly mutter 'We walk by faith and not sight'

He had to wait two years until the next election, but rather than ponderously choring through his duties with a doleful demeanor he feigned gusto to resonate wholesome happiness in the Crockett household.

The Life and Death of My Best Friend, Davy Crockett

During these two years, we saw very little of each other. I visited on only a couple of occasions and Davy reciprocated however, whilst the family was still illiterate it was evident, with Davy's patience they had developed into competent farmers and hunters capable of managing the household without additional paid support.

Finally it came as no surprise when during one of our hunting trips Davy confirmed to me that the two years of farming life had not dulled his spirit for returning to Washington and that he intended to seek re-election, furthermost it was also no surprise when, within a few months he had regained his position in Congress.

After a few month's absence from the homestead, a messenger lettered me with a request from Davy. The few lines of words stated that his return to Washington had been successful and once again he had the ear of the house, but recently had suffered a bout of melancholy and his doctor had advised a period of rest away from the stresses of politics. He informed me that even though he had footed many a mile in the south he had never seen any of the northern cities and so he would like me to accompany him on a tour of the north and east regions. He did not enquire if I favored a visitation, instead, he assumed correctly that I would want to accompany him and he finished the petition by enquiring how quickly could I reach Washington?

Chapter 16 - The Grand Tour

I assumed I could reach Washington before my replied transcription, so leaving the animals and land in the trusted keep of John Wesley Crockett, I saddled up my most resilient horse and left Tennessee forthwith.

I followed the same route as Davy took to Washington, occupying both a saddle and a carriage for over a week. Walking stiff-back with travel, sore and feeling awkward dressed in poor man's skins amongst the well suited Washingtonians, I also found myself dumbfounded when I encountered a man with a very distinct semblance to Davy.

Standing behind a cart full of books on a bustling street corner, donned in a full frontiersman jacket with ornate tassels and an oversized coonskin hat, the man was shouting exaggerated details and falsehoods concerning my friend from Tennessee. I listened and watched for a few minutes as the man claimed boisterously to all passersby that he was Davy Crockett and for thirty cents they could buy his authenticated and signed biography.

As the hawker shouted out quotations "If you know it to be true then just go right ahead and do it," and "Sometimes you've just got to go right down a path to see where it leads you," I gave him an offended stare and distanced myself from his pitching to sped with agitation to Mrs Ball's boarding house where Davy was renting lodgings, whereupon after a great deal of conversation he kindly sent out for his manservant to supply me with more suitable city wearables.

The Life and Death of My Best Friend, Davy Crockett

I told Davy about the fraudulent bookselling braggart, but unconcerned he just laughed stating the man was only trying to earn a few dollars albeit mischievously, and as I would later find out we came across many others copying his likeness and giving speeches in brew houses for free drinks and a couple of actors who were characterizing him in stage performances. Davy had become fashionable, and the public was intrigued.

After plenty more catch up chatter he revealed to me his intentions to tour the north east, and although he never implicated otherwise I could tell by the glint in his eye the prescription of rest was a ruse manufactured purely for the opportunity to travel.

Amongst the boardwalks and in the restaurants of our capital city Davy's appearance attracted the eyes of all and never once due to his instinctive geniality did he refuse to pass a few moments with the inquisitive, shake a friendly hand, or initiate dialect with those too embarrassed to approach.

In the bars, drinks were liberally offered by the many hospitable fellows and his name was toasted and chanted when it was time for him to make a polite excuse to retire.

After a few days recuperating from the long horse ride, we left Washington and by evening we were dining with the prominent business gentlemen of Baltimore. Politics and amusing banter spread from lips to ears faster than a spooked squirrel, but Davy did not mind, he was completely blush-free, at ease and although he was by no means an intellectual or had wealth, he was naturally blessed with a sharp tongue which bettered any baiters and enthralled the dinner guests.

The Life and Death of My Best Friend, Davy Crockett

Some, a minority around the large tables, being well mannered and not accustomed to honest backwoodsmen's tongue considered Davy rude and vulgar, whilst the others found him amusing and his tales appealing. Whilst Davy revelled in all the attention I often feared humiliation, and so I would disengage from most of the converse and enjoy the evenings with my eyes and mouth engaged entirely upon the huge portions of exotic fare.

A few days later, we experienced our first ever steam-powered vessel when we boarded a steamboat bound for Philadelphia, a place until the previous day I had never heard of. Davy admitted after a lengthy bout of silent considerations that he was looking forward to a town where he had no regard and going amongst people, who being taken up by their own affairs and pleasures could pass him by in the street without knowing or caring who he was.

After a pleasant passage down Chesapeake Bay, we disembarked to board a rail car. With a dozen carriages attached, and pulled by a huge wheezing steel beast, this was a new sight which set upon our eyes, and another new experience for us. After a brief moment of dubious hesitation, an attentive railroader escorted us to a comfortable bench next to a wide window, where once the huffing and puffing commenced we could watch the towns and countryside pass us by in utter comfort.

Leaving a dark grey streak behind us we astonishingly travelled seventeen miles in only fifty-seven minutes and we needed no rest to ease travel weary limbs and no water to swill off travel dust.

The Life and Death of My Best Friend, Davy Crockett

Another reception was arranged in Delaware where we experienced wine for the first time. The rouge vinegar, called wine did not appeal to our taste, but it ensured Davy gave the most vehement toast to end another pleasant evening which had contained more eye-enticing amounts of hot fanciful food, brandy, and afterwards, the softest of beds which delivered to my stuffed body the most comfortable night's sleep I had ever experienced.

After eggs and bacon the following morning we boarded another steamboat and stood on deck in the mild breeze to watch the city of Philadelphia come into our view. To our bewilderment, it appeared as if a mass army had gathered to stand shoulder-to-shoulder on the wharf. Davy asked the Captain why there was such congestion and to the Captain's delight he announced to everyone who was preparing to disembark that the city folk of Philadelphia had gathered to greet the famous Wildman into their city.

As Davy stepped onto the docking platform, the Captain hailed loudly Davy Crockett's arrival to an eruption of instantaneous applause. Davy saluted, removed his hat, and tilted his head to acknowledge the crowd, and although his face displayed a slight embarrassment, his eyes narrowed and his mouth curled to betray his modesty. I recall again being astonished to see such a welcoming exhibition of joy, hurrahing, and a strong desire to meet the Colonel this far away from Tennessee.

Although, Davy had no idea that he was going to attract such adulation, he stepped onto the wharf and into the throng without any nervousness or hesitation. The cheers sounded, his name was called, hats were thrown, and slaps on the shoulder and handshakes met him in every direction he stepped.

The Life and Death of My Best Friend, Davy Crockett

Never considering snubbing an open hand of the greeters, it took us quite a considerable time to reach our awaiting carriage which patiently waited only yards away.

Pressing on through the compacted crowd, our host led us into an elegant barouche which was drawn by four huge and shiny horses, the size and strength I never knew existed. Davy, awed by all the fuss and the ear-throbbing joyous din posed for a while on the carriage steps, and smiling, he waved to all expressing his gratitude for such a welcome.

Once inside he expelled a huge sigh confessing he did not think the folks this far north would have even heard his name and never had he anticipated drawing any kind of attention. Wiping the sweat from his brow he admitted he had been extremely humbled by the assemblage, and he did not know exactly what to do or say. Our hosts laughed and unconcerned by the lack of his gentlemanship and the rawness of his tones they urged Davy just to do what he always does, act natural with true honesty.

Our arrival at the United States Hotel was no less extraordinary. The side walkers waved as we passed them by and upon our exit from the carriage another large and enthusiastic crowd blocked our passageway. Friendly and politely Davy led the way through the blockade of bodies, shaking each and every clasping hand which was thrust out in front of him. Another speech was demanded and duly given from the lavish stairwell inside the crammed reception hall where Davy, again removed his hat to thank the citizens of Philadelphia for such an unexpected, but warm welcome, then making his obeisance clear he promised he would again address the audience in full at midday the following day.

The Life and Death of My Best Friend, Davy Crockett

True to his word after breakfast Davy emerged from the hotel to address the awaiting huge gathering. Without letters nor any recital, he spoke with genuine conviction regarding his role in the political office. He stated boldly that he would only support his president if the president conducted himself with proper dignity and true loyalty toward all the people. Previously being a staunch supporter of President Jackson he admitted the president's recent affairs concerned him and he would not continue to offer his allegiance through just pure loyalty. His conscience would not allow him to betray the constituents who had put their faith in him to represent them when they had no voice of their own.

After the official business was favorably conducted we were taken by carriage for a tour of the city. We had heard tales from travelers of concrete forests with buildings that seared into the clouds, but now we saw them with our own eyes. Wide cobble streets all bustling with stalls and traders selling all aspects of wares and consumables in bright colors that we never knew existed. Red vegetables, yellow fruit, fancy pants, and polished boots accompanied by bartering lined our route throughout the maze of flat, root-free roads. Davy likened the city to a big clearing of all forestation with only dead trees remaining standing on a dull and foggy day.

Gifts were presented at two unexpected and hastily arranged ceremonies, one being a highly polished and decorated rifle inscribed with 'Go ahead' which amused and appealed to Davy, but in private he doubted its accuracy and the other being a cut glass decanter of which he confessed he had nothing of worth to furnish within its belly. By the time we retired to our rooms three crates of the region's finest liquors had been delivered to Davy's door.

The Life and Death of My Best Friend, Davy Crockett

Being kin to only the sounds of the forest creatures, the smell of fresh pine, and the vastness of the wilderness far from any populous, I knew Davy found the non-stop bustle and adulation exhausting, and although he was too polite to convey any dissatisfaction to his hosts he was relieved when he could rid himself of the throaty smog and return to the solitude of his room.

The next stop was New York where upon our approach on the water buildings as tall as mountains cricked our necks. Standing in silence amongst the debunkers neither of us found words to describe the sky reaching brick and horizon before us however, our wonderment and Davy's brief anonymity were short-lived as with Philadelphia the loose-jawed Captain of the vessel boastfully announced and pointed Davy to the multitude who had eagerly assembled to catch a glimpse of the folk hero, and again he was feted and treated with the greatest of distinction as he was procession led through the mass waving crowd to the American Hotel.

That evening Davy was guest of honor amongst hundreds of New York's finest dignitaries, businessmen, and politicians who used the event to promote their own self-importance, sway opinions, and bias others with their own political beliefs, however when Davy was announced as ' the undeviating supporter of the constitution and the law' in response to recent propaganda the toast and short speech he delivered confirmed in the clearest of messages that there was a time when he was loyal to the president he once followed and trusted, but now he believed the presidents strategy has been changed by influencers and that his integrity was inclined swayed by personal gain and unethical profit.

The Life and Death of My Best Friend, Davy Crockett

He amused the delegation with a yarn about a young boy and a red cow. He told of a farmer who had instructed the youngster to plough the field by simply following the red cow. He walked on behind the cow and ploughed the field all forenoon without rest and was utterly dismayed when the farmer returned and swore at him for ploughing crooked lines. To laughter and resounding applause Davy added, 'Why sir, you told me to follow the red cow.' The laughter did not hide Davy's serious message regarding gumption and his thoughts about the president's motives and his ability to lead the county with honesty. The thunderous applause had not wearied and the cigar smoke not cleared before calls were raised urging Davy to test his skills against New York's finest shootists. We both knew that Davy was in no position to decline no matter how polity he excused and so with a strangers rifle plunged into his hands and tables cleared he began to take aim at an empty ale keg which someone had hastily marked with a target and fixed against a wall.

With expectant eyes testing his legendary skills he squinted and fired to send the ball thudding into the center of the target one hundred and twenty yards away. As Davy acknowledged the cheers and the hand claps a few disappointed sighs and grumbles could be heard amongst the acclaim, and as he began to lower himself back into his chair another loaded rifle was thrust in his direction.

Again not wanting to insult his host Davy stood, and this time without a pause to firm his aim he impatiently unleashed a blast of thunder which propelled lead direct into the center of the target.

Once more within the cheers from his supporters, there were a few grumbles from those wanting to see him embarrassingly fail and one extremely loud boo resonated above all.

The Life and Death of My Best Friend, Davy Crockett

Our attention was drawn to the cynic and as we turned a short, round-bellied, and red-faced man approached our host.

A brief conversation with much arm gestation commenced, and then our host rather apologetically came close to Davy's side to whisper that the agitated dinner guest had boasted that he could beat the wild man in a one-shot match. Davy handed the rifle back to its owner with a compliment upon its condition then he casually smiled towards the challenger. The worry-free glint seemed to annoy the man who reacted by shouting his challenge loudly across the room for everyone to witness, then he baited.

"Any target, any distance and one hundred dollars to be paid by the loser!"

Without hesitation, Davy calmly turned over his palm to wave the braggart to come closer, and then he instructed him to choose his mark. The overweight man bellowed orders for the keg to be taken back another ten yards, then he pulled out a ten-dollar bill and told our host to pin it to the keg.

Once the target was set, our host stood between the two shootists and flipped a coin to decide who fired first. Davy lost, and he stepped back to allow the stocky man to snatch the rifle out of the hands of its owner, and after a lengthy inspection in which he raised the rifle to his shoulder several times to judge its weight and balance, he proceeded to load the missile. Again, more time passed as the challenger firmed his feet, squatted his knees and peered along the barrel, then holding his breath until finally he was sure of his aim he pulled back on the trigger to unleash his lead.

The Life and Death of My Best Friend, Davy Crockett

Wiping clear the smog before his eyes the ignoramus gloat turned to Davy bearing a huge satisfied grin denoting his pleasure after seeing his lead had plunged deep beneath the body of George Washington.

With belligerent arrogance the stout man tossed the rifle in Davy's direction and breaking the silence in the room Davy caught the rifle and congratulated his nameless challenger upon his shooting skills, then without delay he loaded the weapon, stepped forth, focused down the barrel and pulled the trigger with such speed and deliberation that all the wide-eyed onlookers gasped in disbelief.

As the smoke cleared, foreheads rutted and eyes narrowed towards the target with astonishment.

"He missed!" The fat man shouted. "Missed the god darn keg altogether." His flabby cheeks lined from the gloating grin.

"Best check again." Davy calmly requested casually resting the rifle and taking to his chair

Out host hastened towards the barrel where he had to pull back the shoulders of inquisitive crowd who had reached the target before him and arched down low scrutinizing eyes.

 "I can't believe it." He exclaimed as investigating his eyes stared long at the note.

"Pay up bear hunter." The gloat impatiently demanded planting his knuckles before Davy on the highly polished table.

Davy angled his head so that he could direct his words to our host rather than the fat man's bulk. "Well?" He requested confirmation.

The Life and Death of My Best Friend, Davy Crockett

Laugher mixed with gasps of disbelief boomed around the room as our host erected himself and held the barrel high with both of his hands to display the missile damaged note. "Colonel Crockett's only gone and planted the ball in our foundering father's head." He elatedly announced.

"Whoa, their fella I didn't mean to cause no offence." Davy scraped back his chair and stood with his arms held straight to plead his innocence.

Rapturous cheers and applause immediately followed Davy's joke and filled the room, but ignoring the praise Davy arched slightly to put his face to within one inch of his embarrassed opponent.

"Want to go again for doubles?" He teased.

The beetroot faced man who never formally introduced himself reached inside his jacket and slammed a hand full of screw up notes onto the table, then cursing his bad luck he elbowed his way through the crowd to disappear.

Davy thanked the man for collecting the easiest one hundred dollars he had ever earned and advised him 'that a man's temper is so much a good thing that he should never lose it.' Then returned to the celebrations buying drinks for everyone in the room.

After the affairs in New York were concluded we headed up to Boston to dine and debate with yet more politicians and businessmen, and yet again Davy was greeted with enthusiasm and his speeches and memoirs were received with enormous displays of pleasure.

The Life and Death of My Best Friend, Davy Crockett

During one of our formal lunches, Davy made reference to President Jackson being honored by a Harvard University with the doctorate LLD which he amusingly translated to meaning a lazy lounging dunce. He did not share with the dinner guests that he too had also been offered a title by the University of Cambridge, but he had politely declined it acknowledging that the only degree he had ever taken was the degree of good sense and he had no ambition to receive caps and bells which he had not earned and had no rights to claim.

As with all his after dinner speeches, Davy thanked his hosts for their hospitality and he earnestly offered to repay their kindness by inviting them to visit his home. When he was asked. "And how shall we sir, find where you live?" Davy laughed and replied. "Why sirs, you simply sail down the Mississippi until you reach the Obion, streak up here a mile or two then jump ashore and ask for my name."

Leaving Boston we stayed briefly at a town called Lowell where never before was so much wealth and comfort laid upon our eyes, but even so, still the wild man from the backwoods enjoyed the warmest of receptions and friendliness which was bestowed upon him by all. All throughout the journey, new wonders had unveiled themselves to us, and Davy, trying to educate himself was an earnest learner, and what he did not understand he carefully listened to and mentally absorbed everything worthy of note.

The warm commendation that Davy received, he acknowledged, and on our return journey in his final speech which included a lengthy political attack on President Andrew Jackson. He denounced the president for betraying his voters, many of them being the same men who stood at his side when he was the General who led the fight for freedom with dependable humbleness against the Indians and the British.

The Life and Death of My Best Friend, Davy Crockett

Addressing a huge crowd he silenced the clapping and cheering by stating. "Gentlemen of Boston I came here as a private citizen to see you and not to show myself. I had no idea of attracting such attention, but I feel it is my duty to thank you all. I cannot express my gratitude enough to you all, who have given to a plain man, like me so kind a reception. I came to your county to get a knowledge of what I could not get other than seeing with my own eyes, and coming from a great way off I shall never regret having been persuaded to come and visit here. With great affection, I will take my knowledge of your ways and carry them back home with me to never forget and share with my family. My only aim in office is to do away with prejudice and give our people the correct information for a time will come when honesty in the world of politics will receive its reward.

I hope you, gentleman will excuse my plain straightforward ways which may seem strange to you folk here for I never had, but a few months of schooling in all my life and I confess I consider myself a poor tyke to be here addressing the most intelligent people in the world however, I do believe it is the duty of every delegate of the people that he must when he is called upon to give his opinions honestly and tonight I have tried to give you a little touch of mine.

Gentlemen, I have detained you much longer than intended. Allow me to conclude by thanking you for your attention and kindness to the stranger from the west."

With the fondest of memories, we began our return passing through huge crowds again at Baltimore, Philadelphia, Pittsburg, Cincinnati, Louisville, and finally to Washington where Davy planned to attend the closing of Congress.

The Life and Death of My Best Friend, Davy Crockett

Again he was feasted, received compliments, presented with gifts, and was called upon to give speeches. To our great surprise, his renown through the land was such that every news seller on every street corner displayed gazette headlines quoting his peculiarities and his political speeches. He never purchased a printed page that detailed his accounts and his portrait, but he perused with interest and the utmost diligence the strange surroundings and the scriptures which were shaping his life.

We stayed in Washington for a few days rest, often hearing calls ' Crockett for president!' bellowing out from the boardwalks everywhere we walked, but eventually we left the immense crowds behind us and returned to the simple tranquility of the wilderness and home. Once more filling our lungs with the fragrance of fresh pine and dew-laden grass to which Davy sighed confessing he felt like a weary bird and that he now wanted to settle down on his homestead and shut out the turbulence of the evolving world.

I left Davy to enjoy his homecoming in private and returned to my cabin meeting up with him one week later for a hunting trip. Donning his usual deerskins and fox skin cap he shouldered his rifle with thoughtless zest as we plunged deep into the dark and dank marshy forest.

It didn't take me long to recognize Davy was rather sullen and not enthusiastic for hunting. After a few days back at home he had realized all the excitement of the traveling, the flattery, the applause, and his popularity as the great bear hunter, had marveled him and now it left him listless for his former life as a poor backwoodsman.

The Life and Death of My Best Friend, Davy Crockett

As we sauntered sluggishly with little care for the hunt he spoke of his political visions and the stimulation of political life. The clamor for him to run as president had engrossed his attention and occupied his every thought. By the time the sun had dropped Davy's mood was as dull as the shrouded forest and finally he raised his sullen face up from his feet to announce he was going to challenge Andrew Jackson for the leadership of the party.

I knew it was pointless to try and dissuade him from continuing with his actions even though we both knew Jackson was widely idolized, even in Davy's own district. Davy was fully aware that standing against him, instead of alongside him would be futile for his own political career and as we walked he remonstrated that he could no longer support the man he once served as a soldier and favored in Washington, he had convinced himself after many long sleepless nights to risk everything by following his principles whilst risking political suicide by setting about to become one of the most inveterate opponents of his former leader.

Once again Davy attended political rallies making every effort to sway public opinion and win the voter's mark however, this time the challenge was unsurmountable and he was not equipped with the resources to equal Jackson's political influence or the financial skullduggery to buy votes with bribes and so to his indignation he lost the election.

On our trek homeward after the election Davy was completely void of his usual raillery. The strain on his face revealed bitterness and a resentment that I'd never witnessed before. He could not shake off the disappointment of losing.

The Life and Death of My Best Friend, Davy Crockett

I bemoaned to him that by telling the truth and not bowing down to a man he could not trust had meant that now he must now live with the consequences.

Although still hurting and knowing that his virtues had cost him the chance to be the president he remained resolute, stating over and over again that he would never sacrifice his beliefs and judgment to gratify such a man as Andrew Jackson and that one day he hoped he could return to politics in a time when speaking the truth did not result in being cold shouldered.

The Life and Death of My Best Friend, Davy Crockett

Chapter 17 – Go to Hell

Davy had begun to have notions of visiting Texas, as for some while we'd heard talk of American filibusters setting to wrestle the territory from the Mexicans and annexing it into the United States.

The talk that fell upon our ears consisted of an immense and beautiful land that was prime for growing cotton, however, business opportunities were nonexistent because the land owners had to survive in poverty and they were starved of progression by worthless Mexican tyrants. Gossip mongers and fortune tellers prophesized that if the settlers could get funding for an army from wealthy southern advocates for slavery, then the pioneers could rapidly take over the territory. This would result with newly created political opportunities for those who braved forth to assist the Texans with their quest for freedom.

Davy enthused there was no doubting the Texan's eventual success and he saw a vision of political glory opportune itself before him. Here in this ruthless new territory, he decided that he would either rise or fall to his destiny.

He broke the news to his family cruelly without consideration to their devastation and ignoring their pleas and tears behind his new revelation of duty he attended one final meeting to thank his constituents for their support and loyalty.

He stated one last time he could not go on representing the Whig party whilst those seated around him in Congress chose to forget their responsibilities and simply nod support for something which they did not truly believe.

The Life and Death of My Best Friend, Davy Crockett

He concluded his speech by hailing to the dejected crowd he was done with Congress and the politicians, 'for they will all go to hell for their actions and I will go to Texas'

Once more I hired a local laborer to tend to my place, but this time with sorrow in my heart, due to our stay in Tennessee being all too brief I said farewell to the mountains and I shouldered my rifle to ride alongside my stubborn, famous friend.

Clad in new deerskins made especially for the journey we rode to the Mississippi, then boarded a steamer which delivered us to the mouth of the Arkansas River. From there, we traveled along the windings of the river for over three hundred miles until we came across a cluster of cabins in a place called Little Rock. Here we sought refuge from the elements in a small tavern, but it wasn't too long before a small group of loiterers began to take notice of the two strangers who were supping their local brew and gulping down their steaming broth. Gradually word spread that the famous Colonel was convalescing and the tavern soon filled with gawking onlookers and curious well-wishers. Free drinks were thrust upon us from all directions and once the alcohol had entranced the normal thoughts and bolstered the courage of the locals shooting challenges were repeatedly called for until finally Davy relented and told the opportunists to prime their weapons and wait for him outside.

"Where there is drink there is danger." He forewarned.

The landlord took an empty wooden cask and drew a wide circle, with a piece of burnt wood in the center, and then he wedged the target in a tree about one hundred steps distant.

The Life and Death of My Best Friend, Davy Crockett

Three sharpshooters detonated their lead, each in turn until Davy took the ground. Not one piece of lead had punched the circled target, but Davy respectfully congratulated the men for at least planting all three of their balls deep into the keg, then assuming a poise of general carelessness he leveled Betsy, and without taking care to aim he pulled back on the trigger to deliver his lead dead center of the circle.

Cheers and applause sounded, but one of the men who displayed the manners of someone who had drunk too much liquor shouted.

"The shot is a fluke! No man could hit a target at that distance without taking aim."

Davy calmly smiled at the antagonist and refusing to be irked, he nonchalantly replied.

"Good words cost no less than kinds one fella." Davy smiled.

"Trickster!" The man spat back.

"I can do this five times out of six any day of the week." Still, Davy held his smile. "Night or day."

I knew Davy well enough to see that his teasing boast was deliberately fixed to provoke the man into a wager, for when Davy set about galling someone he didn't do it halfhearted.

"Five out of six!" The man disputed.

Sniggers from all around indicated everyone knew what was coming next.

The Life and Death of My Best Friend, Davy Crockett

"I've got twenty dollars here to say that you can't." He raised his hand clutching a grubby crumpled note.

"Indeed, you have my friend, however my first shot was free. For the hospitality you friendly folks have awarded me." Davy rested casually on his rifle butt. "But now if I'm being paid for my shooting prowess then I'm afraid I don't even load Old Betsy here for less than five times that note you've got crumbled there."

The stranger's eyes bulged wide, he was incensed that Davy was trying his uppermost to avoid the challenge. He turned to face the semi-circle of onlookers and he cussed waving his arms out in front of him furiously. He called Davy a liar and a flee fair attraction, and then he turned his attention to the bemused crowd relentlessly and vehemently, insisting they should contribute some of their hard gained earnings until the one hundred dollar fee was attained. One by one, he grabbed the collars of his fellow drinkers and shook furiously until finally, he turned to Davy clutching the demanded fee.

"Well, all right then." Davy nodded, holding his smile. "I'm really sorry to have to do this to you kind folks, but seeing as you are all so insistent so it be."

Davy reloaded and angled his frame sidewards towards the target. "I give any of you fella's permission to shoot me down if I happen to miss." Setting his footing he deliberated longer than with his first shot, then concentrating he took aim and fired.

As the blast waned and smoke cleared the silence was only interrupted by those who shuffled and squinted for a clearer view of the keg.

The Life and Death of My Best Friend, Davy Crockett

Only four holes could be seen and with eyes flickering between Davy and the keg excitable mutterings began to be heard.

The stranger arched forward to improve his vision of the keg then he expelled a huge roar of laughter and announced with a huge gust of hilarity. "He's missed. The god darn phony has blazed wide."

Davy blew the remaining smoke away from Betsy and threw a glance at me. "You know what to do." He calmly said.

I took a hold of the man's collar and defying his resistance, I led him forcefully towards the keg.

"Can you count?" I asked.

"I can manage up to five." He replied holding up his stretched fingers whilst shaking his head with puzzlement. "And I can see that there are still only four holes."

"You need to be checking again." Davy shouted, using the side of his hand to direct the call.

"Four holes!" The man replied holding up just four fingers as if to confirm his claim to those who may not have heard. "I said it was a fluke. No man can hit the center twice from that distance."

"Ya think." Davy shouted as I tugged down the keg from the tree.

I held the barrel high for all to see then I shook it to listen to the bullets rattle from within.

"Stand aside and let me take a scant." Bullied the gambler. "Four holes."

The Life and Death of My Best Friend, Davy Crockett

He confirmed loudly, his face still angled towards the target.

"Plug your finger in the holes." I invited.

"What?" He frowned.

"You heard me. Stick one in there, same finger in all the holes." I repeated, still holding the keg at an angle for all to see.

By now, the crowd had gathered in tight around us to get a closer inspection of the unconventional proceedings.

Bemusedly and slowly, the man placed his trigger finger on the opening of the first hole. It would not protrude beyond his grubby nail. He obliged my instruction and one by one he tried to force his finger through the rest of the bullet holes each time with the same result until he probed the center hole. This time his finger slid easily inside the barrel only stopping when his knuckle touched the wood. Angrily, the man repeated the test with each hole, again ending with the same result. Cheers and laughter erupted and Davy's name was chanted as the crowd realized that Davy's second shot had centered the target again and protruded direct through his first hole.

Still disbelieving the bear hunter's shot had perfectly followed his first shot the humiliated man grabbed the keg from my grasp and hailed repeatedly for an axe. The weapon was quickly produced and passed from hand to hand until it was Davy himself who displayed great pleasure by stepping between the congested bodies to hold out and offer the axe to the infuriated nonbeliever.

The Life and Death of My Best Friend, Davy Crockett

Throwing the keg to the floor the man took the axe and swung it violently sending chips and shavings high as savagely the barrel was hacked until the lid fell loose. The crowd surged forward and packed in tight for a closer inspection as the man bent low to tilt the barrel to allow the lead balls to slide out onto the mud.

"Impossible! Utterly impossible." He raged as five lead balls rolled clear for everyone to see.

Yet again cheers erupted and Davy was hoisted high onto the shoulders of the jubilant admirers who paraded him on their way back to the tavern for more celebratory drinks and food.

I relieved the sulking stranger of the wager without any resistance, his dejected face tilted downwards, and his dull eyes fixed on the bullets still wondering if or how he had been deceived.

Another uproarious time was had by all within the tavern. Davy returned the wager fee to all those who had been bullied out of their money and he entertained all the enthralled listeners as both tales and whiskey flowed. Later, when the revelry had calmed a little he chose to enlighten everyone with the affairs in Texas and of his intentions to provide aid, either by way of his political influence or by the gun.

Fueled by alcohol and their minds flooded with imaginings of adventure five of the revellers, Edwin 'Pepper' and Napoleon 'Leon' Mitchell, Samuel Edwards, John Garvin, and Ben McRay made an ill-judged decision to volunteer and join us.

The Life and Death of My Best Friend, Davy Crockett

The following morning, to our surprise, waiting for us at the stables was the man who issued the shooting challenge. At first, we thought he had shown himself to make trouble, but to our surprise, he offered his hand to Davy and apologised for his actions adding it had been a great pleasure to meet the Colonel and that he should not have tried to embarrass him. Both men wished each other well and we rode out in the direction of Fulton on the Red River.

After only fifty miles at a ford on the River Washita, we happened upon a preacher who was in a condition of immense peril. Unprepared he had attempted to cross the ford, but halfway across he found he could not progress any further nor make a safe return. Stranded, distressed, and exhausted he had slumped on a mud rise to wait for his fate in the rising waters, his horse and his belongings all long since dragged away by the strong current.

With immeasurable difficulty, the seven of us roped ourselves together to wade deep towards the lost soul and after exhausted efforts, we were rewarded when we dragged his limp and semi-conscious body over the top of the raging water to safety. After retrieving him from the cold ravages, we warmed and fed him with mulled berry juice to the point where he slowly regained his faculties and blessed us for saving his life.

Davy informed him that although we had managed to save his life unfortunately we could not salvage anything else and so he had lost everything.

Seemingly unconcerned the Preacher raised a faint smile and replied. "My wealth lays not within this world my friend."

The Life and Death of My Best Friend, Davy Crockett

Over supper, he informed us that he was a pioneer in the wilderness and his mission was to distribute Christian leaflets and preach gospels in the remotest of hamlets where most people had never seen a clergyman or even considered religion. I could tell by Davy's lined forehead that he was wondering if the Preacher was referring to him direct.

We offered him the use of one of our spare horses and he joined us along the way, and having heard exaggerated tales of Davy Crockett on his travels he shared his opinions and extensive knowledge on politics, religion, farming, and Texas. Then during our mid-day rest he preached, and with much gusto spreading his influence from his soul and out of his lips with a stream of eloquence that seemed to hold the attention of all natures creatures. Birds appeared to fall silent, squirrels and rabbits unfearing looked out from their hiding, the fish bobbed high on top of the waters and faded flowers seemed to bloom spreading a fresh fragrance about us all.

Although we few were utterly alone in the vast wilderness suddenly we felt surrounded by love, courage, hope, and strength. There was no music to help him lead our hearts, but nothing could be more expressive as his voice recited and hailed forth the religious divines without the need for a prayer book.

Every word had its meaning, every description formed a picture, his whole orations breathed over us a powerful and majestic reverberation that never before had any of us witnessed.

After a pause in which we were able to regain our breaths, each of us, one by one pressed and shook the hand of the Preacher and thanked him for warming our weary hearts with a generous swig of throat-burning liquid.

The Life and Death of My Best Friend, Davy Crockett

Davy entertainingly set the example of how to take the drink by holding aloft the cask above his face and directing the flow of liquid from a distance into his mouth without spilling any. With some amusement, the Preacher who had a notable dispensation for our alcohol followed Davy's style until he too was satisfied.

Onwards we progressed merrily encouraged on our journey by the jovial banter, inspiring doctrines, and allocations of the throat lubricant. We rested again at a place called Greenville for a short while, washed off sweat and grime in a stream and then pressed on through vast forests and contradictory treeless prairies until we reached Fulton. Here the Preacher announced that God's work would be required in Texas and he asked if he could continue to travel by our side. Davy reminded him that danger and maybe even peril may find them at their destination, but the Preacher calmly replied.

"It is Gods will and desire that I should go forth and administer his holy comfort to the grieving who up to now had been depraved of a fitting benediction."

And so he became the sixth member of our pack, joining the Mitchell brothers and their friends from Little Rock who were by now displaying nervous signs of regret.

We convalesced for a few nights, again Davy was received with distinction everywhere he revealed himself, and then we sold our horses to purchase a ride on a steamer for a relaxing journey of several hundred miles to a dry hole of a place called Natchitoches, where just a small number of white stone adobe buildings sheltered a few hundred leather faced occupants.

The Life and Death of My Best Friend, Davy Crockett

One night whilst we were enjoying high spirits as a result of sampling the local intoxicant we happened across a skillful magician. For a while we watched the trickster fleece a few of the locals of their scant earnings, but then Davy who was opposed to dishonesty and fraudulence approached the table to get acquainted with the crook. He wasted no time in protesting his dissatisfaction at the evil practice and whilst we who gawked expected a furious confrontation the man calmly invited Davy to sit and elucidate. After a short while a couple of us grabbed our drinks and invited ourselves to join the two some's friendly debate. We listened as Davy told the man it was a sin against all human nature that a man who possessed such creativity and wisdom should disgrace himself and indebt himself to god for practicing such a pitiful livelihood.

Not knowing who Davy was, but being impressed by the way Davy conversed his objections, the man instead of reacting with defending quarrel, and threats of violence or denial placidly answered.

"But what else can I do? I am in the waters of despondency and I have debts right up to my chin. This is the only way I can stop myself from sliding under and drowning in my debts."

Not questioning who he was or why he was in debt Davy responded. "Then brace yourself and hold your chin up before the water reaches your lips."

"My friend there is no use." The man shook his head and sighed. "It is utterly impossible for me to wade through my debts, and even if I could my dishonor would leave me with such a dirty plight that it would defy all the waters in the Mississippi to wash me clean again."

The Life and Death of My Best Friend, Davy Crockett

As we listened, he added in a despondent tone. "No sir. If I try to live like an honest man I would be like an eel in a skillet. All out of my element, turning and writhing without any hope of survival."

Davy smiled. "I deny that my friend. It is never too late to stand proud and become an honest man." Then after a pause to swill his throat, he added. "Even if it is true what you admit to and you cannot live an as honest man, you still have the next best thing in your power which no one can say nay to."

Scowling with confusion the man asked. "And what is that?"

"To die like a brave man for in the eyes of all men a glorious death is preferred and is righteous and remembered whereas the life and death of a sinner is soon lost into obscurity." Davy swigged dry his tankard then continued knowing he had the man's ear.

"Most men are remembered as they died and not how they lived. We all, every one of us gaze with earnest admiration upon the glories of the setting sun and yet we scarcely bestow a passing glance to the noonday spender."

Now completely intrigued the man leaned forwards nearer to Davy and asked. "Your god darn right, but tell me how this can be done."

"Cut free from your degrading habits and leave your past, and your associates right here. Don't look back on your past transgressions and regain your dignity by accompanying me and my friends in fighting for the freedom of Texas."

The Life and Death of My Best Friend, Davy Crockett

Davy's proposal hit the man's inner core and he scooped up all his gambling instruments and thrust them inside his pocket, then he scraped back his chair to rise and stride with his head lowered thoughtfully in circles around the tavern. After a minute or so and with all eyes gazing upon him he returned to the table and exclaimed.

"Your sincerity has convinced me sir and by heaven I will try to be a proud man once again. I will live honestly or die bravely trying." He reached out for his tankard and gulped until it was empty, and then slamming the empty jug on the table, he resoundingly confirmed. "I will go with you sir to Texas and to reclaim my honor."

He held out his hand which was received with Davy's clasped palm, "Lancelot Booth."

"David Crockett from Tennessee."

The juggling card trickster became the seventh member of Davy's freedom fighters.

In Natchitoches, we purchased cheaply some tough, but old Mustangs to transport us along the old Spanish road which spliced vast prairies of boundless orchards of honey trees and wildflowers. It was amongst these parterres at the far boundary of Natchitoches that we enlisted our eight volunteer.

Not long into our journey a poetic tune broke the clopping of our horses and caused us to investigate the source of the beautiful noise which arose from amongst the abundant honey trees in a meadow to our left where bees hummed between the colorful heads of weeds.

The Life and Death of My Best Friend, Davy Crockett

There we found a group of young women and one youthful fella who were occupying themselves by harvesting valuable golden honey.

Not wanting to cause alarm we pulled up our horses and rested on their manes some distance from the laborers to watch and listen to the solitary handsome young male entertain his female companions with his imaginative sweet tongue. We dismounted and chose to relax a while whilst his pleasing renditions continued to breeze over the nearby meadows however, our attentions distracted the group from their exertions, and with an inquisitive scowl, the young man left his casket to approach and ask us if we wanted to buy some honey. Inclined to please the friendly singer we negotiated a fair price and we were about to take our leave when he asked us where we were travelling to and for what purpose.

Davy told him our next stop was Nacogdoches, and then he took great delight in explaining our mission with a lengthy chord of excitement that appealed to the youngster's imagination, and with haste he ran back to his fellow workers to shout something in a language we could not understand. Mounting a small pony and heeling it towards us at a gallop he stated for a small fee he would guide us across the pathless plains and through the dense forests until we reached our destination. However Davy was concerned by the age of the youth and at first he declined any help, but the affluent youth was persistent and he declared that we would never find Nacogdoches without him to show us the correct path.

After a brief consultation, with reservations because of his young age, we decided it would be in all our interest to hire the guide for a small fee, and so after agreeing on the charge, Davy told the youngster that once we had reached our destination he must return to his family.

The Life and Death of My Best Friend, Davy Crockett

Agreeing to the contract the young man, who introduced himself as Ezra Gallardo led the way along the dusty ground cheerfully breathing out pleasing ballads and tuneful odes of fables which merrily alleviated the tedium.

When the singing stopped he told us that the locals in his county had become so accustomed to runaways fleeing north to avoid persecution and injustices in Texas that his sisters became intrigued when they saw us traveling south. They had instructed him to inquire about our concerns, and they forbade him from riding by our side due to the rumors of a huge advancing army, and the impending threat of mass bloodshed.

The trek to Nacogdoches passed without incident worth of note and we were received kindly by the thousand or so local Mexicans and Indians who inhabited the few stone and tent dwellings.

We traded our horses for fresh ones and rested only overnight, setting off early the following morning before the sun peaked over the baron horizon deliberately without disturbing our guide from his slumber. We left his fee next to his bed and instructions with the locals stating that we thanked him and that wished him well on his return journey home.

We were less than one hour into our journey when to our rear we heard the galloping approach of the singer. Our friendly guide had refused to return to his home, and he defied all our threats and all orders to disassociate himself from us. Ignoring his plea, we continued onwards, but suborning he followed our trail some fifty yards behind us until the huge orange ball above eventually sank in the distance and the light became so poor that we made camp, and lit a robust fire on which we could boil a sumptuous evening meal.

The Life and Death of My Best Friend, Davy Crockett

Without words, or any objections, the singer sauntered amongst us to find his place around the fire and pour himself a bowl of steaming nourishment. Later that night he sang us the sweetest lullaby that I'd ever heard. The little Rock boys teased him, but the Preacher hushed them by stating 'he who sings drives away misery and sorrow.'

The Life and Death of My Best Friend, Davy Crockett

Chapter 18 – The Pirate

The following week we continued southwest across the diverse and ever-changing terrain until after about two hundred miles we encountered a vast expanse of cane breaks. Without a tree or any greenery to be seen anywhere we had to cut a small trail through the reeds just wide enough for a single horse to pass through.

So high was the sky reaching reeds, above thirty and forty feet, and having no support they drooped inwards, and the tops arched to form a sun-obscuring canopy. Guessing our route of direction the best we could, exhaustingly onwards we hacked our way through the reeds in almost darkness for three days until finally, we emerged upon an expansive herbage pasture where dragon flies skimmed the surface of sun glistening water and bull frogs merrily croacked.

Here, shielding our eyes from the painful brightness we saw the greenery was abundant with wild turkeys and droves of wild horses. In the far distance, several miles east of our position we viewed an immense herd of grazing buffalos which re-awakened Davy's passion for hunting. He bemoaned that although he had hunted most game and killed several bears he had never had the opportunity to bring down a buffalo. Our singer remonstrated, that although the prairie appeared to be a peaceful garden to our eyes we were still far into the wilderness, and should Davy lose his way or should we get disoriented and separated in the turmoil of the chase then some of us could get lost and easily perish in this vast region of isolation.

The Life and Death of My Best Friend, Davy Crockett

With every mile that we traveled I could sense Davy's temptation growing stronger and stronger, he was unusually fidgety and oddly quiet. Both I and Davy knew we would survive should we happen to get spilt from the group, but giving consideration to the rest of our group we remained silent for our desire to chase the huge beast and eventually Davy returned his attention to the journey ahead.

We crossed the Trinity River without hindrance or delay and in the dimness of another looming night and encouraged by the sight of flickering lantern we approached a lonely hut and called out a friendly greeting stating we were not renegades nor hostiles and that we simply enquired if the occupant would like some company. A crooked back, wizened old woman cracked open the door to state she had nothing of worth and that she could offer nothing, but the cover of her shelter. In his usual affable manner, Davy soon dispelled the women's concerns and she invited us in for a sup of her coffee and a slice of cornbread. And in return for her hospitality, we shared with her our game, a few tales, and Davy played a few chords from the fiddle with an accompaniment of harmonized poetry from our singer's bellowing lungs.

As daylight spliced the ill-fitting wooden planks something disturbed our horses and alerted us to danger. With rifle primed Davy cautiously levered open the door to quell his curiosity.

Two other travelers had tethered their ponies next to ours and were approaching the door when they were suddenly halted by the barrel of old Betsy.

The Life and Death of My Best Friend, Davy Crockett

With their hands stretched high they told us they were accustomed to stopping off at the old woman's cabin to check upon her wellbeing whenever they came within a few miles of her homestead and within an instant we knew these rough and skeletal specimens of humans deemed us no threat, and confirming there account the old women invited them to join us for breakfast. It was obvious from their ragged appearance these two frontiersmen rarely advanced into the realms of the civilized world. The taller of the two had long grey and greasy hair that rested below his bony shoulders and shrouded most of his deep-lined grimy face it tangled in his chest reaching white cheek whiskers. Hanging from his body was the tattered remnants of a sailor's jacket and drooping over his shoulder from a piece of string was a tarpaulin hat. His companion, who could not speak English bore the resemblance of a diminutive Indian, eyes as dark as a wildcat, long black hair as shiny as a bird's wing, and leather-colored skin which was almost entirely covered by a hood of stitched deer skins.

Gnawing on bones the old timer told us he was a former pirate who had in bygone days menaced the merchant ships around the shores and waters of New Orleans until his ship was attacked and captured by the British. Fleeing for his life to avoid the noose he had been living off his scant bounty for the last ten years in the wilderness with his wife whom he introduced to us as 'Dove' and bearing her perfect white teeth with a friendly smile she corrected 'Chenoa' then feeling at ease she lowered the hood and allowed the garment to drop to the floor revealing her slender shoulders and barely covered blemish free skin.

Although we regarded the girls as a savage we felt embarrassed by the scant deerskin cover and quickly we averted our eyes towards the food.

The Life and Death of My Best Friend, Davy Crockett

Noting our embarrassment, the Pirate spat at the girl and signaled instructions with his eyes for her to re-cloak her beauty. Once satisfied he raised his greasy hair from the side of his face to reveal a wide scar and a deformed forehead, then he flipped over his left hand to display a severed palm and half of a thumb, both reminders of a Captain's saber that he had collected during his escape from the attack on his ship.

Once more Davy lectured the wanderer upon the chance of redeeming his sins by the honor and glory of supporting the law-abiding Texans in their fight against persecution and terror.

Intrigued, the man furrowed his brow and narrowed his yellow eyes as he contemplated the proposition. He spoke with a native tongue to the Indian women and after a few exchanges with some snappy gesticulation, he turned to Davy with an acknowledging nod to announce. "Lead me to my redemption and save my soul from the devil."

Once our breakfast lay heavy in our guts we bade the old hag farewell, and leaving her with the hind leg of a deer and a whole turkey as parting gifts we again took to the narrow dirt path that led the way to the dusty naked landscape with another two new recruits.

We ventured forth without rest until mid-noon, whereupon we trod across a huge green baize, dotted with small clusters of waist-high trees and a variety of colored wildflowers which were unbeknown to us. Striking in its verdure, the sloping scene to our front would not have been out of place in one of the large parks in New York or Washington.

The Life and Death of My Best Friend, Davy Crockett

Requiring rest and food we secured our horses and built a fire. Davy, for once took a seat alongside us to relax and with our eyes closed and our faces towards the warm sun we readily allowed the pretty squaw to roast our game and boil us a brew.

At peace, watching a few white clouds drift slowly above our heads we chattered sociably, sang and played the fiddle whilst we awaited our masterfully crafted feast. However, not long into our rest a strange rumble in the distance ceased our playful activities. The squaw ceased from turning the spit and erected herself to stare across the undulating lands before us. One by one we arose to join her and squint over nature's beautiful and bountiful garnishings.

Nothing to be seen concerned us as the gentle breeze swept over the brushwood, its fragrances and refreshing wafts pleasing our faces, yet still the distant rumble could be heard over the faraway hills, its reverberation gradually increasing. With some head scratching and increased concerns as one we strained our eyes towards the far hills from whence the sound came. We tilted our heads towards the rumble and we examined the sky once more. There were no grumbling clouds and no dark rain carriers, just idyllic blue and the occasional bright dapple of white fluff.

The squaw dropped to her knees and touched the soil with her right ear.

"Cannons?" The pirate asked knowing from his own experiences this rumble was not caused by the release of gunpowder.

"You can burn my cap if I know," Davy muttered holding still his examining gaze.

The Life and Death of My Best Friend, Davy Crockett

Suddenly our horses stopped eating and reared up, screaming and distressingly tried to pull free from their tether. As a group, we inhaled large composing breaths and stretched our necks even more as on the horizon an immense black cloud rose from the earth.

"What in darnation." Muttered the magician as the menacing storm manifested and swept across the surface of the loose prairie dirt with immense rapidness.

"Tornado?" One of the fellas from Little Rock suggested.

"Uh." We all wondered.

The cloud of dark dust continued its advance directly toward us at a galloping pace, the strange phenomenon expanding wider and higher with every passing second. The flowers before our eyes began to flutter, then like one of the waves I'd seen in Baltimore they seemed to roll towards us until the ground trembled under our feet and a thunderous din burdened our hearing.

The Indian woman leaped to her feet and pointed towards the rolling mass, and screamed words we could not understand.

"Stampede!" The pirate translated. "Stampede!" He yelled over and over pointing at the intensifying uproar.

Immediately we spun on our heels and as fast as we could, we sped toward our horses as behind our backs the thunder grew louder.

Davy glimpsed the Preacher had decided not to run and put his faith in God to protect him. He stood motionless with eyes clamped tight and his bible clutched against his chest.

The Life and Death of My Best Friend, Davy Crockett

I swerved my stride and joined Davy to grab the Preacher by his collar and drag him out from his trancelike state and towards his horse. Faster and faster we ran, but beneath our scampering feet, the ground shuddered, making it difficult for us to keep upright. With the greatest of haste, we struck out the horse's hobbles and leaped onto their unsaddled backs, then without even the quickest of rear glances, we heeled our horses hard into an immediate gallop.

"Buffalo!" I heard Davy exclaim as he pulled alongside, and this time impelled by fear, my curiosity forced me to quickly turn my head. My mind could not comprehend the vision my eyes relayed as amongst the dense black cloud of thick dust, rampaging behind us were thousands of wild snorting, hoof thundering black beasts, all charging down upon us with the speed of a gale. Bellowing and roaring, with terrifying deafening tones the immense herd thundered across the once peaceful pastures obliterating all in their path.

Frantically bouncing high, bare-arsed on the back of my Mustang, I urged him on faster and faster with my heels. Water blurred my vision and I could not see any of my companions, and sensing the innumerable thongs gaining upon my back I lowered myself over my Mustang's mane and kicked in my heels harder, and sharing my fear my trusted companion obliged to give his all and he did not let up.

I could feel the heat of their sour breaths swirling around my neck and I felt the fervor of the devil on my shoulder as he began to claw me into the grasp of the unrestrained monsters.

The Life and Death of My Best Friend, Davy Crockett

Suddenly the brightness before me dimmed and my horse drew to an immediate halt dismounting me in the process. I bounced and flipped several times on the hard surface and rolled through several small bushes, but uninjured I managed to coil myself until I could stop the motion and prevent my body from colliding against a wide tree. Wiping the grit and water from my eyes to my great relief my trusty horse had entered a small thicket of cedars and saved me from certain doom. Twenty or so strides to my side I could see Davy and the others, they too were disheveled and in the process of regaining their faculties.

I straightened and cracked out a pain in my back then with an uncontrollable shaking in my legs, with awe I watched a huge black buffalo who in advance of the rest of the herd swerved his thong of followers around our sanctuary of small obstructing cedar trunks. Roaring with deafening fury, his tail rigid and his head near to the ground, his solid bulk furiously thundered passed us being immediately followed by a mass commotion of earth destroying stompers.

From the dullness of the trees, a brief flash and a blast of powder caught my eye. Davy had leveled his rifle and took aim at one of the passing beasts. If his lead struck with accuracy we do not know for through the swirling thick dust no beast was felled and they continued to charge on undeterred.

After a few minutes, we braved to peep between the trees to watch the ground trembling mass once more turn into a large black cloud on the horizon. With enormous sighs of relief, we wiped the muddy sweat from our brows and drew in close to recount the tale of the unexpected encounter with death.

The Life and Death of My Best Friend, Davy Crockett

Suddenly screams from the squaw penetrated through the buzzing in our ears and ranting in a high-pitched delirium, she frantically looked amongst the trees. Running from stump to stump she pulled her hair and slapped her head with the flat of her hands as her eyes flickered in all directions. She shouted and pleaded to us in words we could not translate, but we were soon to know the meaning of. The pirate was missing, and so were the young singer and also one of the Little Rock fellas, Ben McRay.

We sped from the shadows of the forest and out into the cloud of settling dust to scan across the trampled horizon and call out their names. We ran in all directions, but there was nothing to be seen except battled soil and trampled plants. The scene of devastation was in total contrast to the serene garden of which we scampered from only minutes sooner and due to the destruction the landscape was unrecognizable to our eyes. Our camp, our saddles, and all of our possessions that we could not carry had been trampled beyond any salvation, and more importantly three of our companions were missing.

The Preacher took the squaw's hand, kissed it, and knelt at her side to pray, but thanking him for his consolation by patting his shoulder she pulled free her hand and joined us by taking to her horse to search for signs of life. Pepper Mitchell cussed our luck and blamed the Indian by claiming she was a bad omen.

For a few seconds, I thought he was going to reach for his knife, but his older brother Leon defended her and told him to hold his tongue and judgments until his senses settled. He then, rigorously rubbed his fingers through his brothers hair to shake out the muddy dust until his locks returned back to ginger.

The Life and Death of My Best Friend, Davy Crockett

With the frustration temporally diverted, we searched all afternoon knowing but daring not to say that we knew all three of the men had been trampled into obliteration.

All we could see was miles of mud, deep ruts, beast prints, and crushed shrubbery, then just as the light began to fade and we were contemplating ending our search one of Chenoa pulled from the mud the remnants of the pirate's tarp hat.

Unexpectedly no screams or wailing were released by the Indian woman, as already fearing her husband's death she examined the tatter of cloth and pressed it against her breast. Lowering her head, she silently sobbed allowing grief-flowing tears to drop onto the crumpled keepsake.

With sympathy, we led our horses very slowly until darkness once again prevented our safe passage. The huge moon had replaced the sun, but its slivery glow was intermittent as slow passing clouds drifted and the resulting periods of darkness risked our mount's safe footing on the now uneven surface. Without the sweet renditions of Ezra, our journey had been taken with an unwholesome anxious silence. The three deaths had affected our morale and regret, and restlessness was exhibited in the conduct of the Little Rock boys who trailed sluggishly at our rear.

The Life and Death of My Best Friend, Davy Crockett

Chapter 19 – The Cougar and the Squaw

Amongst the barrenness of the destroyed prairie, we found a large isolated tree that lay upon the ground. Still fresh in its demise, most of its branches were still thick with busy leaves. Without exchanging many words we agreed the tree would be ideal for a camp and so we tethered our horses and whilst the fella's built a fire the Preacher once again tried to console the young widow with whispered words of sympathy and prayers from the book of God, meanwhile, I scavenged for food whilst Davy collected foliage. He was in the process of weaving the leafage between some of the higher branches to make the widow a comfortable bed when a heart-stopping roar turned all of our heads to his direction.

"Looks like this bed is already taken fella." Davy calmly announced as before him on the tree poised a large cougar.

For the longest of moments, neither the human nor the beast moved, both bravely held their posturing in defiance. The beast angered by the disturbance growling with its demonic glaring eyes glistening from the intermittent brilliance of the moon, Davy rooted knowing to turn away would ensure his death.

"Hold still everyone, it looks like we got ourselves a little dispute over whose tree this belongs to." Davy slowly held up his arm to emphasize his warning and signal for us not to move.

"Looks like he's found his supper." The Pepper quipped.

The cougar snarled, its eyes widened, and it showed its huge reflecting teeth, and then slowly it crouched on its haunches, readying to launch an attack.

The Life and Death of My Best Friend, Davy Crockett

To all who gazed on with fearing rigidness, it was obvious there would be no retreat from the savage beast, and not only Davy's life, but all our lives were in peril.

Davy carefully took a step back, and I slowly and soundlessly stretched out my hand in vain for my rifle, which was propped against the tree. It was just out of my reach. Lifting very slowly one foot from a branch and placing it onto another Davy managed to take three steps backwards when the cougar leaped with its legs extended in his direction. Ducking low Davy met the leap by slamming his head into the wild cat's rib cage and wrapping his arms around its muscular back both the aggressor and the defendant thudded from the tree and into the soil. With teeth snapping furiously they rolled and flipped together and Davy held tight his arms around the beast with all his strength until it gave a fierce shake which flung him loose and high.

Without hesitation or reflection, I discharged my rifle hoping that my stinging lead would distract the cougar and render it breathless. However my lead just splintered wood and snarling with increased fury it once again leaped at Davy, who now on the rise had managed to pull free his knife, enabling him to strike it handle deep into the savage's gullet.

Blood sprayed high and wide, but we knew not if it was man or beast. Even so, the cougar snapped and clawed with rabid severity. Fighting for his life in equal measures, Davy pulled free his knife and desperately stabbed it repeatedly into the body of the snarling beast until its breath wavered and it withdrew from the fight.

The Life and Death of My Best Friend, Davy Crockett

For the briefest of moments the beast eyes leered upon the prostate and gasping man, their intense ferociousness slightly dimmed it snarled again and glanced around as if considering its next victim, but then slowly and very cautiously with a whimper it astonishingly began to turn and holding its head so that its eyes remained on Davy the beast shook away drool and blood and limped away into the darkness.

The squaw was the first to reach Davy's side and wiping away blood from his face with her hand with a heave from her supporting shoulder, he was raised up onto his weary feet.

My priority was to reload and I keep my aim in the direction of the retreating cougar. The others also primed their weapons and once composed the magician blindly took a few steps into the pitch to ensure the cat was not about to return.

Panting from breath and shaking from the exertion Davy was aided away from the tree and lowered to rest and whilst we kept watch for the returning predator the Indian made several compresses from leaves, moss, and bark to stop the blood from oozing out from Davy's deep lacerations.

Having regained his senses Davy hollered his disapproval across to the Little Rock gang. "I'm really grateful for the help you fellas gave me back there."

Pepper broke away from his thoughts and raised his face from the mesmerizing flames. "Figured you wouldn't be needing any help." He sniped to accompanying sniggers from his miserable brother, Leon.

"Why so?" Davy replied.

The Life and Death of My Best Friend, Davy Crockett

"B'cos we heard you could wrestle an alligator and skin a leopard with no trouble at all." Pepper laughed.

"Nothing wrong with your hearing then." Davy quickly replied. "Just your scruples."

The Indian woman hissed at Davy urging him to rest and she pressed the flat of her hands hard against his shoulders to prevent him from rising and inflaming the agitation.

"Yeah. Listen to her Colonel and rest up before you exhaust yourself." Pepper continued.

I heeled the hammer on my rifle and its click prompted everyone's eyes to fix in my direction. I held my wordless gaze on Pepper for longer than two men should look at one another and the silence was only broken when the magician returned into the orange hue to enthusiastically announce the cougar had fled into the darkness.

"Hell of a day eh." The magician expressed, sensing the emerging hostility.

"Yeah. Just one hell of a bad day." Leon bemoaned.

"Come on and get a sup of this fine coffee." The magician dunked a mug into the coffee skillet and held it out in Pepper's direction. "Everyone's just a little itchy that's all." He said.

"And very tired." Pepper seemed to settle reaching out to accept the cup then slumping back against his rest.

The Life and Death of My Best Friend, Davy Crockett

With the spat dusted we hankered down to rest, but an uneasiness set within me that prevented any sleep that night, born not from the stampede, the attack from the cougar nor from the sobs of the Indian women, my mind was alert with a feeling of tragic inevitability, how many more times could we walk away from deaths calling.

By sun up we were moving again. Davy in great pain studied the actions and the mood of the Little Rock gang, the Preacher periodically closed his eyes and leaned back his head to address his God in the sky, the widow continued weeping and I scouting far and wide in search of abnormal disturbances.

After a short while we turned away from the trampled ground and once again led our mustangs onto a scene of greenery and sporadic forestry that stretched as far as the eye could see. Here there was no evidence that neither man's footsteps nor his axe-welding destruction had disturbed this remote paradise and progress without saddles over pathless lands was tedious and painful. Also, being sullen and due to the stampede incident, it was becoming recognizable that our time spent traveling together would be soon coming to an end. Whispers and meaningful glances were exchanged between the brothers, Leon and Pepper making it obvious they now regretted their impetuous decision to join the politician and his friend on the quest to assist the Texans.

The uneasy silence loomed over us throughout supper and we smoked the fire with greens to intentionally keep away the little biters and blood sucking nippers. Come shut eye in a haze of woody smoke we all laid our beds intentionally further apart than we had previously done.

The Life and Death of My Best Friend, Davy Crockett

For the second continuous night, I rested uneasily, allowing the calls of the night screechers in the far distance to penetrate my slumber and keep me alert. However, it was not the night beasts that disturbed me, but a rustling close by. Without displaying any signs of alertness and keeping my legs and arms still, I cracked open an eyelid to see a shadowy figure kneeling on top of the Chenoa. Nevertheless, I remained completely still until my vision cleared enough to see Pepper holding down the woman with the weight of his body pressing down on her petite frame. He had one hand pressed hard against her mouth whilst his other ruffled arduously under her tunic.

Slowly and quietly I stretched out my arm for my rifle, but as I did so I saw Davy rise from his semi-recumbent position and hobble quickly to kick his foot with such force into Pepper's back that it dislodged him from on top of the vulnerable woman.

"You need to control your urges, Mister Mitchell." Davy advised.

By now everyone had been roused and rubbing the tiredness from their eyes with accompanying gasps they watched Pepper roll over and pull free his hunting knife.

"And you need to mind your own, hog hunter." He threatened with a glare that equaled the wildcat.

Flicking glances between Pepper's face and the knife Davy warned. "I think you better revisit your intentions boy." Then he withdrew his own knife to match Pepper's fighting stance.

The Life and Death of My Best Friend, Davy Crockett

"The squaw needs more comfort than just a blanket." Pepper menacingly waved his knife signaling his intentions. "And this is none of your mind."

"That just ain't so, but there ain't nothing so low as a man who defiles a woman in her sorrowing." Davy held his poise.

"Return to your cot." Pepper took one step forward and stretched out his arm holding the knife within six inches of Davy's chest. "All of you. Get back and bury your heads." He swung the knife in an arc. "You hear me! Get back to your sleeping."

"I think our time together is at an end." Davy rocked from one foot to another and angled his body sidewards.

"Come on fellas, put away the blades." The Preacher took a step forward and held out hands signally and urging for peace.

"Pepper quit your fooling and drop the blade." Shouted his older brother.

"You stay out of this. The sassy has overstepped his mark by protecting a savage."

Looking at young Pepper I could sense that he was shamed by his undisciplined morals and his sinful weakness. I thought he had carelessly relented to his urges and had exposed himself to humiliation from which anger now resonated, and even though I knew that his fire could not be contained from just words alone I too pleaded with him. "The devil got you for a moment boy, that's all. Now take it easy, drop the knife, and turn in."

The Life and Death of My Best Friend, Davy Crockett

Ignoring all pleas for calm, Pepper aimed to plunge his knife deep into my injured friend and he lunged quickly forward. Conversely aware of his intentions, Davy clenched his teeth and effortlessly sidestepped the attack, and as the moonlight flashed on his blade, he dragged it decisively across Pepper's forearm causing him to scream and with his hand rendered useless by the depth of the laceration into his muscle, drop the knife. Clasping his hand over the gaping crevice to restrict squirting blood he fell to his knees, lowered his head, and cried.

Davy hobbled towards him and kicked away the knife then continuing his advance passed the fire he arched over to lift Betsy. Through short panting breaths of exhaustion, he demanded. "Get your horse and get out of camp." He demanded.

As wide eyes gaped on from around the dying hue of the campfire I fixed my grip tight around my rifle studying the intentions of the Little Rock fellas, however unconcerned Davy sheathed his knife and disappeared into the darkness.

For what seemed an eternity, no one else moved and no one spoke. The Indian sobbed, Pepper emitted pained grunts through his clamped teeth and his brother shook his head and cussed his disgust so quietly that only those next to him could hear his words.

Eventually, Pepper raised his head and called for help until the Preacher apprehensively wandered to his side and knelt beside him.

There was no fond farewell party for Pepper nor words of sorrow for his departure. In near silence, his wound was strapped, but no one helped him arise and no one objected to his ejection.

The Life and Death of My Best Friend, Davy Crockett

Leon, still shaking his head, seemed to dissociate himself from his brother and he somberly wandered off into the darkness as Davy proceeded to use Betsy to lever to ensure the abuser climbed onto the back of his horse. Hauled up to an accompaniment of insults and cusses direct from the devil's tongue, Pepper said that he hoped Davy would be rewarded with a slow and painful death at the end of an Indian's knife.

Leon stepped out of the darkness holding in one hand his rifle and in the other some ammunition to appeal to the injustice of his brother's treatment. "Davy, although I don't agree with what my foolish brother has done and I honor your uprightness, my conscience will not permit me to just let him be expelled without a furnishment to hunt for food."

Davy, remaining faithful to his principles, walked over to Leon and took the rifle and ammunition out of his hands, then he returned to his former friend and placed the rifle strap over his shoulder and the ammunition in his hand. Turning away from Pepper, Davy issued him a warning forbidding him to return to camp, and then he slapped the horse's hind to send it away into the pitch of somberness.

There was a general nervousness around the camp that night, the widow continually sobbed under her blanket, Leon was unable to find any comfort and he twitched and fidgeted, the preacher angled the pages of his prayer book to the dying ambers, and I being tormented by what had just occurred failed to calm my pulse enough to sleep. Yet that night Davy seemed at peace in no time at all, however I have no doubts at all, whilst his eyes were at rest his ears would have remained alert to the sounds of danger.

The Life and Death of My Best Friend, Davy Crockett

Sunrise cast away the cold evening chill and seemed to ease the morbid tension and immediately after breakfast, we embarked on the unobstructed expanse of nature's beauty once more.

The huge orange ball to our right had not yet fully peaked above the distant swell of the horizon when again we were alarmed once more by faint rumbles of hooves, then our concerns increased as rhythmically the clip-clopping grew louder and louder.

We scanned our whereabouts, looking for a place of sanctuary amongst the treeless prairie, fearing another enormous herd of buffalos was heading in our direction, but appearing on a distant summit and sweeping into our view were about fifty Indians. Our fears were not relieved.

Charging forth and gaining upon us with the uttermost speed, the band of painted and plumed warriors screamed garrulous yells and divided into two columns with military precision to circle around us.

With no retreat or seclusion possible, Davy urged us not to show our weapons, to remain calm, and not to display any signs of fear. Although my body trembled and sweat from fear trickled on my brow and down my back, I could not help but admire the magnificent yet appalling spectacle of these half-naked savages with long flowing hair and decorated spears that dazzled against the morning sun.

Slowly, the Indians steadied their horses and, as the dust settled, the lead warrior slid down to the soil from his blanket to stride forward with a determined and assuming pace. Without a word, his narrow deep eyes examined us, paying great attention to the squaw.

The Life and Death of My Best Friend, Davy Crockett

Davy flicked a concerning glance towards me which I registered and acknowledged with a subtle nod. As the Chief postured in front of us I noticed that swinging from his spear were two fresh scalps, so fresh was the hair that Pepper's blood still dripped from the ginger hair and remaining segments of ripped flesh.

The warrior shouted something to the girl and answering in a native dialect, she dismounted to approach him. The incomprehensible exchange continued with a volatile accompaniment of many gestures and animated scowls until eventually, the young widow turned to Davy and to our immense surprise told him in perfect English, that the Chief wanted to talk to him.

For a brief period of time, we were stunned by the widow's articulation for previous to this incident, we naively and foolishly had no inkling that she possessed the ability to speak our language.

Davy dismounted and met the fearful warrior face to face. Our interpreter explained that we were dishonoring the Comanche by trespassing on their lands and he demanded to know where we were travelling to.

Poised and tremor-free, Davy replied that we had not meant to cause insult and that we were merely passing through and then he equaled the Chiefs dispute with courage by asking why the Comanche's had blocked his passage when they were friends with the white man who in the past had supplied them with rifles, blankets, and steel to make spears.

The Chief did not seem to react well to the retort and with a lined forehead, he ranted at the squaw and shook his spear at Davy.

The Life and Death of My Best Friend, Davy Crockett

She seemed unwilling to translate his reaction and so consciously maintaining the bravado Davy added that if the Comanche passed through American territory would they want to be treated with respect and be allowed to pass through without facing hostility and being threatened.

The warrior's face raised in our direction and he intimidatingly stared at us one by one until his eyes once again settled upon Davy. He then took a few steps forward, moving so close to Davy that their breaths warmed each other faces. Still, Davy remained poised and blinklessly bold as he held the Chief's menacing stare.

Suddenly with a swiftness that gave no time for any reaction, the Chief reached down and grabbed at Davy's sheaf to pull free his knife. Defensively Davy stepped back and raising both his arms to signal he was merely intent on a peaceful resolution he calmly mouthed. "Whoa there, friend. There ain't any need for you to be unfriendly." but ignoring the call the warrior secured the knife in his belt and grabbed tight the women to drag her back towards his horse.

Resisting his will she heeled her feet into the soil and pulled back from his hold. With many warriors surrounding us, we knew it would be futile for us to intervene so hopelessly we all watched on feeling foolishly inadequate, then further humiliated as cheers and laughter erupted from the savages as the struggle began to amuse them.

Comanche shouts were exchanged between the Chief, the woman, and some of the warriors as the tussle continued, but still, neither Davy nor any of us dared object knowing our interference would result in our own savage and tortuous deaths.

The Life and Death of My Best Friend, Davy Crockett

Undeterred the squaw fought back and kicking and slapping at the warrior she broke free from his grasp and ran to wrap her arms around Davy's shoulders.

"I must go." We heard her cry.

"No! We will defend you." Davy gallantly replied.

"No." The squaw's eyes bulged fear. "You must not."

"Stand behind me." He commanded, maneuvering the girl behind him.

Our eyes gaped wide and our hearts thundered hard within our chests. Expecting a deathly onslaught and to meet out doom we feathered our fingers on our weapons and braced ourselves, however to our amazement the Chief simply threw back his head and released a heinous laugh to which the entire group of savages copied.

"No." She resisted and refused to move her feet. "This is the only way."

Then she whispered in Davy's ear and after a moment's embrace the squaw detached herself from Davy, cast a lamentable smile in our direction, and walked back towards the Chief who with his arms waiting for her swooped her up and onto his horse.

Holding a leering stare at Davy, the Chief mounted his horse and wrapped one arm around his captive, then with yells and screams that chilled our spines the warriors turned away with speed and charged from whence they came.

The Life and Death of My Best Friend, Davy Crockett

As I watched their trailing dust cloud disappear over the distant ridge I braced all my muscles hard and held one long deep breath to regain my composure and to stop my legs from quivering, then without further delay, I followed Davy's lead and heeled my mustang in the opposite direction to the far ridge where hoof dust lingered.

Fearful of further hostilities we travelled all day, often walking miles to rest our weary mounts and once within a suitable sanctuary of dense woodlands we dejectedly made a small camp and hid behind our shame by making small talk until Davy made it plain there was nothing we could do to stop the hostiles from taking the widow and that she had made him promise he must not risk any of our lives by initiating a foolish and futile attempt to prevent her from being abducted.

Around the dancing flames of our little fire both the Preacher and McRay admitted they had never seen an Indian warrior before and that they had been presented with such a fearful sight nor had they ever been more intimidated as when they heard that shrieking war cry.

No one mentioned the death of Pepper, Leon concealed his thoughts and silently occupied himself by stoking the fire.

After a while, Davy informed us the squaw told him the warrior wanted to know if his wounds were from fighting with another white trespasser they had killed earlier that morning. She admitted the man had been part of the group, but due to his dishonor, they had abandoned him. Then she told the Chief the wounds were inflicted by a cougar that the brave white man he had fought with his knife.

The Life and Death of My Best Friend, Davy Crockett

The Chief disclosed he had found and skinned a dead cougar and the deadly wound upon it had been inflicted by the knife of a brave man, and not the bullet of a coward which had been discharged from a safe distance upon an animal which cannot defend itself.

The Chief told the squaw it would offend their ancestors in the sky should the warriors take the life of such a brave man without provocation however he considered it a great honor to own the brave man's knife and parade it as a trophy in front of his people. Then he demanded to know if she had been stolen and abused by the traveling white men to which she answered no, the brave man accompanied her and saved her from the Cougar had been friends with her dead husband and once their affairs had been conducted in Texas, they were going to help return her back to her homeland.

Together with the preacher, we all asked the Lord to guide her spirit and we thanked him for giving her the ability to communicate with the Chief for had it not been for her dialect and her melodramatics we would have seen our last sunrise for no doubt we would have been butchered and scalped.

The rest of the evening again, we sat in near silence contemplating the events which had concluded in the previous twenty-four hours. In the dark expanse into which our eyes cannot see no matter how hard we scowl or fix a stare our pitiful reminisces and wild imaginations vexed us, our losses had been considerable and utterly hurtful.

The Life and Death of My Best Friend, Davy Crockett

Davy noted our soured inclinations, and he endeavored to distract us from our depression and charm the atmosphere by recounting some narratives in Washington and the time he dined at the White House with the president. Only being a kin to eating with his hunting knife and scooping food from a wooden bowl, he recalled being dumfounded by the oversized sparking silver cutlery that surrounded the finest porcelain, all of which was laid before him on the biggest table he had ever seen.

He told how he had to wait and watch the other guests to see which implements to use and how to use them and he laughed recalling he found the use of a fork impossible and he caused consternation amongst the country's elitist social gentry by eating his entire meal with just a knife, and afterward such was the sweetness of the food he did not sleep for three days. Davy's humorous recollections eventually distracted our morbidity just enough to allow our eyelids to grow heavy and force upon us the requisite of sleep.

The Life and Death of My Best Friend, Davy Crockett

Chapter 20 – The Bandits

By dusk the following day we had reached the banks of the Colorado River and we settled down to eat with a Texan who had been travelling in the opposite direction. Introducing himself as Juan Luis, he then concerned us by stating he had heard rumors from the local Latinos that Santa Anna, the fearsome Mexican president, was leading his vast army through the region to eradicate the Texan's uprising. Not being a family man nor a fighter, Juan had resigned himself to leave the combat to the skilled and the brave and flee to his cousin's homestead across the border until peace was restored. Not enquiring about our business, Juan kindly shared his provisions with us, and simply refraining from prying, he hankered down with us for the night finding shelter from the chilling wind on a slope amongst some large boulders.

After morning coffee, Juan pointed to rivulet and departed, telling us that if we followed its passage for about four hours, we would reach a large gathering of freedom fighters in a small village called Bexar.

The plume had not dispersed from our dying fire when we heard the distinct sound of gunfire. We terminated our duties and turned our heads to the distant explosion, and listened as several more shots echo around us. Apprehensively, we reached for and checked our weapons, then frowning and using our hands to shield our eyes from the low sun on a distant embankment, the rising dust of a galloping rider was revealed to us.

"Juan?" I asked Davy.

The Life and Death of My Best Friend, Davy Crockett

"Guess so." He replied, throwing me a confused glance. Before I had time to question his speedy return, the larger dust cloud of four chasing riders came into our view.

"Darn it." Cussed Davy.

"Indians?" Wondered McRay

"Thieves!" Davy leveled his rifle and eyed down the barrel. "Maybe this will put them off." He said, knowing that due to their speed and the distance, administering a successful shot would be impossible.

The thunder and the revolving ball had the desired effect. As it thudded into the ground close to the lead horse, the riders pulled tight on their reins, allowing the fleeing rider to reach our camp amongst the large boulders.

"Banditos!" Juan shouted as he leaped from his saddle to land in a crouch behind a giant rock. "Four of them." He warned, pressing his palm hard on his red-drenched shoulder.

"Well, if they come at us from this distance there'll soon be none of them." Davy admonished. "Take cover fellas and hold your nerve." He advised as he climbed onto a boulder the size of his cabin.

From our guarded position, we watched the attackers circle each other as they deliberated their next actions and then after much deliberation, they formed a straight line spacing themselves about ten feet apart from each other. Slowly, with an open display of rifles and pistols, they inched their way forward scanning for their foes on the hillside and amongst the many obscuring boulders.

The Life and Death of My Best Friend, Davy Crockett

One man shouted something in Mexican and when there was no reply, another one of the gunmen shouted in English that if we gave them everything we had, they would not kill us.

Not wanting to reveal our position again no answer was given, but Davy whispered. "Looks like we are going to have a dust-up with these blackards." Then he told us to take aim at one man each adding if they were fool enough to continue their charge upon us then we would have enough time to reload and fire off another shot.

The Preacher pressed his back up against a rock and closing his eyes and clasping tight his hands he quietly recited God's words. Along with our three Little Rock companions, we spread out and hunkered low enough to shield our bodies whilst permitting us a clear view of the lay below us.

The English-speaking Mexican shouted again that we should surrender and if we didn't they would fire upon us and show us no mercy. The threat irritated Davy's patience and provoked him into a response.

"Fire away gringo!"

The Mexican laughed and whooped, then he spurred his horse into an immediate charge towards us.

Remaining calm, Davy called out to us. "If I take down the one with the loose mouth, maybe the other will flee." We all nodded for him to go ahead and shoot again and he replied by telling us to fix up our aim on the other. He then pulled back on the trigger to blast the antagonist backward and out of the saddle.

The Life and Death of My Best Friend, Davy Crockett

The remaining outlaws did not heed the warning and now determined to seek vengeance for the death of their friend they too released a yell and heeled their mounts into an attack which we instantly met with a salute of lead that left two more of the bandits slumped dead in their saddles. The third bandit pulled tight on his reins and turned his horse as quickly as he could to make his escape.

"You can't let him get away," Juan warned. "He will return with many others."

Having quickly reloaded, Davy exposed himself on the rock to clear himself of the thick smoke and took aim at the diminutive galloping figure. He held taught his body and once more pulled back on the trigger to halt the speeding horse with such force that in its fall it tossed the fugitive high into the air.

Quickly once more Davy reloaded old Betsy all the time keeping his eyes fixed on the man who by now slowly staggered up onto his knees. Leaning to his left he fell onto his side once more and then rubbing both his hands near his rib cage he hauled himself up onto his unsteady legs to staggered forwards. By now Davy had levelled Betsy and fixed his aim with such accuracy the fatal shot shattered the man's skull and felled him instantly.

As Davy held his stance on the rock to survey the scene for any further movements, the Little Rock boys withdrew their knives and ran through the boulders to extradite any last breath that the robbers may have contained. A few minutes later they returned with blooded blades and full arms of pistols, rifles, and ammunition.

The Life and Death of My Best Friend, Davy Crockett

Wasting no time, I returned to the fragments of our campfire and selected a charred piece of wood, then using my fingers to hook the lead ball out of Juan's shoulder, I commenced to seal the hole with the searing heat. Thankfully, our friend soon succumbed to the pain and fainted, enabling me to complete the task without his resisting struggles and ear-paining screams.

Not wanting to spend another night in these wild parts we collected our meager belongings and headed out from the boulders where the salubrious air refreshed our lungs and the crystal cool waters of the streams enabled us to swill out the dust from our throats and wash the travel grime from our faces.

Juan was in an utter state of delirium. His right arm was incapable of holding the reins and he could not make his journey to his cousins as expected, so we secured him tight in his saddle and his horse to mine.

Over the next few miles we collected three of the bandit's stray horses which we talked to kindly and persuaded them into yielding to us another rifle, ammunition, and several purses containing silver coins, then slowly and without further incident we continued on our way across hedges of wild camellias and vanilla plants which scented the air with perfumed wafts until finally, we caught sight of the small adobe buildings which shaped Bexar, and across to its left another half mile distant across strangely infertile fields was a stone missionary which displayed in the breeze a Mexican tri-colored flag.

Hitching our horses to the rails we smiled and nodded acknowledgments to the few half-hidden faces of the greeters who gawked curiously down at us from the boardwalks.

The Life and Death of My Best Friend, Davy Crockett

It appeared our arrival failed to cause any great arousal as we had expected and only a few innocent and playful youngsters gathered about us and our horses in the desolate, dusty street.

Void of all macho's and elders the children led away our horses to the stable yard whilst we allowed our attentions to be drawn towards the beckoning clamor of mirth which exuded from the several cantinas and spilled out into the streets. Doors flung open and music and laughter spilled out everywhere as ladies began to appear, teasing us with sultry pretenses and shouting and waving for us to join them in making merriment.

In desperate need of wholesome food, we pounded through the swinging doors of the nearest cantina. Trade was brisk, Texans, Mexicans, senorita's old and young crowded the fetid smoke-filled room. Shoulder to shoulder with each other reveling with intoxication, their gaiety and conversations fused with the chords of several fiddles into an inaudible din. We muscled our way through the debauchery to sample the local brew and order a bowl of greasy food and before the first mouthful had burned our dry throats, a leather-faced stranger struck up a polite introduction and conversation which included an inquiry to our sudden appearance.

With his newly acquired knowledge and his inquisitiveness satisfied the stranger excused himself and disappeared amongst the wall of backs and shoulders with a friendly gesture that included leaving a pile of coins on the plank for us to purchase more refreshments, however just a few minutes later.

The Life and Death of My Best Friend, Davy Crockett

"Crockett! Colonel Davy Crockett!" Was repeatedly shouted above the din and emerging through the readily parting bodies were a couple of Americans whose appearance attracted the eyes and attention of the revelers.

"David ..... David Crockett." Davy corrected.

A powerful-shouldered man examined our appearances and then stretched out his hand to demand an introduction. "Crockett. Colonel Crockett. We'd heard rumors you were heading this way." He announced. "And may I say how pleased we are to welcome another man who is no stranger to the smell of gunpowder."

Davy obliged without hesitation, stretching his hand in the man's direction to find it was received with a firm shake and a cordial smile.

Suddenly the fiddles stopped playing, and the din silenced. Everyone in the room angled their faces and fixed their gazes in our direction, then cheers, whoopee's, and applause spontaneously erupted from all directions and a surge of bodies clamored around us.

"Jim Bowie and James Bonham." Said the shorter wide-shouldered man with the formidable presence as he turned over his left palm to introduce his companion.

"Davy Crockett from Tennessee and my friends." Davy's head tilted towards the six of us who had formed a semi-circle to listen to the three men's dialogue.

The Life and Death of My Best Friend, Davy Crockett

The man named Bowie held out his arms as if to make a barrier and called for everyone to return to their preoccupations, then he asked us what news we conveyed and how far behind us were the reinforcements.

Never before have I seen as many joyous faces suddenly turn ashen, nor have I ever witnessed a rapturous crowd collapse into such a startling silence when Davy carelessly replied that the seven of us had traveled alone and he knew nothing of the whereabouts of further troops. It gave me the impression that in a single sentence, Davy had dashed all their hopes and commanded them to the gates of hell.

Aware of the disenchanted mutterings Bowie stated that he wanted to introduce Davy to Colonel Neill, the commander of the regular troops, and hastening us out of the cantina Davy was barracked with calls demanding to know where his legions of followers were stationed and what had happened to the huge assembly of troops from Tennessee whom he was commanding.

Bowie told Davy to ignore the disenchanted heckles stating that his men 'are just kinda desperate for some good news', then Bonham added 'been too many insincere words and false pretenses'.

Our introduction to Colonel Neill did little to ease the commander's obvious state of agitation and our lack of news regarding aid vexed him to the point of reaching for his decanter of brandy, at which point he downed himself two quick shots.

After a moment's contemplation where he simply stared at the bare wall he sighed, and without an offer of an invitation to his guests he absentmindedly helped himself to another dose of the medicine, then he

The Life and Death of My Best Friend, Davy Crockett

forlornly slumped back in his chair and apologized for what we had already deduced. He had been expecting cheering news regarding the supply of armed and trained unit fighting men.

Depressingly, he explained that he desperately needed reinforcements because many of his current outfit of paid troopers were at the end of their enlisted service, and without additional fighters, food, clothing and ammunition he feared they would soon disband on mass.

Followed by several deep sighs and a severe bout of head scratching he announced that he would like to assemble the troops the following morning when they had sobered up and introduce them to the famed politician. He hoped that a rousing speech from the legendary orator would increase their waning spirits and dissuade deserters.

Bowie worried the propaganda hoodwinking would not have the desired effect upon the fearing soldiers. He warned that daily they were receiving reports from their whores of a huge advancing Mexican army and without news of support from Sam Houston or Stephen Austin he thought it would be ill-advised to hold an assembly because he said the disenchanted men would shout the loudest. After a short consideration of his options, Neill concluded that with no additional support, he felt duty bound to exploit, with Crockett's permission, his fame to bolster the morale of the soldiers by claiming with Crockett now in Bexar many more volunteers will want to fight by his side and he was convinced many more men are now sure to follow.

Jim Bowie knew his men well, and his assumptions were proven correct. Although Davy's introduction was received with cheers and some initial optimism, it became evident afterward that his rallying address did not

The Life and Death of My Best Friend, Davy Crockett

appease nor inspire the desperate troopers to stay beyond the expiration of their enlistment period and during the second night of our stay about half of the soldiers disappeared into the black vastness beyond the hue and smell of the cantinas.

For those whose principles and convictions bound them to stay and defend the town with honor, they simply caroused the dull days and cold nights by exploiting all forms of local hospitality. Wild parties and debauchery spilled out everywhere from cantinas to brothels as the fighters determinedly enjoyed their final days of liberty before the arrival of the guns and cannons would force them to seek protection in the old missionary the locals called the Alamo.

Three days later, citing a family illness urgently beckoned him, Colonel Neill followed most of his men and left the town to return home. His final act as commander was to delegate his position, however failing to be decisive he divided the authority and nominated Lieutenant Colonel Travis, a tall, immaculately clad, and clean-shaved lawyer with a tongue akin to the higher classes of the social gentry to command the remaining paid troopers whilst, Bowie the forthright rough cut Texan was to command the volunteers, many of whom had already followed him to San Antonio.

The two men who both demanded and received respect from natural, but contrasting styles were both unhappy with the orders given by Neill.

William Barrett 'Buck' Travis commanded through the power of his grammar, he was eloquent and authoritative with a direct presence and demeanor that seemed more aligned to the training fields of West Point rather than the crudeness of this insignificant little town, whilst James

The Life and Death of My Best Friend, Davy Crockett

Bowie, a veteran of fighting skirmishes with the Mexicans, was a man of his people who earned his respect through his actions and his ability to coerce his requests without raising condescending demands. Habitually, he drank and socialized with his subordinates and this ritual behavior was considered abhorrent by Travis who conducted his affairs independently and in isolation without the requirement of correlation or interaction with his subjects.

Friction existed and all cooperation between the two leaders was none existent. Often both the men disagreed and argued in front of their subjects, causing agitation and rifts to divide amongst the ranks.

Davy knew their discourtesy and disrespect were none constructive and being void of any prejudice he often acted as a regulator and peacemaker using his diplomatic elegancies to abate the often heated arguments and temporarily unite the men towards the mission's common purpose, but day after day the two leaders harassed and barracked each other without suspension.

Travis wrote appeals to Sam Houston and sent out dispatch riders daily, stating his forces urgently needed more provisions. He gave orders to stock the old mission with anything of worth that they could appropriate from the locals.

The defenses around the crumbling mission were strengthened and cannons were positioned strategically to cause maximum destruction upon those who chose to assault the rudimentary fortress.

The Life and Death of My Best Friend, Davy Crockett

Bowie and his loyal volunteers patrolled and scouted the area for news, pillaged livestock, and reconnoitered terrain for escape routes. He had ambitions to join forces with Sam Houston at Washington-on-the-Brazos and he urged Travis to abandon the area and join him however, Travis was resolute stating repeatedly that Houston needed time to build an army and he was duty-bound to defend the town against the might of the Mexican army and give Houston as much of the precious gift as possible.

Without warning, one late afternoon the town fell eerie silent. The locals hurriedly and desperately packed from view all of their belongings closed their shutters, and loaded up their carts to flee from the town. The signs of advancing Mexican soldiers were ominously obvious and knowing the danger was now nearing we too fled the town to take our position on the walls of the Alamo.

From the distant walls, we watched and listened to a roar like nothing I'd heard before as regal horsemen, richly adorned with velvet capes and silvery gleaming helmets, led hundreds of straight-backed marching military men gracefully into the town.

Arriving with the pageantry of trumpets and a roll of beating drums, the vast army, splendored in scarlet, blue, and white uniforms crowded the once empty street their gold trim and bayonets strikingly resplendent in the low sun.

For months I'd listened to gossip and alarmist talk which I'd mainly considered exaggerated fabrications from long-winded cowardly skedaddlers, but now before my eyes and no more than a thousand strides away assembled a force of desolation which dried my mouth, rendered me speechless and made me feel queasy.

The Life and Death of My Best Friend, Davy Crockett

Together and admiringly silent, we peered and focused hard to search for and glimpse the dreaded imperial General, but there were so many squat men attired with regality that none of us could be sure which one of the killers he was.

In ghastly silence, our eyes remained beset upon the enemy's splendor and our minds despondingly occupied with the prospect of doom until Travis and Bowie roused us from our speculative misery with lung-bursting orders, which set us to work in preparedness for an attack.

Davy told me that Bowie had secretly sent out an envoy to discuss terms for surrender under a white flag which angered Travis and when the rider returned with the grim news that surrender would only be accepted under General Santa Anna's personal discretion and that any clemency would only be considered if a list of his demands were fully adhered to, immediately he dispatched his own rider to inform the General that neither he nor any of his soldiers would humiliate themselves by bowing to his demands. As we watched Travis's rider return with haste to his rear we saw the rising of a red flag.

"Guess that concludes matters," Davy said turning to walk from the gantry.

"What?" I chased after him.

"Vengeance without mercy." He stopped, sighed, and nodded in the direction of the flag. "Death to all."

The Life and Death of My Best Friend, Davy Crockett

Chapter 21 - Victory or Death

On the second day of the siege Bowie took ill, and he had to be carried to his bed by his slave, Ben. Suspicions led us to believe his condition was due to excess consumption of the devil's brew, but when his condition did not ease and he deteriorated quickly throughout the day an herbalist informed Travis that he suspected typhoid or tuberculosis and he feared the man would be a burden rather than a desirable.

Lengthy discussions were held between Travis, Davy, and Bonham with considerations for surrendering the vulnerable man to the Mexicans, and after much debate, they reluctantly agreed that submitting Bowie to the fate of the Mexicans without a fight would adversely affect the morale of his volunteers. To ensure there was no spread of disease, they arranged for Bowie to be confined in isolation in one of the bunkhouses and they assigned his manservant to care for his welfare.

Later that day Davy confided to me that Travis had dispatched a courier named Albert Martin with a rousing and notable plea for aid which he felt was sure to appeal to the conscience of all Texans. Although he did not reveal the details of the wording contained in the letter, he did tell me that on the envelope written in striking bold letters were the words 'VICTORY OR DEATH'. That evening Davy took to his fiddle seemingly buoyed by believing the call to arms would succeed and the arrival of reinforcements would displace the ever-increasing Mexican army. In the early hours of the morning quiet, our rest was broken by a series of sharp bugle calls that spliced the chilly air like some sinister sermon that kept us edgy all day. From that day forth every sunrise was greeted with the same foreboding strain.

The Life and Death of My Best Friend, Davy Crockett

The following day, we spent our time strengthening the palisade near the low barracks and we witnessed the arrival of dozens of Mexican cannons. Later, we counted our rations, sixty bushels, thirty beavers, four barrels of flour, one butt of dried beans, two casks of whiskey, two boney cows, and ten pigs. More meat was required if Travis's objectives were to be achieved.

Sometime in the afternoon, the Mexicans large assembly of musicians picked up their instruments and harmonized us with a dramatic serenade. At first, the entertainment startled us from our lethargic tedium, then we began to wave our caps because the music cheered our spirits and relieved some of the boredom. As the long fanfare of trumpets, drum rolls, stringed melodies recessed we hollered for more renditions until Travis informed us the Mexicans were taunting us with death serenades.

The infamous El dequello whose notes ordained blood and death with the promise of 'no quarter given' continued and as one serenade finished immediately another one was struck up and by rotating the musicians, the chords tormented us both day and night without interruption, lull nor let up.

At sun up the next morning we discovered the Mexicans had completely surrounded us with cannons at no more than six hundred yards away. Fearful knowing looks, silence and shaking heads confirmed all our thoughts, we now knew there was no way out and that our existence upon this soil relied solely on the arrival of reinforcements.

Travis pomped bravado, but we knew he was just trying to allay the trooper's fears. We enquired to the condition of Bowie, but Susanna Dickinson our Lieutenant's wife who had been assisting the slave,

The Life and Death of My Best Friend, Davy Crockett

regretfully confirmed that there was no improvement and that he was now delirious with the fever and only whiskey eased his suffering. She feared that he would never walk free from the bunkhouse.

Travis ordered a head count, one hundred and fifty-four fit and able fighting men, two slaves, one incapacitated, and half a dozen family members who had chosen to stay by their husbands, brothers, and fathers.

In the afternoon more Mexicans arrived, too many to positively identify, but we estimated well over another one thousand infantry, then much deliberation ensued when one of our fella's brought to our attention a huge cannon that was being drawn through the town and positioned brazenly in our eye line.

"This big boy is going to be a might inconvenient." Davy said, watching the soldiers position the cannon some fifty or so strides closer than the rest of the artillery. "Gonna have to do something about it." He added without removing his eyes from the Mexicans, who chocked the wheel and began to assemble a supply of cannon balls. "Load me up some rifles boys." He said, leveling Betsy and concentrating down the barrel.

After the explosion of gunpowder, the fall of a soldier a rapid cowering ensued for a few moments, however a further scurry of activity signaled the Mexicans determination to continue and sighing, Davy asked for another rifle. Again the lead dispatched another Mexican direct to his god, but fearing reprisals from their commander the soldiers continued to follow orders and they began to prime the cannon.

The Life and Death of My Best Friend, Davy Crockett

Davy was handed another five loaded rifles and he unleashed another five shots killing or wounding another four Mexicans and preventing them from loading the mighty wall destroyer, yet cowering low and undeterred by the accuracy of the shooter they still obeyed their orders.

By the eighth slain Mexican Davy changed tact and aimed for the mounted officer who had ridden across the plain to investigate the holdup, however after the officer cowardly positioned himself a further ten paces behind the cannon Davy took a while longer than usual with his aim which when it was delivered blew the officers gleaming hat high into the air and thrust his instantly limp body out from the saddle.

After a frantic bout of arm waving and gesticulating, the three remaining soldiers cast away their tools and fled amongst the cover of the knee-height scrub.

Hearing the discharge of shot followed by cheers, Travis had taken up a position on the gantry to observe the shooting proficiency, and when the slaughter had concluded he gave orders for a lookout to be posted solely on that cannon night and day.

Santa Anna's revenge was immediate and before we had time to climb down from the wall cannonade from all four sides was unleashed upon us. At first, we sped for cover and ducked down low under anything solid we could find, however after a short while we mercifully asserted the bombardment from distance was more of a nuisance than a catastrophe because the inadequate force of the balls made little impact upon our thick walls.

The Life and Death of My Best Friend, Davy Crockett

Travis replied to the assault with a short barrage from our own cannons until he decided to preserve ammunition and gave orders to cease the retaliation. Santa Anna's anger had not abated and his bombardment did not ease and it continued to nuisance us intermittently for the rest of the day and throughout the night.

The ensuing day was a repeat, with the continuous bombardment accompanied by the horns and drums. Only fatigue concerned us until eventually, we mastered how to rest amongst the cacophony of harmony and thunder. Later in the day, we suffered our first casualty when a man called Harrison had to be treated by Missus Dickinson for a shrapnel blast that lacerated his left forearm and the defenders enthusiasm was wounded when cannon ball destroyed the liquor wagon causing much consternation and an immediate tirade of cusses and retaliatory threats. The Preacher took to the wall and tried to calm the agitation by delivering a rousing sermon in which he alleged the missile had been diverted by god to prevent abuse and he stated to the bewildered listeners that 'Drunken men cannot stand brave and tall, they are unstable and good for only staggering in their own vomit' he then raised his fist defiantly to hail. 'Samson only drank water '

On the fourth day howling cold winds shivered us and added to our misery it brought along with it another force of Mexican soldiers. Davy tried to rouse our spirits with speeches of promised aid and funny recitals which told of ants wisely cutting paths around stone buildings whilst donkeys would try and bang the door down with their heads. Yet concealed behind our brief smiles we knew these ants would not be allowed to venture off track and there were infinite numbers of willing donkeys prepared to suffer bruised heads.

The Life and Death of My Best Friend, Davy Crockett

We all fully understood the Alamo had to be taken at all costs and that vengeance must be served as a message to all Texans. None of his speeches were answered with noisy hurrahs or jovial bluster, on this occasion just solemn and somber faces engulfed with dread simply stared back at the vigorous optimist.

Infuriated by the relentless bombardment and wanting to cause a decoy, Travis ordered another volley of our own cannonade, and whilst the Mexicans took temporary cover from the assault he dispatched Bonham to Sam Houston's headquarters with another written plea for immediate assistance.

That night we shivered under our furs and huddled close around the fires, this time the trembles were not born from the fear of death, they were a consequence of the swirling gusts that whipped across the hard soil and howled through the swaying brush to chill our bones.

Davy always said there's nothing like the warm flames of a fire to inspire conversation and distraction. Never was it more strangely true and recognized by all who were trapped in here alongside us as we huddled around to admire the hot dancing flames which seemed to ease our pains, relieve our suffering, and temporary alleviated the torturous fear as if in some magical way the flames threw more than comfort into our faces.

That night my eyes swept across the relaxed defenders as they played their fiddles, dealt cards, snoozed, and attended to their pipes whilst spreading tales of past glories and exaggerated reminisces.

The Life and Death of My Best Friend, Davy Crockett

"Come on Leander, let us get a piece of pleasure from that o'l cheerful fire," Davy pointed to three silhouetted figures huddled around a luminous blaze. "Let's get squat down with those boys over there."

"Are you in Colonel?" The dealer raised his eyebrows in Davy's direction.

"No, thank you. I've found trouble follows gambling." He shook his head, still abiding by his principles, even in this gloomiest of situations.

"Well, ok then, but then sit ya self down and warm up ya paws."

Davy accepted the offer, and he shuffled in on the opposite side of the fire to the gamblers and alongside two pipe-smoking old timers.

"Am I dealing ya in fella?" Asked one of the glowing faced men with puerile eagerness.

"Sure...... What's the tender." I asked.

"Corn, beans and a bucket of spit is all we have." Laughed the card dealer.

Civilly accepting the newcomers to their fire the men shuffled to open up a space for us to sit and as they did they began to introduce themselves as Private John W Baylor, Private Daniel Cloud, Lieutenant Jacob Darst, and Private Rich Ballentine from Scotland and Captain Philip Dimmitt.

Davy tucked in and held out his palms to enjoy the warmth as he listened to the gambler's incessant babble and immature ridicule. We were soon joined by the Magician and understanding the brave soldiers needed their minds occupying with a cheery distraction to temporarily displace their thoughts of approaching doom Davy withheld to himself his opinions on gambling.

The Life and Death of My Best Friend, Davy Crockett

In the spread of yellow hue Davy noticed Captain Dimmitt's right arm bore a faint tattoo with the message, 'Any fate, but no surrender' and later he told me that he wondered how many times the Kentuckian had lipped the words to strengthen his resolution and beliefs.

As the hours passed and as the flames spread their solace amongst the gathered it wasn't long before the cards were folded and banter and yarns became the only traded amusement. This became our nightly routine, we'd take turns to keep watch, feed, and then warm, hunkering down to listen to fables and embellished tales ranging from morbid recounts and haunting truths to beautiful memories and auspicious recollections.

For the next two days, the intense bombardment eased, but we were still unable to fully rest our leaden eye lids due to the periodic forays of the Mexicans who encroached upon us to deliver more misery by firing off shots at our lookouts on the walls. In order to repel the nuisances we were obliged to stand at our posts and return fire both day and night for prolonged and exhausting periods. The Mexicans, being vast in numbers once weary were able to retreat and attack again with fresh and eager murderers where as we were compelled to stay at our stations eventually learning how to eat and slumber against the walls, never again were we able to return to the friendly campfire frivolity.

Come darkness on the seventh day Davy led a group of volunteers out from the protection of our fortified walls to flame and destroy a number of timber outbuildings, stockades, and some dense areas of thicket that had provided cover for the sneaky Mexican sharpshooters.

The Life and Death of My Best Friend, Davy Crockett

Unable to obtain permission to leave my post and volunteer, from my position on the wall I could hear shots discharged, yells, and screams for over one hour, then isolated furnaces lit up expanding circles of amber, and in the shadows, I saw scurrying silhouettes of combatants from both sides emerged in and out of the darkness to fire off desperate defending and attacking shots.

Finally, a couple of hours later Davy returned, displaying a beaming smile that indicated he was satisfied, yet relived with the mission's outcome. In the debrief to Travis he estimated they had killed over thirty Mexican marksmen, whilst only two of our Texans fellas had received minor injuries which were soon remedied by Missus Dickinson. In addition to destroying the Mexican's concealment, our skirmishers retrieved eighty bushels of corn in one of the abandoned buildings.

As the flames raged high displaying our success the distant band struck up again, its horns and drums beating loudly and relentlessly the unnerving requiem. During these long cold nights as we leaned against the barricades and stared out towards the distant glow of campfires we were at our most despondent, as the minute's slowly dragged doubts tortured our thoughts, we were hopelessly captive in a living grave unable to rid the constant shadow of terror as we waited for death.

Day seven tediously faded with no significant events to record. Bowie's condition was reported as being stable, but still perilous and our food rations and ammunition were double-checked. In a far corner there was a lot of head scratching by Travis and his secondary's and hailing from the distance beyond the walls the orchestra continued to irritate. Every few minutes the odd cannon's blast continued to menace our defenses, but it was the cold wind which shivered our spines more than the threat beyond

The Life and Death of My Best Friend, Davy Crockett

the walls. That night the sky was clear and the air frigid and, although the icy wind hurt our bones and watered our eyes on any other night the uproar which lit up the darkness might have been viewed as a thing of beauty contrary to the warning of destruction.

On mid-morning the following day, 1st March Travis assembled us to inform that during the night Bowie's condition had deteriorated further and that he was not expected to recuperate any time soon therefore he was taking full command of the garrison and its defenders. There were a few sighs and shakes of the head from both the disgruntled who were only loyal to Bowie and those who were saddened by his sudden demise, but no one objected.

Once more, Travis and Davy tried to raise the morale by insisting we had not been abandoned by our leaders and they were sure that many more troopers would soon arrive. At dawn, we discovered that Captain Seguin had been dispatched under cover of the darkness by Travis with yet another plea for help.

However, that night as the long night shadows set and the dullness provided cover we found some fleeting cheer to repel our wind numbed faces and fingers. Rifle discharge from the Mexican lines blasted above the monotonous chords of the band and seized our attention towards a group of riders who sped passed the lines of our foe and swerved to evade all attempts to bring them down.

Cheers, hand clapping and hat waving accompanied their hasty approach towards our gates, but in order to repel a pursuing and enraged unit of Mexican cavalry two dozen or so of us leaped up onto the walls to send a volley of halting lead in their direction.

The Life and Death of My Best Friend, Davy Crockett

Pulling up to an immediate halt and turning the Mexican's swagger quickly vanished when they realized their danger and they hastily heeled out of range to face the wrath of Santa Anna.

With great eagerness for news, we all besieged our new compatriots, our ears angled for inspiring news. None forth came. The thirty-two men from Gonzales despondently quashed our brief optimism by confirming no further troops would be arriving and they had disobeyed orders and left base camp to join us knowing there would be no heroic return.

How ungrateful we must have looked when their valiant actions had only been received with melancholic eyes and dour words of hopelessness as now we realized as defenders of the Alamo garrison there was to be no salvation and no escaping the final bitter embrace of the dark angels.

Later that same evening under the shroud of darkness and guided by the intermittent glint of moonlight Bonham returned from Sam Houston to confirm that our fate lay between ourselves and Santa Anna, regrettably, he confirmed no assistance was to be dispatched and our doom could not be prevented.

Although we were relieved to welcome the volunteers their arrival disposed of the problem increased rationing. We had corn and flour, but to keep up our strength additional meat would be required, and very soon.

The men openly discussed that malnutrition and starvation would eventually lead to our dishonorable surrender. Slaughtering the horses was vigorously debated with stout objections reasoning that our four-legged friends may be our only route to freedom.

The Life and Death of My Best Friend, Davy Crockett

Finally, it was agreed that before any of the horses was slaughtered a small parry of volunteers led by Davy would, under the cover of darkness raid the Mexican livestock. The lives of our trusty horses depended on the mission success or failure, but either way, Travis declared our desperate act would reveal to Santa Anna the desperateness of our situation and probably persuade him to continue with the siege for a while longer and postpone any immediate plans for an attack. Travis said that whilst Santa Anna would seek to starve us into submission we were able to gift more time to Sam Houston thus enabling him to gather more troopers.

Clear skies prevented an immediate raid and we had to wait another two nights until drifting clouds shielded the low moon's silvery glow. Over the next day three more volunteers defied Sam Houston's orders and sneaked their way into the Alamo to increase our numbers to one hundred and eighty-seven. That night for the first time the music suddenly stopped to alarm us, now the silence tormented us day and night.

With the moon finally obscured Davy signaled it was time for us to cautiously creep through the gates and crawl our way across the soil towards an old fandango's stockade. At the far edge of town, it was known amongst the Texans that a local farmer had a supply of pigs, chicken and goats which he incompetently secured behind a waist-high two-piled fence. It was Davy's plan to send six men over the fence to grab whatever they could carry and flee back towards the fortress whilst two banks of four shooters spilt by a distance of twenty strides were to lay low with their weapons primed ready to provide cover. Fitness and speed was of equal importance as was the sure aim and a steady finger and whilst the best shooters took up their positions the youngest and fastest progressed quietly towards the pitiful fence.

The Life and Death of My Best Friend, Davy Crockett

Painstakingly rising over the fence without detection the six men grabbed and clutched tight their grips a haul of chickens and one pig, with lung bursting speed they scampered for their lives.

Less than a minute had ticked by before the notifying squeals and squawks alerted the enemy troops and rushing forwards to investigate they squinted into the pitch and discharged aimlessly a dozen or so hopeful shots in the direction of the high pitched noises. Following the discharge of shot with a Mexican war cry they lunged forwards with their bayonets fixed to hunt down the thieves until their reactionary advance was halted by Davy, who was in the first row arose with his companions to discharge a volley of lead in the direction of their calamity.

The intermittent burst of moon glow through the clouds did little to illuminate the surrounding area and with the bellows of thick smoke I could not ascertain if any of the chasing pack had been felled.

As the six chicken and pig carriers passed us by, immediately followed by a dashing Davy and the other three shootists, I arose from behind a cluster of sage and along with my fellow gunmen fired upon the shadowy figures who had once again begun their charge upon the rustlers. Without waiting to judge the accuracy of our aim we too turned and ran as fast as we could in the direction of the Alamo. Several paces in front of me Davy and his accompaniment had dropped to their knees and were quickly reloading as we scurried passed them at speed. Excitedly I shouted to Davy 'Give 'em hell' to which he grinned and nodded.

Again, now to my rear, blasts of thunder were unleased into the faces of the faltering chargers and after striding over another hundred yards my group once more dropped to our knees and we reloaded as quickly as our

The Life and Death of My Best Friend, Davy Crockett

fingers would allow, and once Davy and his group had sped passed us we again arose to release our deathly wrath of lead. With our defense now over, I sprang from the smoke and turned to make my final sprint back to camp when suddenly, an explosion of pain in my back rendered my leg useless and I stumbled into a ditch. I struggled to rise and staggered, my legs detained by deep mud, but then I realized it was not the mud that hampered my progress, and I fell.

I gasped hard over and over again trying to fill my pained lungs with fresh air and I pressed my body down flat and hard into the depths of the undergrowth praying I had not been seen. Distorted lights whirled and I began to lose my vision, all sense of direction, and my presence of mind. I managed to reach behind me and placed the back of my hand on the burning sensation and it became flooded with hot liquid.

Monstrous agony forced me to clamp my teeth as hard as I could to prevent myself from squealing out loud, then for what seemed an eternity I held my hands over my ears tight as if to block out the taunts of the death hunters until finally cramping pain bereft me of most of my senses. I spat out a mouthful of bile into the soil as an unbearable burning surged and ravaged throughout my entire body and I could do nothing to repress it beyond readily accepting the dullness of nihility, and the serenity of unconsciousness.

Unable to determine whether I was in heaven or hell, I slowly became aware of vermin scurrying around my ankles. Slowly I cracked open an eyelid, but my reflexes resisted the brightness of daylight and I immediately returned my eyes to the darkness.

The Life and Death of My Best Friend, Davy Crockett

With enormous effort, I tried to kick out at the rats, but immediate billowing pain ceased my entire body and within seconds I had returned to the painless unconsciousness.

When I roused myself again darkness had descended once more, but flashes as bright as lightning dazzled me and I was incapable establishing my location. With all my strength, I raised onto my knees and began to crawl along the base of the dyke, not knowing or caring which direction I traveled.

Pain dictated my every move and my every breath, allowing me only to intake shallow repeating pants. I dragged along my stiffened body for a while all the time praying for the infliction to end quickly, and with no clarity or reasoning within my thoughts I cared little how I met my demise. Oh, how at that moment I would have welcomed the swiftness of a Mexican bayonet.

I have no knowledge how far I dragged my wrecked body before I once more submitted into blackness and headed for the pit of Hades nor I have no sense of how long I laid in the dirt unconscious, but at some point in my stupor I became conscious of familiar pleasant fragrance, a redolence of sweet flowers and herbs. Slowly I became aware of a presence and I felt the warmness of breath upon my face. Cold water trickled on my burning brow. I felt my collar loosen and more water cool around my neck and shoulders. Overwhelming agony decreed that I could not open my eyes and thank my angel for the kindness and so the words I struggled to summon were released as only groans. Fatigue became again an unbearable weight in every muscle and finally, the slight exertion debilitated me once more and I slipped into the dark world of emptiness, waiting impatiently to accept death.

The Life and Death of My Best Friend, Davy Crockett

Bright light penetrating through my closed eyelids irritated me so much that I was stirred once more from my unconscious state. Death did not come, and I slowly became aware of muffled noises and I felt a soothing, feather-like swab brush across my forehead. Gentle whispering slowly replaced the inaudible din, but again, no matter how determinedly I tried, I could not force open my eyelids.

Some while later I finally blinked out of my sleep and keeping my head rested I slanted my eyes from side to side trying to adjust them to the vivid shafts of sunlight that spliced the wild brush and cane shelter and illuminated my surroundings. Tentatively I rolled my head just enough to glimpse thick foliage beneath my shoulders which comforted my body as I lay, then slowly I became aware of a shadow on my legs that originated from a slender framed woman who was standing in the makeshift's entrance shelter. With light-footed steps, the silhouette approached to kneel by my side and tenderly dampen my forehead with a cool compress.

My eyes felt heavy, and I struggled to keep them open, as all before me was still a blur. Water dripped onto my lips and into my mouth, easing the sore dryness. I shook my head to dispel the lethargy and clear the haze, but bolts of pain rendered me useless. Confusion muddled my thoughts. Was I dead? Journeying to heaven with an angel at my side to ease me through my time of passing. Seeing my distress, the woman tilted my head and with the cup of her palm, she ladled more water into my mouth. The liberation was instantaneous and rousing, and I tasted a salty linctus on my lips.

"You are healing well." I recognized the low-toned voice. "But you need more rest."

The Life and Death of My Best Friend, Davy Crockett

"Anna?" A conflagration held my tongue and tried to prevent me from talking. "Is that you?" I winced.

"Don't move." The woman whispered, holding her palm gently but firmly on my chest to forbid me from trying to rise.

"Chenoa?" I confusedly rasped.

"Yes. Is it I." The Indian calmed me. "Just one more day of rest and you will be well enough to travel."

"What?" I could hear her words, but I was too confused to unscramble a meaning. "Travel?"

"Yes, to Jacinto." As she spoke once more, she dampened my brow with a cold herbal pulp. "I have been given news that there is someone there who wants to talk to us."

"Davy?" I wheezed.

"I have no name, but what I do know is that we have little time. That is why we must move tomorrow." She warned me.

"Jacinto?"

"A soldier who passed us by told me that a dying man there shouted out many names in his hallucinations and yours was one of them."

"Dying?" My jaw locked due to the waves spiralling pain and the effort of speech fatigued me and I closed my eyes as I listened to Chenoa describe her dreadful tale.

The Life and Death of My Best Friend, Davy Crockett

Slowly and with hushed tones she explained that a troop of twenty Texan soldiers who were searching for Mexican runaways told her that there had been a huge battle at a place called Jacinto and that the Texans had slaughtered the army of Santa Anna. I heard and digested her words, but I was too exhausted to seek answers to my many questions. Fearful of rape she avoided all eye contact with the fervent gawkers and being careful to keep her distance, she dare not speak.

One of the soldiers suspected that she was taking care of a Mexican soldier and using his bayonet, he forced his way into the tiny shelter only to appear seconds later ashen-faced and slack-jawed. Swilling his throat clean with fresh water from the steam he reported to his Captain that a white man lay dying under the canes and he claims to be Leander Staxton from Tennessee. Shaking his head in almost disbelief, the Captain sighed and cussed stating they didn't have time to waste surveying the undertakings of a squaw, however, his curiosity willed him to dismount and investigate the soldier's declaration. Scowling at me whilst he quickly examined my condition, he impatiently asked me my name, to which I confirmed, and then without another word, he quickly exited the cover to address Chenoa. With hurried tones, the Captain informed her there was a dying Mexican in a field tent hollering out some names and that Leander Staxton was one of them and so if you know this fella you should hurry across over there before he meets his maker.

Chenoa asked the Captain which direction we should travel and he pointed east, then heeling away his horse at speed one of his men following on behind shouted 'two hundred miles, you can't miss it, there'll be buzzards everywhere.'

The Life and Death of My Best Friend, Davy Crockett

The next day we arose with the chorus of the morning birdsong and after a potent herbal drink she doused me in a crafted fragrance that kept the flies away. Finally, after weeks of lying on my back with hesitant steps, Chenoa supported me onto a travois she had crafted, and without any words she led her pony in the direction the Captain had pointed. In silence, we traveled for hours. I intermittently managed to doze, but bone-shaking pain was a constant companion. We rested briefly and often, each stop just long enough to take some water and feed the pony, then we continued slowly on with our backs to the descending sun until sheer darkness hindered Chenoa's inclinations.

Finally recovering my senses over a roasted supper of rabbit Chenoa made it known to me that she had fled from her Comanche abductors and tried to pick up our trail, and then by chance she found me face down and close to death in an arroyo. As daylight began to shine on a thousand or more uniformed soldiers, she circled back several miles into desolateness, dragging me with her pony until she felt it was safe enough to build a comfortable bed and a small shelter robust enough to aid rest and recovery.

Removing the lead from my shoulder with a charred poke of wood, she used traditional remedies to heal my wretched body and care for me until my vigor returned. She stated I had been in a state of delirium and the notches she had carved into the roof support to mark the break of my fever indicated a period over thirty days.

Somberly she added that only a couple of days later, just before the sun peeked through the remnants of the night clouds, hundreds of bugles sounded in the far distance, and then for over two hours thousands and thousands of chilling shots were fired.

The Life and Death of My Best Friend, Davy Crockett

By early morning, the inherent sounds of spring had returned and she heard nothing more.

Now my mind was tortured with the fate of my friend and our comrades within the old mission and for the following nights, I was void of all sleep and solace. Thankfully, my recovery progressed well and by the third day, I was able to walk with the aid of a carved branch for bodily support. This gave me much relief from the pain I was suffering because of the bumpy travois and by the fourth day, I could eat and rest well.

The Life and Death of My Best Friend, Davy Crockett

Chapter 22 – Old Friend

Emerging from a cluster of dense oaks grove where foul air soured a light breeze our eyes appalled upon barbaric carnage. Spawn across a wide field, large birds of many breeds tore upon the flesh and feasted from hundreds of slain bodies. The pleasant spring freshness had been replaced with the acridness of discharged powder and the repulsive thick stench of charred and rotting flesh.

Grief immediately beset us as we morosely observed a handful of white men drag and throw dead bodies on funeral pyres whilst others stacked lifeless corpses onto a couple of farm carts. Many men, however just sat around fires at the edge of the camp smoking their pipes, drinking and laughing, no doubt boasting and reminiscing about the vengeance which had brought about their glory.

Eventually one of the loitering gloaters took an interest in the squaw and her crippled friend and he became intrigued enough to ask about our concerns. Upon our reply he told us that most of the injured Mexicans and those who had surrendered had been butchered by the revenge-fevered Texans, he did add after a long scratch of his beard and a damnable grin, that few of the younger boys, musicians, and such like had been saved from the blood drunk maniacs and they were festering away at the edge of the field.

He raised a blood-crusted finger and, laughing he pointed the way to some tents over yonder telling us to follow the stink. We knew the men who fought here at Jacinto could not be reasoned with, along with many others they had lost loved ones to the Mexican butchers, so we ignored his shameful contempt and silently moved on.

The Life and Death of My Best Friend, Davy Crockett

We ignored the glassy-eyed and swollen death grimaces, the moans from the wounded, and the cries of the inconsolable as carefully we placed our feet between the dead and dying to walk furtively unobserved amongst the solemn presence of death until we reached a thick line of tall oaks.

No one else gave a second glance to the two strangers who inspected the rows of the weak, the needy, and the dying who lay in the shady grass eagerly waiting for the eternal darkness to finally embrace them and cease their pain.

We arched low to peer at the many prostrate bodies and nothing else. Putrid air seared our nostrils and often we had to turn our heads towards the trees to refresh our lungs and draw breath from the brown and green foliage before we once again scoured amongst the decaying.

We turned over limp bodies, raised limbs, and lifted bloody face coverings for some considerable time until eventually, I heard Chenoa gasp.

"Ezra!"

Sharpe eyed and alert as ever. Her eyes had locked upon the swollen and blackened face of the young singer. Quickly she opened her water cask and carefully she poured droplets of water through his swollen purple lips, as his eyelids flickered, tenderly she washed away his mask of dry blood.

 With her fingers, she feathered his blood-soaked clothing until he winced whereupon she tore open his shirt to reveal a crevice of green and purple which furrowed deep into his stomach.

"May your god help him." She said with little faith whilst glancing a despairing look in my detection.

The Life and Death of My Best Friend, Davy Crockett

Her eyes warned that we needed to get him away from the foulness of disease immediately and so with great effort and without any objection, she raised his limp shoulders and I his feet, and together we staggered a couple hundred yards through the trees until we reached the purity of a cold river. Here Chenoa collected herbs and attempted to bathe his wound, but the sweet smell of rotting flesh would not be flushed away, and nor could she prevent the seeping of dark blood. Unyielding to the singer's impending fate she applied the same compassionate care and curatives that she had administered on my injured body weeks earlier and by nightfall Ezra had rallied enough courage and regained consciousness enough to mutter his tale of woe.

Though sips of water, he rasped barely audible words into our lowered ears, tearfully informing us that somehow he got carried away with the stampeding buffalo until eventually he was barged out of his saddle and into unconsciousness.

When he regathered partial consciousness several hours later, he found his horse had been trampled to death, and in a state of utter delirium for the next few hours, he wandered aimlessly until finally his brain lifted from the mind fog and his vision and thoughts cleared. The following day he picked up our trail in the freshly trampled soil, but without a horse, he could not gain upon us.

Eventually, desperate for food and water, he wandered into a small settlement where he was harassed by a group of American mercenaries. Noting his ability to speak in their tongue and Mexican they shackled him and traded him for cash to a Mexican scouting party who in turn told him that if he did not agree to be their translator they would kill him.

The Life and Death of My Best Friend, Davy Crockett

After a couple of weeks and still bound, the scouts dragged him into Bexar where he was conscripted against his will into the vast forces of Santa Anna.

The story he told ripped open my soul so wide I could not breathe and my heart beat so hard it pained my entire body. He told us that from the small town, he could see the Alamo and occasionally he saw the brave defenders on the walls.

He informed us that the Mexican fighters were intrigued and excited when they found out that a famous congressman, whom they called Crockerty, and the legendary Texas revolutionist, James Bowie were trapped inside. The soldiers were eager for the siege to end and the battle to commence, but when the relentless cannonade and the music stopped for them to assemble the impending attack seemed to surprise most of them.

At one hour before dawn, every available bugle bellowed, and bugle answered bugle, there tones imperious and cruel and they blew forth an evil command. The call to arms signaled in unison the vast force to level their weapons and purposely set forth towards the Alamo knowing many of them would be sent delivered to heaven before the sun had fully brightened the new day. Cannons were ordered to fire once again, and they briefly lightened up the sky, then rifles bellowed, and thick smoke, agonizing wails, screams, and calls for bravado filled the dull morning air.

He described the sickening horror of the conflict, the merciless shrieks, curses, deathly wails, and then the dreadful silence as the dawn broke through the darkness in the east, spreading its calefacience over the battle-ravaged slaughter.

The Life and Death of My Best Friend, Davy Crockett

The explosion of powder had calmed and now the final intermittent death screams fell silent.

Tears wetted Ezra's cheeks as he explained through rapid shallow pants how he was dragged through blood and carnage on his knees to translate the final words of a few Texan prisoners before they were sent to their destiny.

He told how he heard the Mexicans praising the Texans for their bravery right until the end. Hand to hand they fought with despairing valor until they were finally conquered, yard by yard and room by room, finally the missionary succumbed to incredible carnage. He said that he could still hear the drip, drip, drip of flowing blood which reddened the walls and pooled in the dirt.

He was dragged on his knees over lifeless limbs, guts, and blood until from a distance of only a few yards, through the shoulders of encircled soldiers, he glimpsed the encircled prisoners.

Six doomed men with Davy amongst them, holding his head defiantly high and proud as he struggled to keep his weary body upright.

He told how his services as a translator were not required and the glance that flashed across his eyes was only brief as smoke from the executioner's blast ended the deplorable view. He said the image of the heroic souls who pained their last breath would remain with the witnesses, haunting their rest whenever they closed their eyes.

The Life and Death of My Best Friend, Davy Crockett

With a tremor in his weak voice, he described that Davy's body swayed in front of the rifles that were pointed at him. He was so exhausted that he was scarcely alive and almost unrecognizable from the feral man whom he had met on the prairie only a few months earlier.

He paused as his mind drifted a while, and then he revealed Davy's horrific afflictions, his left arm was smashed with shot and hung loose by his side with blood pooling at his feet, his forehead was lacerated so deep that skin flapped below his eye and blood and smoke-blackened his face from which yellow exhausted eyes valiantly stared at his conquers who had been instructed to take their aim.

There was a moment's macabre silence before the rifles granted him relief to instantly end his suffering, and then he was gone amongst the smoke and under the bodies of his dead comrades, who had been executed alongside him.

That was the last Ezra saw of Davy as once more he was dragged across hell's dirt and shackled to a hitch rail whilst the Mexicans cleared the dead, lit funeral pyres, and celebrated their victory.

His final recall was being hauled behind a supply cart for endless miles until the Mexicans were unexpectedly confronted and massacred by a feverish Texan force. Here, as his captures abandoned him and fled in panic due to lead and blade swirling amongst them, he was felled by the force of a bayonet and he could recall nothing other than incessant pain and harrowing apparitions.

The Life and Death of My Best Friend, Davy Crockett

We stayed on the watery banks of Buffalo Bay for two more days and became friendly with a couple of the Texas fellas who remained on the battlefield to clear away the rotting bodies. Intrigued by our truths, they supplied us with ample food, a basic rifle, and two healthy geldings. Chenoa attentively tended to Ezra's wound with fresh water and shrub potions.

She tried hard to rally him with words spoken with soft melodious tones like a lullaby, yet somehow all of her determination proved to be futile and free from his suffering, Ezra eventually succumbed to the eternal sleep from which he never awoke. My agony that damp day did not ease by knowing that amongst the angles in heaven, there would be sorrow and anger. God had been merciless and his heart empty and desolate of conveying compassion to those who fate was cruelly decided in Texas.

Now as the flame flickers dull on my candle of life I still reflect and grieve for great the man I was proud and privileged to know for over half of my life. From being born into a world of poverty at the very edge of civilization, he soon learned how to provide earthen riches and revel in adventures that men above his stature could only dream of.

He was a man of fearless courage ingrained with pure honesty and a stubborn loyalty to both those he served and those who were endeared by him.

He was humble, yet he held a natural charm for humor. His converse enthralled everyone by means of amusing narratives that he used often to deliver serious messages and sentiments. His truths were never lame and boring, and he had a fanciful imagination. His memories enriched the lives of many and his presence captivated everyone from backwoodsmen to

The Life and Death of My Best Friend, Davy Crockett

presidents, and still he never considered himself as having superior rights to any man or woman, regardless of their social status, beliefs, or ethnicity. He did not dwell on his failures and he did not boast of his triumphs, that being said he was not perfect. He claimed he abided by the will of god, yet the beast sometimes possessed him.

His flaw for adventure resulted in him neglecting his duties as a family man and his long absences from home stole the love of a needed son, husband, and father. Often he was driven only by his own convictions and he put his perceived sense of duty before the word of any other man or the devotion of any woman.

As the long dark and cold nights deliver there wintery tranquility upon the surrounding forest and dampen my humble cabin, it is with extreme proudness, albeit tinged with some regrets and heaps of sadness that I gather my grandchildren, Bright Star, and Snow Moon around my satisfying hearth to reminisce about the fortunes and tragedies of my best friend, Davy Crockett.

The Life and Death of My Best Friend, Davy Crockett

Other Westerns by Daniel Carlson include;

The Vengeance Trail

The Return

Life Taker - The Story of the Gun

A Kiss for the Cursed

Printed in Great Britain
by Amazon